Y0-DKO-077

THE MERRY-GO-ROUND

Other Books by Carroll Hofeling Morris

The Broken Covenant
The Bonsai
Saddle Shoe Blues

THE MERRY-GO-ROUND

Carroll Hofeling Morris

Deseret Book Company
Salt Lake City, Utah

©1988 Carroll Hofeling Morris
All rights reserved
Printed in the United States of America

No part of this book may be reproduced in any form or by any means without permission in writing from the publisher, Deseret Book Company, P.O. Box 30178, Salt Lake City, Utah 84130. Deseret Book is a registered trademark of Deseret Book Company.

First printing August 1988

Library of Congress Cataloging-in-Publication Data

Morris, Carroll Hofeling.
The merry-go-round / Carroll Hofeling Morris.
p. cm.
ISBN 0-87579-152-2 : $10.95 (est.)
I. Title.
PS3563.087398M47 1988
813'.54–dc19 88-14885
CIP

For Gary

THE MERRY-GO-ROUND

The little girl sat on the front steps of her house, a two-story stucco three blocks from the jewel of Minneapolis, Lake Harriet. She was waiting for her father to come home. She had been waiting since before suppertime. Her mother, watching the parade of trikes, bikes, and occasional scooters going around the block, encouraged her to join it. She refused. "I want to be here when Daddy comes," she said primly, smoothing the ruffled skirt of her dress. Again she looked down the elm-shaded street in hopes of seeing her father's 1949 Buick turn the corner, her lips moving in a silent incantation.

She had never told anyone, but she always thought of that car as a big black whale with silver teeth showing in its gaping mouth and a row of round, shining gills on either side. Her father she thought of as Jonah. Every morning the car would swallow him and bear him away from her. Every afternoon at about five o'clock, she would begin praying for his return. She was convinced that her prayers alone beached the whale in the Martin driveway and made it disgorge William H. Martin, a young but already successful builder.

This night, the shadows were already advancing to the east side of the street, and there was a clear, evening quality to the calls of neighborhood children before the massive, low-set car glided up the street.

"He's here!" Maxine Martin cried, flying down the steps and across the lawn. Her father bent down and scooped her up into his arms.

"I've been waiting, Daddy," she said.

"For what?"

She giggled, patting his shoulders with her pudgy hands. "You know."

"Of course I know," he said, grinning. "Just wait until I give your momma a kiss."

The little girl's mother accepted the kiss, then said, "It's already past her bedtime. If you take her now, she'll get all worked up. She always does, and then it's impossible to get her to sleep."

"But she's been waiting, haven't you, Button-Nose?"

"Uh-huh."

"We won't be long, dear," he told his wife. Then he took his daughter's small, sweet hand in his, and she skipped beside him the four blocks to the playground of the neighborhood school.

He watched as she climbed the ladder to the top of the slide and whizzed down it. Then he pushed her on a low swing. "Higher! Higher!" she commanded in her bright tremolo. When she was satisfied, he stepped back to wait until the arc of the swing shrank to stillness. "Now let's climb the monkey bars," she called to him, already on her way.

During all this time an exquisite anticipation had been building, for there was really only one reason they came to the school playground in the evenings, and they always left it until last.

"I guess we can go now," he said with mock seriousness when she tired of the monkey bars.

"Silly Daddy. We can't go yet," she giggled, pointing to the merry-go-round.

"Oh, my goodness! I almost forgot," he gasped, surprise broadly drawn on his face.

It was an old piece of equipment that she now ran toward, one set slightly apart from the rest and encircled by a moat that countless childish feet had dug. The flat metal disc with spokes leading from the center post to horseshoe-shaped handgrips on the outer rim listed to one side. Once it had been a proud red, but legions of passengers had worn all the paint off except for random chips that were dull and lifeless.

Bill Martin picked up his daughter and placed her near the center post. She sat down, drawing her knees up and putting her arms around them to hold down her dress. "Okay. I'm ready," she said.

He began pushing. The merry-go-round moved slowly at first, then picked up speed, creating a wind that ballooned an unsecured part of Maxine's skirt and lifted her fine brown hair. Faster and faster the merry-go-round went, pulling the trees on the edge of the playground and the brilliant colors of the sunset behind it as her cry of delight spiraled into the darkening sky.

THE PUSH-OFF

The midlife crisis came on overnight, the way a wrinkle appears during sleep.

At least that was the way Maxine Martin Heffelfinger thought about it afterward. And, in fact, she did attribute the vague feeling of malaise she had one morning in early September to the appearance of a small new wrinkle extending from the corner of her nose to her upper lip.

Others would not have seen it. They would have noticed instead the healthy glow of her lightly freckled skin, the unusually clear green of her eyes, and the beautiful cheekbones that defined her heart-shaped face. To Maxine, however, the wrinkle was ugly, disfiguring. It was the kind of wrinkle that, when joined by others of its ilk, causes the mouth to fall in on itself like crumpled tissue paper.

Scowling, she reached for the small 2.5-ounce bottle of Ever Youthful, the new anti-aging cream put out by her company, Pure Organics. It was based on a formula worked out in Switzerland that was purported to be a truly new concept in cell regeneration.

At thirty dollars an ounce, it better work, Maxine thought, smoothing the rich cream on her upper lip, then moving her attention to the area around her eyes. But she really had no doubts: Maxine Heffelfinger was a true believer.

She believed that Pure Organics, the multilevel marketing company she was currently signed up with, would make her fortune while giving her better health and wrinkle-free skin. Already she was Pure Organics' top money-maker in the Twin Cities area.

She believed that *Fit for Life* was *the* dietary plan to follow, and that the world would be a better place if everyone ate only fruit up until noon.

She believed that discipline a la Dreikurs would solve every problem she had with her son; if not, it was only because she herself had failed to follow through with logical consequences.

After putting one last pat of Ever Youthful between her eyebrows, she combed her Lightest Auburn hair. Thanks to Clairol, the vibrant image reflected in the mirror agreed with the inner image she had of herself. This congruence of images was something she worked at. She had no patience with people who sat around mewling about the hand nature had dealt them. If they didn't like it, they could do something about it.

When she was satisfied with what she saw in the mirror, she started downstairs. She still felt oddly disquieted, but since that feeling didn't fit into her scenario, she wielded her determination against it like a broom against a cobweb.

So much for that! she thought.

In the master bedroom, Ernie Heffelfinger still sat on the edge of the king-size bed, his regular, ordinary features softened and blurred by sleep. His was the kind of face that is easily overlooked, but, when once really seen, is engaging, endearing even. He rubbed his hand over the stubble of his slightly rounded cheeks and sighed.

It was hard for him to get going in the morning; he had always envied Maxine's early-morning vigor. The moment she woke up, she was ready to move. And move she always did, leaving him to lie in bed like a slug. The sounds of her purposeful progress from bathroom to closet and then down to the kitchen (the routine was the same every morning) infused him with just enough guilt to ruin any enjoyment he could otherwise have had in the last, warm moments before crawling out from under the covers.

Hunched on the edge of the bed, Ernie looked at his hands. He inspected them often, feeling as he did so that he was reading the course of his life. In a way, he was. Each of the scars on them told a tale, from the thin, white scar on his thumb – acquired while carving his first pumpkin – to the newest, tenderly pink one, which was the result of carelessness on the job. And the yellow line of thick calluses on his palms indicated the kind of work he was doing.

They were big hands, useful hands, but they were neither graceful nor elegant. The reason was easily apparent. Their size was the result of a large palm rather than long fingers. His relatively short fingers, attached as they were to his blocky palms, reminded him of Vienna sausages. The image seemed appropriate, considering the rhetorical question asked once by his father, Helmut H. Heffelfinger: "Where did you get hands like that? They look more like the butcher's than mine."

He wondered again if there was any connection between his feelings about his hands and his decision (made fifteen years earlier) to drop out of law school and become a cabinetmaker. He had always had the uncomfortable feeling of masquerading as a law student. He had even had nightmares of someone pointing an accusatory finger at his hands and crying, "You there! What are you doing in this class?"

But something had happened a few evenings earlier, something that was beginning to change the way he felt about his hands. He had seen Isaac Stern playing the violin on TV and had been mesmerized by Stern's fingers, which were not long and narrow, but more like his own. For the first time, he looked at his square palms and short fingers without hearing his father's words.

"They're good hands," he said with emphasis as he rose from the edge of the bed. "Cabinetmaking is an honorable occupation, and one heck of a lot more useful than making a closing argument before a jury."

Still, he couldn't get out of his mind the proposal his friend and fellow employee at Anderson Homes had made. Carl Gregory, master carpenter, had approached him with the idea that the two of them should start a building company of their own. "We're part of the reason people want Anderson homes. Why shouldn't we be getting more of the profit?"

At first he had resisted the idea, knowing that they would also have to take more of the risk. Also, he had a very clear recollection of the trouble his decision to drop out of law school had caused between himself and Maxine. Carl was persistent, however. And the more he talked, the better Heffelfinger and Gregory, Fine Homes sounded to Ernie.

I do want to do something more than build cabinets, he thought, as he ran his thick fingers through his sandy hair. *And if I want to do it, I have to do it now.*

Pete Heffelfinger, age sixteen-and-a-half, shaved that morning without once meeting his own gaze in the mirror. He knew what he would see if he did: nothing.

Nothing and nobody.

It would only confirm the conclusion he had arrived at in the last few days: He, Peter Heffelfinger, was one of the Invisibles.

Walking the halls of Wayzata North Senior High, a suburban school west of Minneapolis, were several easily recognizable groups. There were the Jocks and the Nerds, the Punks and the Preps, the Motorheads, the Potheads, and the Airheads. The Invisibles were a group as well, but nobody recognized them. They didn't even recognize each other.

He forced his gaze up from the spot on his chin he was shaving, past his wide, full-lipped mouth, past the tip of his short, fleshy nose. Then, looking directly into his steady, brown eyes, he promised himself that that would change. He would do something to make himself visible—he just wasn't sure what.

When the idea came to him, he burst out laughing. He could imagine what his mother would say about it. Never in his life had he done anything that she wouldn't have approved. At least nothing major. He had had rebellious feelings now and again, but with Maxine for a mother, rebellion wasn't practical.

The idea stuck with him, though. And the more he thought about it, the more he thought, *Maybe* . . .

The date was September 23, 1987. It was not a date any of the Heffelfingers would be able to point to afterward, saying, "That was when it began." They might have, if they had given real attention to their own early-morning thoughts, or if each had known what the others were thinking.

But they didn't, so they had no way of knowing that they were on a merry-go-round. A merry-go-round that was slowly, slowly beginning to turn.

PETE'S GO-ROUND

1

Pete Heffelfinger stared at his reflection. He was thinking, That's *not* what Lightest Auburn looks like on the package.

On the package, the model's hair wasn't obscenely red. His hair was. Words like *carrot* and *pumpkin* kept popping into his mind, but they didn't come close to describing the visual shock the new color of his hair caused. Or the visceral reaction.

I'm going to puke! he thought, but he didn't. He sat down on the stool, the wet towel still draped around his neck, his hands drooping down between his legs, and his head following. Every so often he looked in the mirror, just to see if it was really that bad.

It was.

What happened? he wondered. *Lightest Auburn doesn't look like this on Mom.*

Well, maybe it does. Come to think of it, I've always thought her hair was a bit much. It makes her look too pale.

Makes me look too pale.

I got what I wanted, that's for sure. Everybody will stare at me the minute I walk into school tomorrow. The minute I get on the bus, for Pete's sake!

It always seemed funny to him when he used that expression. For Pete's sake he had applied the hair coloring. Now, for Pete's sake, he wished he hadn't. He started to comb his coarsened hair so he could go to the drugstore for a new shade of Clairol – Invisible Brown.

He hadn't gone to the drugstore for the Lightest Auburn. His mother had enough boxes of it on the top shelf of the linen closet. She always kept a stock of it, although it was easily available. Even the grocery stores had it. When he had asked her about it once, she had replied, "I don't like being caught without some when I want it."

Pete understood. His mother was a compulsive sort. When she wanted to do something, she wanted to do it—now! It didn't matter if it was twelve o'clock midnight. Her stock of Clairol was necessary for those occasions when coloring her hair became a matter of survival, something that couldn't wait ten minutes, much less ten hours.

Once he had decided to dye his hair, he felt the same urgency. He didn't want to wait until he had the chance to buy a kit of his own. It was easier and simpler to use one of his mother's. Besides, it saved him the embarrassment of presenting himself at the checkout counter with hair coloring in hand.

"And I was worried about *that,*" he said to himself with a short laugh. "It's nothing compared to how stupid I'm going to feel walking in like this."

But Pete Heffelfinger never made the trip to the drugstore. In the middle of combing his hair, he pulled some strands straight up—and discovered that spikes were exactly what his new red hair demanded. He stared at the spikes, absolutely fascinated. Then he pulled a few more strands up.

"Hmmm," he murmured, looking at the result with a speculative gaze. "Now the only problem is making it stay up. That shouldn't be too hard. Punks do it all the time."

Punks? Startled, he stared at himself. "Is that what I'm going to be? Peter Heffelfinger, Punk?"

"Naw."

Then, "Maybe."

And finally, as he made his decision, "Yeaaaaah!"

But while he rubbed gel toothpaste into his hair, he wondered if he could pull it off. Looking punk on the outside was one thing, but what were punks like on the inside? He had never talked to any, so he didn't know.

He knew for sure what his mom thought about them. "Why would anybody want to walk around looking like that?" she asked once. He had had no idea. In the years since she had asked that question, the punk craze had peaked and ebbed, and he still had no idea.

"I should have done this years ago," he mused. "If I were like Mom, I would have been the first punk to walk the hallowed halls of Wayzata North." He shrugged. "So I'm a little late—so what? I'm not on the ground floor, Mom, but I've joined up."

He couldn't help chuckling as he realized he had used the phrasing of his mother's famous "ground floor" speech, the one she gave when she was trying to get her prospects signed up with the multilevel marketing organization she currently was pushing.

When he finally got his hair standing straight up, he realized that for this new look to really work, the hair above his ears and around the back of his head had to be shorter, lots shorter. He opened the linen closet and rummaged around in the back until he found the Wahl clippers his mother had used back in the days when she could get him to sit still long enough for her to cut his hair. In the days before he locked himself in his room and refused to come out while she still had her clippers in hand.

"If you don't let me cut your hair, you'll have to pay to have someone else do it. I won't," she had threatened.

Which had suited Pete just fine.

Now he put on the clippers the attachment meant to keep the hair from getting cut too short, took a deep breath, and went at it. He had a crazy urge to close his eyes until it was over, but he forced himself to keep looking as he moved the clippers around his head and the brilliant hair dropped in clumps on the soggy towel.

His hair, when he was finished, was just awful enough to be quite wonderful.

Not bad, he thought, pulling the towel away and shaking the hair into the trash can. Being neat by nature, he also swept up the floor and cleaned off the counter before taking another look in the mirror.

The hair was right, but now his sober, unremarkable shirt and pants were not. What he needed was something from Ragstock, which sold everything from Swedish army uniforms to old flannel pajamas. If you didn't find what you wanted hanging from the racks or stacked on the tables (and if you could stand the smell of mothballs), you could fish through the barrels and boxes on the floor. He took a quick look at his watch, which he had taken off before starting the operation. It was almost five, too late to drive downtown even if there were a car available, which there wasn't.

When the idea came to him, he snapped his fingers in a "got it" gesture. "Mom took all that old stuff over to Will's. All I have to do is ask him."

Besides, he told himself as he bounded down the steps from the patio to the lawn, *Will, of all people, should understand.*

Will Martin, Pete's maternal grandfather (in a manner of speaking), lived in a renovated barn behind the Heffelfinger house on Rockford Road in Plymouth, Minnesota. Maxine had spent weeks looking for a place that had two houses on the property, one for the Heffelfingers and one for Will, with no luck. When she finally found the old homestead west of Minneapolis, she knew it was the place for them.

The property was only five minutes from Interstate 494, which was part of the freeway system encircling the twin cities of Minneapolis and St. Paul. It was about the same distance from Highway 12 (soon to become Interstate 394), which led east from Wayzata's pricy shops and gold coast of mansions on the shores of Lake Minnetonka to the center of Minneapolis. The proximity to these highways meant easy access to all the areas of the Twin Cities, and the surge of commercial development and new neighborhoods along them meant the value of the property would only increase. Those developments would one day surround the old homestead in their inexorable move westward, but it was, in the meantime, still definitely country.

The house nestled in a hollow near a pond, with a rise of oak and maple trees forming a bucolic backdrop. Geese and ducks frequented the pond during the day, and in the evenings, deer stepped timidly from the grove to drink. Across the street, the neighbors' farmyard was full of equipment, and their twin blue silos stood sentry by the big white barn decorated with Pennsylvania Dutch hex symbols. In the spring, the smell of warm, plowed earth sweetened the air, and in the fall, the raucous voices of crows could be heard in the fields of drying corn.

Such advantages overrode the fact that both buildings on the property were in need of a good deal of repair, something even the real-estate agent acknowledged—the listing had borne the words "Handyman's Special." But Ernie was up to the challenge.

The main house was what he called a "classic Minnesota farmhouse." It was a two-story building, well constructed but unadorned except for a modest front porch. The original floor plan was functional as well. When the Heffelfingers bought it, the house consisted of a small living room, a huge kitchen, a bedroom, and a bath on the first floor, three bedrooms and a bath upstairs.

Ernie had gone to work on it right after they closed the deal. He had redone the outside with narrow white clapboard and complemented the windows with shutters and flowerboxes of Federal Blue. He had extended the porch across the whole front of the house and installed a new front door, a reproduction with an oval etched-glass window.

That accomplished, he completely reconstructed the inside. With Maxine and Pete as his crew, he created an entryway and built a completely new staircase with a gentle curve and beautiful newel at the bottom. He tore out the wall between the existing living room and the small bedroom to make one large, gracious room whose focal point was a classic mantel of his own design. He gutted the kitchen and created a warm country kitchen/family room with maple cabinetry and bookcases and a brick fireplace. Upstairs, he built a separate bath and walk-in closet in the huge bedroom that was to be his and Maxine's and redid the other bath and bedrooms.

While he was busy in the main house, his buddies Carl Gregory and Henry Levering created a large garage and a two-bedroom in-law apartment out of the still-sound barn. Before painting the finished building, Carl whimsically added a cupola and weathervane to the roof.

The work completed, the Heffelfingers and Will had moved in. It had been almost a year since then. Almost a year since Will Martin's recovery from the dreadful accident that took the life of his wife (and Maxine's mother), Helen.

Physical recovery, that is. The man who miraculously woke up after being in a coma for months was not the person who had lost control of his car in a furious deluge and skidded into the path of a semitrailer truck. He knew nothing of William (Bill) Martin, developer, patron of the arts, high councilor in the Minneapolis Stake of The Church of Jesus Christ of Latter-day Saints, also known as the Mormons.

Nor did he know Bill Martin's daughter, Maxine, who had come sobbing to the hospital, expecting to fling herself into the arms of the father whom she had loved and who had returned to her.

The months following the first meeting between Maxine Martin Heffelfinger and Will Martin were even more difficult than the months preceding. Maxine never accepted the fact that her father was gone and in his place was an irascible man/child who needed to be taught virtually everything.

It was different for Pete. Once he got used to the idea, he found it easy to accept the new personality of his grandfather. He had spent many hours in the hospital helping Will learn such simple things as The Importance of Brushing Teeth After Meals and Making Sure Your Shoes Are on the Right Feet.

Pete was glad his mother had insisted upon bringing Will home instead of sending him to an institution. Although he knew better than to admit it, he liked Will better than he had ever liked his grandfather, Bill. Will didn't always question him about why he was doing something he shouldn't do, or why he wasn't doing something he should do.

So it was with a grin that Pete Heffelfinger crossed the lawn between the Heffelfinger house and Will's barn and knocked on the door.

A man of sixty opened it. He was as tall as Pete, five foot eleven. His eyes, a disconcertingly bright blue, were set in a face marked by broad, beefy cheeks and a nose worthy of a prize fighter. Only the intelligent eyes and surprisingly sweet smile redeemed Will Martin's face from homeliness.

When he saw Pete, Will burst into laughter. Pete laughed too, partly out of nervousness, partly because of what Will was wearing.

"Looks like we're both playing dress-up," the older man chuckled. "But your hair wins out over my costume."

He stood back to let Pete in, then struck a pose in the middle of the living room. "What do you think? It's my army uniform. At least that's what your mother says."

"You still fit into it. Great!"

"*She* says I look like this in the pictures."

"You do, except you were younger then."

"I suppose so. How old am I supposed to be?"

"Sixty."

"I'm still in good shape for being sixty," Will said, looking at himself in the mirror over the fireplace. "Of course, that's assuming your mother is telling the truth about my age." He straightened the collar absently. "I don't remember a thing about being in the army, you know."

"I know."

"So what can I do for you, Pete my boy?" Will asked. He grinned slyly, adding, " . . . that you haven't already done."

"I, uh, I want to try on some of your old clothes."

"Why? Don't you remember who you are? Do you have a cranial contusion too?"

"Nothing like that. I just want to try something different for a change."

"That's the way." Will jabbed the index finger of his right hand in Pete's direction. "If you don't know who you are, you have to playact a bit. Try on different roles."

Still talking, Will led the way to the second bedroom, where the boxes of memorabilia and clothes were stored. Many of the boxes were opened. Clothing hung over the sides of some and lay in heaps on the floor, as if thrown there in disgust.

"I can see it's been one of those days, Grandpa," said Pete, slipping into his old form of address.

"Don't call me Grandpa," said Will shortly. "You're a person, I'm a person. That's all I know. Call me Will."

"You *are* my grandpa. Sort of."

"That's what your mother says, but I don't believe it just because she says so." Will dragged a Hawaiian shirt from one box, then rejected it. "She's a bossy one, isn't she? Flounces right in and announces she's my daughter. Huh! I don't know her from Elizabeth Taylor. Anyway, if I had my choice I'd take Liz. She'd make a fine daughter."

"There's the pictures, Will."

"A pox on the pictures. Can't recognize a single person."

Will had been roaming from box to box as he spoke. Now he dropped down on the one clear chair. "It would be all right if everyone would just let me be myself, instead of insisting that I act like *he* used to. I'm fine the way I am. I can read, I can write, I know a little history. I can find my way around town, too. If only Maxine would stop pushing me to remember the past. I don't need to. I'm a real person without it."

"She just wants her daddy back."

"She's not getting him back!"

"Hey, don't yell at me. I'm not the one you're mad at."

Will nodded. "Right. So what do you want to try on?"

"Something outrageous."

Will resumed rummaging. "I don't know if I can help you. Bill doesn't seem to have been outrageous. He was probably quite boring."

"It doesn't matter. Anything that looked boring thirty years ago will look outrageous on me."

"Lucky for you he grew up in the depression. He saved everything, so that woman says. I guess he must have, there's enough of it. How about this?"

Will held up an old leather flight jacket.

"Great. What else you got there?"

Between the two of them, they ferreted out two pairs of double-pleated twill pants, some suspenders, a striped vest with satin brocade back, a huge overcoat with padded shoulders and several buttons missing, a pair of ratty overalls, and numerous shirts ranging from a virulent mustard to a dark plaid, from small collars to long, pointed collars.

"I wouldn't have worn those," said Will, pushing his lips out belligerently.

"Do you ever miss being the person you were before the accident?"

"How could I miss him? I don't even remember him. If you've never had something, you don't feel sorry when it's gone." Will fingered the shirts. "Sometimes I do wonder about him. Sometimes, like today, I want to find him, just so I'll know. I put on these clothes and look in the mirror. Then I look at the pictures . . . " Will shook his head. "It never works."

"I'm sorry."

"I'm not. I don't think I'd like him anyway. He was probably a wimp. Must have been if he let Maxine boss him around."

"He didn't. If anything, Grandpa ran Mom's life." Pete grinned. "Maybe that's why she tries to run yours now."

"She may think she's running it, but I'm just biding my time. When I know enough that I won't make a fool of myself doing something even a kid knows better than to do, I'm going to split."

"Do you mean it?"

"You bet your boots. I'm not hanging around here."

"But Grandpa . . . Will . . . where'll you go? What'll you live on?"

"I've got plenty of money. That wimp made enough. I've seen his bankbook. Maxine has been keeping a mighty tight hold on it, what with this trust and all, but if I can ever get her to relax her grip, I'll pry enough loose to see the world on."

"By yourself?"

"Why not?"

"No reason. I just thought you might want some company."

"Well, well. Maybe we are related, after all. When I make up my mind to leave, you'll be the first to know." He thrust the clothes into Pete's arms. "Go try your new duds on."

Pete experimented with several combinations, then settled on his own undershirt, a pair of black, moth-eaten, double-pleated pants, and black suspenders. Even though it was late September, it was too hot to put on the flight jacket, but he slung it over his shoulders. His own tennis shoes, the ones his mother had thrown out, would look all right with his ensemble, he figured. At least they would do until he could get down to Ragstock or over to the Army Surplus store to buy some boots.

"Doesn't look half-bad," he murmured to himself. "Maybe if I let my beard grow out a little . . . just enough to look scruffy . . . "

"Get out here and let me see you," Will commanded from the living room.

"What do you think?"

Will peered at him through narrowed eyes, his head cocked at a questioning angle. Then he straightened the suspender on Pete's left shoulder and passed his judgment. "If what you wanted was to look like a punk, you've succeeded."

Grinning, Pete picked up his clothes and started for the door.

"You're not going home like that, are you?"

"I was planning on it."

"Then I'm coming with."

"You don't want to miss the fun, huh?"

"Who said anything about fun? One look at you and she'll make you change."

"How? I don't think good ol' Mom is up to tackling me and undressing me by force."

"She'll take away your privileges. Last time I went into town on the bus without telling her, she kept me under her thumb for a month."

"I would, too, if I were Mom. You're too trusting. You could end up on a slab in the morgue one of these times."

"I doubt it. But one thing's for sure. After she sees you like this, she won't be spending as much time and energy on me."

Pete smiled, but his smile faded when he saw Maxine's dark blue Cadillac pull into the driveway. He took a deep breath and said, "Here goes."

He and Will stood in the doorway watching Maxine get out of the car. She put her suit jacket over her arm, then reached back in the car for her attaché case and her large leather purse. Glancing perfunctorily in their direction, she started for the house. Three steps later she stopped, turned, and stared. Pete shifted uneasily as she strode purposefully toward them.

"Hang on to your horses, boy," Will said. "It's going to be a rough ride."

Pete smiled weakly at Will's words. Will was now in his Western Colloquial mode. In the process of recovering his speech, he had absorbed an odd collection of verbal expressions from the books and movies he studied. He might just as well have said, "Chin up, Boyo. The Mater looks a bit peeved." Either way, he would have been right.

2

Maxine started talking even before she reached them.

"I see you've got a visitor, Will," she said, looking at Pete without any recognition. She pointed to the curved bench that surrounded the huge oak tree in the middle of the backyard. "Would you mind waiting over there for a minute, young man?"

Pete opened his mouth to say, "Hi, Mom," but she stopped him with her raised hand. "Please, I would like to talk to my father."

Swallowing a chuckle, Pete sat down on the circular bench. She hadn't even looked at his face, he realized. She had seen only the spiked hair and the bizarre clothes, and on that basis had identified him with the Hennepin Avenue weirdos that Will had been known to bring home on occasion.

That was what had set her off, he knew. She hated Will's excursions. She especially regretted the day he had learned how to catch the Metrolink bus that went by their house and connected with a downtown bus that took him to the heart of the city, where the distance between the fashionable Nicolette Mall and the questionable Hennepin Avenue was a mere block.

Pete didn't blame her. From the time Will learned how to use the bus system, they never knew if he was going to be home when they got back at the end of a day. After his first expedition, Maxine hired a nurse to baby-sit him. The woman didn't even last until noon of her first day. Maxine found a male nurse next, but ended up firing him herself after discovering bruises on Will's arm.

Distressed, she conferred with Will's neurologist, who told her to stop thinking of Will as a child. She reluctantly agreed to allow him a reasonable amount of freedom, if he would obey house rules.

The very next day, Will went downtown again.

He went often after that, never seeming to mind that he was causing a crisis when he did. Maxine, imagining the worst, would threaten to call the police, and Ernie would try to stall her just a bit longer with the logic, "He always shows up." And he would, brimming with tales of his adventures on Hennepin Avenue, at Lake Calhoun, and in the Uptown district.

That was bad enough, but it was even worse when he showed up with someone in tow, expecting Maxine to feed them supper. He had brought home punks, runaways, street people, bag ladies, disoriented releases from the state hospital, and, Pete suspected, more than one druggie. Maxine had refused to let them into her house, but that hadn't deterred Will. He could open cans with the best of them, and he knew how to cook a few simple things like omelets, hamburger soup, and spaghetti. So he had begun taking his guests to his barn instead.

Pete knew his mother thought he was another one of Will's charity cases, and it was obvious she was not happy about it. She didn't even try to keep her voice from carrying in Pete's direction as she said, "Will, don't you remember what I told you about checking with me first before bringing people home?"

"I didn't bring him home. He came to me."

"I knew this would happen sooner or later! Bring enough of them home to feed, and they'll spread the word. We'll have to start a soup kitchen—if we don't get killed in our beds first."

"You don't have to worry about him. He's harmless," Will said, sending a wink and a grin Pete's way.

Maxine caught Will's expression. She looked in Pete's direction, squinting her eyes. Pete smiled sheepishly and waved at her. "Hi, Mom," he said.

Maxine's double take turned into a triple take. "Pete?"

"I told you I didn't bring him home," Will said.

"Pete! What have you done to yourself?" she cried, dropping her attaché case and jacket and starting toward him.

"Nothing much."

"Nothing much? Look at your hair!" She reached out to touch it, then recoiled in horror. "And those clothes! Where in the world did you dig those up, out of a garbage can?"

"Garbage can!" protested Will in an offended tone. "Those wonderful clothes came from Bill's boxes. See those pants? You'd have to pay fifty dollars for pleats like that. First-quality stuff, and there's more where they came from."

A flicker of humor lit Maxine's eyes. "Dad did have good taste," she said. Then she sobered. "You and I have some talking to do, son."

"Whatever. See you later, Will."

"You want I should bring the rest of your things over?" Will asked.

"Naw. I'll pick them up later," said Pete. Then he followed his mother into the house. He could tell by the set of her shoulders that she was ticked-off, but she didn't say anything until they were seated in the family room.

"All right, Pete, what's going on here?"

He slouched in his chair. "Nothing."

"Don't push it. My initial response to this is an urge to scream and then to squeeze your neck. But if you talk to me, I might be able to avoid either one."

"What's to say? I got tired of seeing the same face in the mirror every morning."

"You certainly took care of that. Only it seems to me you've also made a pretty strong statement against the standards we've established in our family."

"I just changed the color of my hair, Mom."

"When are you planning to change it back?"

"Not in the next five minutes, if that's what you're hinting at. I like it the way it is. I'm going to school like this to-morrow."

"You'll get laughed at if you do."

"You haven't been to North lately, or you'd know there are lots of kids who look worse."

"How other kids look doesn't have anything to do with it. You're my son, and what you've done is entirely unacceptable."

Pete was silent.

"I don't want to have a confrontation over this, but I do think you should try to get yourself back to normal before you go to bed tonight."

"What if I say no?"

Maxine's voice betrayed by its controlled quietness the level of anger she felt. "Go to your room, Pete, and stay there until your father gets back from work."

Pete wasn't worried as he lay on his bed, waiting for Ernie Heffelfinger to come home. His dad took things a lot easier than his mother did. The real trouble over this would be between himself and his mother.

That was the unwritten rule. But Pete had not been very old when he realized that his father would let him do pretty much what he wanted to do as long as he was, first of all, safe, and second, happy. It was his mother who had Great Expectations. She was also the one with the power. Pete couldn't remember a time when his father had overruled his mother. He knew that Ernie would be shocked, but that he would try to smooth things over between his son and his wife. That failing, he would withdraw and leave them on the battlefield alone.

It happened the way Pete had known it would. The minute his dad's pickup pulled into the driveway, Maxine called for Pete to come down. With a sigh, he obeyed. He was standing on the stairs when she pulled his father into the living room.

"Slow down," Ernie was saying. "What's the big surprise?"

Maxine pointed in Pete's direction.

Ernie's eyes traveled from the red spikes standing up on Pete's otherwise shorn head to the old clothes and down to the worn-out tennis shoes. It was only as he focused on the shoes that his mind identified the person standing there. His eyes flashed back up to his son's face.

"Pete!"

"Dad!" Pete echoed, flinging out his arms. He walked down the rest of the stairs with his arms outstretched. It was a nice comic touch, he thought, but his mother wasn't amused.

"How do you like your son's new image?" she asked, her hands on her hips.

Ernie, who was staring at Pete, cleared his throat before speaking. "What have you done to your hair?"

"I dyed it."

"And buzzed it," Maxine added. "I'm so mad, I could shake his teeth out!"

"Why?" Ernie asked Pete, more bemused than angry.

"I wanted to."

Ernie hung his carpenter's belt over the newel. Maxine automatically removed it as he rubbed one hand over his scraggly cheeks. "Let me get this straight. You *wanted* to look like that?"

Pete nodded.

"He says he's going to school that way," said Maxine.

"He's not going to do that. He's just saying it to get at you." Ernie hesitated as Pete grinned. "Aren't you?"

Pete shook his head. "No. I'm serious."

"He is, believe me. We've already been through this. I told him he couldn't go to school looking like he does."

"Heck, I thought I looked pretty good," said Pete.

But Ernie wasn't listening to him. He was staring at the spiked red-orange hair.

"Dad, stop staring at my hair. It makes me nervous."

"Get used to it, because everybody's going to stare at it," said Maxine.

"Where did you get that color?" asked Ernie suddenly.

"Out of a bottle. I dipped into Mom's stockpile in the linen closet upstairs."

A wide smile lit up Ernie's face. "I thought I recognized that particular shade," he chuckled, looking from Pete's hair to Maxine's and back again.

"What are you laughing at?" demanded Maxine. "This is anything but funny!"

"I'm not laughing," Ernie protested. "It is amusing though. Matching hair color . . . "

"I'm glad you think it's amusing, but I certainly don't. It's one thing for me to color my hair, but it's another thing for Pete to."

"If you can do it, why can't I?" Pete asked.

"For one thing, you look terrible in that color. It makes your face too pale."

"Did you ever stop to think that you might not look so hot in it either?"

Maxine bit her lip, and tears glistened in the corners of her eyes.

"Now you've gone too far, son," Ernie said. "I won't have you talking to your mother that way."

"I'm sorry, Mom. I didn't mean that. I only said it because I was mad. I like the way you look. Really."

"It doesn't matter either way," she said tightly. "I don't color it for you, you know."

"I didn't color mine for you, either."

"At least I don't skin mine off on the sides."

With the tension escalating, Ernie stepped back, as he always did, leaving Pete in an uncomfortable but familiar position, nose-to-nose with his mother. For a moment, they glared at each other. Then Maxine turned to Ernie.

"I think we can repair the damage. We can take him to my hairdresser and have her trim the top so it blends in with the sides. It'll be a bit short for a while, but it'll grow out. We can pick up some brown wash-in color on the way home."

"Well . . . I guess it'd work," Ernie said.

"Please get in the car, Pete," Maxine said, picking up her purse.

"No."

"Come on, son." Ernie's voice held the plea, Let's not cause any more trouble than necessary, please.

Pete ignored it. "Look, Mom, Dad, it's not that big a deal. Don't get bent out of shape about it. I'm just doing what Will does, trying on a part. I'm only going to keep my hair this way and wear Will's old clothes for a while."

"Why?" asked Maxine. "You've got a dresser full of good school clothes."

"I'm just doing it for fun, Mom. Look at it this way: The stuff you buy me is generic, except for the preppy pants and shirts you got over at The Foursome in Wayzata. Half the time, I'm decked out like a good little prep, and the other half, I'm sporting Sears' Special Purchase. I look stupid."

"And you don't think you look stupid like this?"

"At least it all fits. I'm the same thing from top to bottom. Better get used to it, because this is how I'm going to look from now on."

"Even on Sunday?" asked Ernie.

Pete took a deep breath. Now things were getting serious. "Especially on Sunday," he answered.

"Oh, no, you don't," said Maxine. "That's where I draw the line. You know how the bishop feels about the way the young men dress. It's a suit, white shirt, and tie, or you won't be able to bless the sacrament."

"So? If the bishop is dumb enough to think how I look changes who I am, that's tough."

"Looks aren't everything, but—" Ernie began.

Pete interrupted him. "No buts. If looks aren't everything, it shouldn't make any difference *how* I look."

"It does. Don't ever think it doesn't," Maxine said.

"You're just worried about your reputation. Everybody's going to look at me, and then they're going to look at you and Dad. I know just what they'll be thinking. 'Why don't the Heffelfingers *do* something about Pete?' Well, there's nothing you can do."

"I can ground you," Maxine threatened.

"So do it."

"You're grounded. Go to your room."

"Big deal. I never go anywhere anyway. I'll just get more studying done," said Pete defiantly.

He stomped back up to his room, slammed the door shut, and deliberately put on a head-banger record, one he knew drove his mother nuts. Then he flung himself on the bed and stared dourly at the ceiling.

3

Pete felt nervous the next day as he waited for Bradley McEntyre to pick him up for early-morning seminary. He wasn't sure he wanted to go looking the way he did, but his mother had pushed him into a position he couldn't back down from. If it had just been between himself and his dad, the whole thing could have been made into a joke. He would have felt okay about going back to the house and saying, "I've changed my mind."

But it wasn't just himself and Ernie. And for some reason, the fact that his mother was probably wishing at this very moment that he would disappear from the face of the earth was enough to make spiting her worth his trouble.

"Why couldn't you just leave it alone, Mom?" he muttered to himself. "It wasn't the end of the world."

He felt torn. He wanted to give it all up, yet there was still that inner need to *be* that hadn't changed, and if he went back to his old self, that need would still be there. So he decided to ride it out. He only hoped the kids in seminary wouldn't make a big deal out of it. A vain hope, he knew, but he hoped nonetheless.

Just then, Bradley's old Honda pulled up. Pete opened the door and got in. Bradley, whose short dark hair, dark-rimmed glasses, and serious mien perfectly matched his name, stared at him.

"What happened to you?" he blurted out. "Get mugged by a gang of punkers?"

Pete shook his head.

"Are you going to start hanging out with them?"

"I dunno. Probably not. I don't know any."

"If you're not going to hang out with them, why do *that* to yourself?"

"I felt like it. Looks pretty good, don't you think? I mean, I got my spikes to stand straight up."

Bradley shook his head as he shifted into first. "Just wait till Sister Arnold sees you. She'll probably kick you out of class."

"No, she won't. She puts up with all kinds of junk because 'Seminary Is Important.' Besides, I'm not going to be rude or do my homework while she's talking. All I'm going to do is sit there looking funny."

"Okay, so you make it through seminary. How are you going to make it past Mr. Springer? You look at him cross-eyed, and he'll haul you off to his office before you even have a chance to put your stuff in your locker."

"No, he won't."

"You forget that Springer likes guys that don't make any waves. He's not going to be too happy when he sees you've broken ranks."

"Well, he doesn't need to worry. I'm not going to cause him any trouble."

Pete meant what he said, but he hadn't reckoned with the fact that his very appearance would cause a disturbance. All through seminary, Heather Donovan and Julianna Radke kept looking at him and giggling, while Sister Arnold persevered.

And although there wasn't anything unique about seeing a punk in the halls of Wayzata North, seeing Pete Heffelfinger, Punk, was unusual. Wherever he walked, kids turned to stare. More than once, somebody would call, "Hey, is that you, Heffelfinger?" At first it bothered him, but after a while he decided it wasn't that bad. At least he wasn't invisible. Even his teachers took more notice of him than usual.

"That is quite an impressive display, Mr. Heffelfinger," said Mr. Longfellow, Pete's geometry teacher. "How long did it take you to figure that effect out?"

"Not long."

"Let's hope it won't take you long to reverse it."

Pete ignored the comment. He and Longfellow had never gotten along; it didn't make any difference to him that Longfellow didn't approve of how he looked.

However, Ann Johnson's opinion did matter to him. He had had her for Western Civilization as a sophomore and had her this year for American history. She was a tall woman with a face that had an uncanny resemblance to a Basset hound and a broad-shouldered physique that would have been more suited to a man. Her appearance didn't stand in the way of her teaching, though. Her honesty and sense of humor drew students to her and kept her classes filled.

"See me after class," she said to him just before the bell rang.

She was smiling as he approached her desk, her wide mouth pushing back the cheeks that otherwise hung like flaps. "You've got a new persona, I see," she said. "Any particular reason for it?"

He found he could tell her easily. "I, you know, I just wanted to be somebody."

"You already were somebody."

"Really? Not as far as anybody in this school was concerned."

"You were to me." She raised her hands and said with mock dejection, "I know. I don't count."

Pete grinned.

"Being somebody takes time, Pete. It's a whole life's work. We don't get to be our real selves until we've lived long enough to figure out what's important to us."

"Yeah, well, there are some people in this school who have made it already."

"Do you think so?" Ann settled her large body on the edge of her desk and crossed her ankles. "I'm not sure I agree with you."

"How about Greg Hoffman, our president? And Randy Tullgren, star quarterback? They know who they are."

"It seems so, doesn't it? But they might not, in a few years. They might discover that they're just one of the crowd, with nothing particular to recommend them. They may not be as ready to deal with life as you are."

"Right."

"I mean it. Those two boys haven't had to struggle for much so far. They don't know what kind of people they are inside, because they've never had their backs to the wall. They've never even given it a second thought."

"Then I'm not different from them. I haven't given it a second thought, either. At least, not until now. I've spent my whole life being my mom's boy. I mean, I've measured everything I've said or done according to whether Mom would like it or not."

"I don't suppose she's too thrilled about what you've done."

"Are you kidding? She hates it. But that's just too bad. I'm not changing back."

"Why did you decide to go punk?"

"It was the hair," Pete confessed, grinning wryly. "Besides, what were my choices. Even if I wanted to, I couldn't turn into a jock overnight. I'm lousy at sports. I could have turned myself into a nerd, I guess. All I'd need to do is wear dark-framed glasses and some white socks, get a plastic pocket protector, and go around spouting theorems all the time. But who wants to be a nerd?"

He thought for a moment, then added, "I don't smoke, so being a Pit-dweller is out." He was referring to the students who flocked between classes to the Pit, the designated smoking area just outside one of the doors.

"Now that's an idea," Ann said. "If you really want to rebel, that would be the way to do it. Start smoking."

"Yeah, but that would be dumb."

Ann raised her eyebrows. "I see. You want to rebel, but only a little, and only in a way that won't be too destructive."

"Maybe," said Pete, looking down at his sneakers.

"But do you really want to be labeled as a punker? You've

assumed the identity of a group that doesn't have a particularly good reputation. Did you think about the fact that when you identified yourself with them, you also assumed their reputation?"

"I'm not any different than I was yesterday."

"You're not?"

"Okay, so I don't even look like the same person. Inside I am."

"I know that. But I think you're going to see a big difference in the way people react to you. And the way you deal with that could make you into a different person."

Before Pete had a chance to consider what she had said, the bell rang.

"Great. I'm tardy for my chem study. Can you write me a slip?"

Slip in hand, Pete loped down the hall, thinking about his talk with Mrs. Johnson. He was unaware that someone was following him until he was hit from behind. He sprawled on the floor, his books flying. Before he had a chance to pick himself up, somebody dragged him up by the shirt.

It was Knuckles Price, a fierce loner whose anger always hovered near the flash point. His dead-black hair was streaked with green on the right side. He wore combat boots, torn jeans threaded together with straightened-out paper clips, a muscle shirt, and a black leather jacket with silver studs. His belt was studded as well, and around his neck he wore a crude necklace fashioned of wire.

Before Pete could open his mouth, Knuckles slammed him against the bank of lockers lining the hall. "What's the story, Heffelfinger?"

"What do you mean?" Pete asked, gritting his teeth against the pain in the back of his head. "I don't know what you're talking about."

"Your new getup, Louse Bait. Who gave you permission to walk around like this?"

"What's it to you?"

Knuckles slammed him into the lockers again. The hand against Pete's throat almost cut off his breath. "You don't just wake up one morning and decide to go punk, Slime Bucket," Knuckles hissed into his face. "You ask me. And if I feel like it, I give you permission."

Pete gasped. "I didn't know."

"You do now," Knuckles said, then stepped back, waiting for Pete to ask.

"Look, I don't want any trouble," said Pete, rubbing his throat. "If you stay out of my way, I'll stay out of yours."

In one swift move, Knuckles had him back against the lockers, his fist against Pete's Adam's apple. "So that's how it is. You want to look like a punk, but you don't want to have anything to do with them."

"More or less," Pete managed to squeak out.

"It don't work that way, Maggot Brain. You come to school like this, and you're mine. Got it?"

"Got it."

"So what's it going to be?"

"I don't know . . . "

Another slam. Pete's ears started to ring, and the pressure on his throat was becoming intolerable. Then Knuckles let go, and Pete dropped to the hall floor.

"I give you a day to decide. No, I'll be a good guy. I give you till Monday. Got that?"

Pete nodded. Even that slight action made his head hurt. He swore softly as Knuckles disappeared around the corner, then struggled to his feet and began picking up his books and papers. He felt lousy. On top of that, he was now fifteen minutes late to class, and there wasn't any way he could slip into his seat unobtrusively.

Forget chem study, he told himself. *Forget the whole thing.*

For the first time in his life, Pete Heffelfinger went truant. Without a backward look, he left the building and started walking home. He stopped once at a Burger King to get something to drink, but he ended up dumping it in the trash. His throat hurt too much to swallow.

He had a lot to think about as he trudged the rest of the way home. Like how his mom and dad were going to react to the two hours of detention he was going to have to fill on account of skipping the last two classes of the day. And how the bishop of Maple Hills First Ward was going to react when he showed up on Sunday looking like he did. And whether his other grandpa, Helmut Heffelfinger, was ever going to talk to him again.

To say nothing of what he was going to tell Knuckles Price on Monday.

4

It was Pete's good fortune that Maxine had Pure Organics "Afternoon Opportunities" (as she called her sales/recruitment meetings) lined up for the next two days. It was also his good fortune that he could get a ride home with another kid who had had to stay after school. Because of that, she never found out about the truancy, and he didn't tell her.

It was a good thing. If she had known, Sunday would have been even more of a disaster than it was.

He knew the way he looked was driving her crazy, so he had taken special care getting ready that morning. He had opted for a thatched look. Instead of sporting spikes, his blow-dried hair stood out dry and brittle from the shaved area. He had put on the best-preserved twill pants he could find in Will's boxes, an old white shirt, a narrow tie, and black suspenders. His sockless feet were inside his shoes, which he had taken care to polish.

Okay, so I don't look like the bishop's son, he thought. *I do look pretty good. I mean, the requirements for blessing the sacrament are a dress shirt and a tie. As far as I'm concerned, this fills the requirement.*

The moment he walked into the kitchen, he could tell that his mother didn't agree. She didn't say so right off, however. She started out complimenting him on what he had done with his hair.

"It's not the greatest, but at least it's better than spikes," she said, giving his thatched roof a little ruffle.

"Thanks."

He poured himself a glass of milk, wondering when she was going to say the rest of what was on her mind.

"Uh . . . Pete?"

"Yeah?"

"I know you're trying to create a new image, but I think you should be wearing your suit."

He laughed. "Do you know how dumb I'd look wearing a suit when my hair looks like this?"

"I can see your point," she said with a slight smile. Then her resolve hardened. "Let's put it this way: I'm not going to go to church with you looking like that."

"Then don't go."

"That's not the solution to the problem."

"How about, you go to church, and I'll stay home?" Pete asked innocently.

"That's not it either."

"You're the one with the problem, Mom. You figure out the solution."

"I have. Go upstairs and change."

"I don't think so."

Maxine took a deep breath and tried again. "Pete, dear," she cajoled, putting her arm around his shoulder, "will you *please* go up and dress yourself appropriately, so that I can go to church feeling proud about the way you look?"

If only she hadn't said that bit about being proud of how I look, thought Pete, *I might have done it.* But she didn't want him to change for his sake. She wanted him to change for hers.

"No," he said.

"I don't know what's got into you!" she said in a tone of pure frustration.

At that moment, Ernie walked into the kitchen. "Will's ready to go, so we can leave any time," he said to Maxine.

"No we can't. Not with that Pete looking like he does. Do something, will you?"

"Maxine, there's not much we can do about his hair."

"I'm not talking about his hair."

"What then?"

"He's not wearing a suit."

"I don't see that's any big deal."

"You're not going to do anything about it, are you."

"What do suggest, that I drag him upstairs and forcibly change his clothes?"

"For starters."

"Do it yourself. I won't. Now, I'm going to church, and whoever wants to come with me is welcome."

In the end, they all went to church and spent the next three hours wishing they hadn't.

The Maple Hills First Ward building was located in Maple Grove. It was a long, low building that to the trained eye was unmistakably a Mormon church. It housed two wards of the growing Minneapolis Stake. Pete's ward habitually used the doors leading to the east half of the building, where the bishop's and clerk's offices were located.

The minute they pulled into the parking lot, Pete could tell that word of his changed appearance had spread. A group of kids stood clustered around the door—waiting for him, he was sure. He felt a flutter of anxiety, but he knew that he couldn't show it, or his mother would never let him live it down. Without waiting for the rest of his family, he got out of the car and walked toward the building.

As he approached, someone called, "Hey, outrageous!" And another, "Who did your hair?" The tone of the comments wasn't mean or negative, Pete realized with relief. He winked at his mother as she walked by, her face set grimly.

Then Drew Conzet stepped to the front of the group. Drew, whose jacket hung from his shoulders with Gentleman's Quarterly ease and whose hair was precision-cut, had a very selective circle of friends. Those who didn't belong to the circle were subject to his cutting sarcasm and verbal jabs.

He walked slowly around Pete, sneering as he did. Then

he pulled on Pete's suspenders from behind and let them go. They slapped into his back, leaving an *X* of stinging flesh. "Oh, excellent, Peetie. You've done a good job. You look even worse than before," he said. He giggled, a high-pitched, irritating sound that made Pete want to punch him in the nose.

Pete felt a hand on his arm. "Forget it," Bradley said quietly. "He's not worth it."

Pete gritted his teeth. He was shaking inside, but he knew Bradley was right. He drew a deep breath. "Thanks, buddy." He put his arm around his friend, and they walked into the church together.

Because they were scheduled to help with the sacrament, they started toward the front of the chapel. Partway up the aisle, Bradley elbowed Pete. "Oh-oh. Here comes Brother Markham, and somehow I don't think it's me he wants to talk to."

Pete nodded, noting the scowl on the face of the priests quorum leader.

"Uh, Pete. I need a word with you," Brother Markham said.

"Yeah?"

Brother Markham shoved his ubiquitous wad of gum to the side of his mouth. "You're supposed to bless the sacrament this morning, right?"

"Yeah."

"Uh . . . let's schedule for another week. I can ask someone else to substitute."

"Why?"

Brother Markham's round, brown eyes were unblinking. "Now, Pete, you know what the problem is. We can't have you up there looking like that."

"Why?"

"It would set a bad example."

Pete snorted. "Don't you think it sets a bad example when you let certain guys bless the sacrament when they've been out drinking the night before?"

"Who are you talking about?"

"I'm not going to say. But I'm going to be ticked if you tell me I can't go up there when you've let guys who have done lots worse stuff."

"I have no idea what you're talking about. But I do know it would be highly inappropriate for you to be at the sacrament table today."

"Are you saying I'm not worthy?"

"I'm saying you aren't dressed according to standards."

"I'm wearing a white shirt. I've got a tie on. What's missing?"

Markham lowered his head—and his voice—and said, "I'm not going to have an argument right here in the chapel. Go sit by your parents, and I'll talk to you later."

"Don't count on it."

Pete walked back to the bench his parents and Will occupied and sat down by his father. All through the service, he could feel the gaze of curious eyes on him. It didn't bother him that much, but he knew what it was doing to his mother. It had always been important to her that they look like a happy, successful Mormon family. The image she had worked to create had just been destroyed, and by him. Even with his father between them, he could feel the resentment, humiliation, and anger she directed toward him.

He stayed through the opening exercises. Then, without telling his parents what he was doing, he got up and left. Will found him out in the parking lot after sacrament meeting.

"Not too comfortable in there, eh?"

"Nope."

"Sorry about what happened."

Pete shrugged. "No problem."

"I think it is a problem. You have to see it from their point of view, Pete, my boy. The church is two things at once: a social organization and the repository of the ordinances of salvation."

"You've lost me already," said Pete, surprised to hear Will using such complicated language. He had had the feeling lately that there was more to Will than Will let on. Now he knew he was right.

"Listen, it's simple," Will said. "Any organization is committed to its own growth 'in perpetuity and throughout the universe.' "

When Pete didn't laugh at his attempted humor, Will explained, "That's lawyer talk. It means forever. I learned that listening to some early-morning classes on cable.

"Anyway, the best way to insure that growth is conformity to certain standards. It keeps the next generation coming up the pike, ready to take over when necessary. You are a potential danger. You might block the flow."

"Hardly. I'm not important enough for anybody to pay any attention to. They'd just step over the top of me."

"Maybe not, if there were more like you."

"What are you planning, Will?" asked Pete, suspiciously.

"Nothing. Don't let it get you down. Things aren't as bad as they seem." Then Will grinned, opened his arms wide, and, with a beatific smile, said, "Remember, God loves you and so do I."

5

The incidents at church were only the beginning of Pete's Sunday trial. He was still facing the arrival of Helmut H. Heffelfinger, his grandfather.

This H. H. H. (who had once been called "Stillwater's answer to Hubert H. Humphrey") would pull his Mercedes into the Heffelfinger driveway at exactly 1:29 and would knock on the door at precisely 1:30. He would greet his son with a handshake, brush his lips against Maxine's cheek, and give Pete a heartfelt, if fleshless, hug. He would sit in the wingback chair, the one he considered as having the most authority, and pull out his burled oak pipe. Then he would hold forth on the state of the world, America, and Minnesota, in that order. That settled, he would inquire into the well-being of his son's family. When Maxine called them to the table, he would eat his meal slowly, cutting his meat with elegant, precise motions and complimenting her at the appropriate moment. At the sounding of some inner clock, he would rise, thank Maxine for inviting him, admonish Pete to do well in school, and shake hands with his son at the door. Helmut's visits followed the same pattern every third Sunday. They might well have been choreographed.

But this Sunday was going to be different, thanks to Pete's transformation, and the whole family knew it. The uncertainty about how Helmut was going to react made all of them nervous. As soon as they arrived home from church, Will disappeared into his barn and Maxine into her kitchen, while Pete and Ernie sat in the living room, each trying to find something interesting in the Sunday paper. It wasn't working. Both of them were too edgy and anxious to concentrate.

Finally Ernie set the sports page down and walked over to one of the Pella windows that he had set in on either side of his elegant mantle. He stood there a long time, gazing at the road down which his father would drive any minute. Then he sighed heavily.

At that moment, Pete would have been willing to give up his punkdom in a flash, if it weren't for the power-struggle with his mother.

"Hey, Dad, if you don't want Grandpa to see me like this, call him and tell him not to come."

"I can't," Ernie said.

"Why not?"

"That's what he would ask. These Sunday visits are a part of his ritual. Besides, he's probably turning off of I-494 right now."

Pete looked at his watch. "Probably."

"Look, would you at least consider combing your hair flat and putting on some of your other clothes? For me?"

"He's going to see me like this sooner or later, Dad. Might as well get it over with."

"I suppose so," said Ernie, looking back out the window. "Tell me why this is so important to you."

"You wouldn't understand."

"Give me a chance. Listen, Pete, I know there's something going on inside, or you never would have put yourself through what you went through today. Or your mother and me either."

Pete shoved at the newspapers that were scattered on the floor with the toe of his shoe. "I dunno. This whole thing's crazy. It started out as one thing, and it's ended up as something else. At first, I only wanted to do something different. You know, I got tired of combing my hair the same way, and putting on the same clothes, and saying the same words. I felt like I was going to go nuts if I didn't break away from myself."

"I know that feeling."

There was a quality in Ernie's voice that drew Pete's eyes to his father's face. "You do?"

"I . . . uh, don't tell your mother, but I've almost decided to go into business with Carl."

"Great, Dad!" Pete was on his feet in an instant, shaking his father's hand and clapping him on the back. He was genuinely happy to hear the news, for he knew that in spite of his father's love for working with his hands, Ernie felt inadequate in a family of achievers.

Ernie's smile was oddly shy. "Thanks. Now this is between us, okay? I haven't figured out how to tell Maxine yet, but we're already getting cranked up. Carl has been talking to a couple who want to build a pretty big house somewhere west of us."

"Sounds great!"

"I just hope we can pull it off. There's a lot of stuff we've got to get settled before we can even start."

"You will, Dad." The pride Pete felt in his father showed itself in a cheek-stretching smile. "Guess you and I are sort of in the same place."

"Only *you* can always go back to being the way you were. Once we make the break with Anderson Builders, we're on our own. It's sink or swim."

Pete's smile faded. "Wrong, Dad. I wasn't planning on looking like this the rest of my life, but I can't go back to the way I looked before. Not now. Everybody's made it into an issue. Mom. The guys at school. My teachers."

"I don't suppose the reaction at church was any help."

"You'd think I'd killed somebody."

"It wasn't that bad," said Maxine in a studiously light voice as she entered the room. "But it was close. I've never sat through a more uncomfortable meeting."

"Why was it uncomfortable?"

"You did make us look pretty silly, Pete. You have to admit that."

"It could have been worse."

"Really? I don't see how."

"I could have thrown up in the foyer. Or started to sing during the talks. Or mouthed off in class. As it was, all I did was spoil your image."

Maxine's laugh was strained. "You did that, all right. Nobody else has a son who looks like you. Everyone was staring."

"How do you know they weren't staring at you?" asked Pete with a disarming smile. "You look real good today."

Caught between frustration and pleased surprise, Maxine was still searching for an answer when the doorbell rang. Pete's eyes flew to the clock. It was 1:30. Helmut H. Heffelfinger had arrived.

"Oh, no. I'm not ready," said Maxine. She started for the kitchen. "You answer the door and explain what's going on here. He's your father, and *that's* your son."

"Why couldn't he have had a flat tire? Or run out of gas? Better yet, somebody could have stolen that car of his," murmured Ernie disconsolately.

"No they couldn't," said Pete. "Remember, he's got one of those alarms. Half the country would know the minute someone even brushed the door handle by accident."

"It was a thought."

Pete put his hand on Ernie's arm. "Hey, Dad," he said in a conciliatory tone, "what about if I go get Will? While I'm out there, I'll try to paste down my hair and find something else to put on. Okay?"

"I'd appreciate that, son."

Pete never did comb down his hair. He had told his dad he would, and he had meant it at the time, but something happened in between that changed his plans.

"Are you sure you want to do this?" he asked Will as they started back to the main house.

"Talley ho! Into the breach!" cried Will. "Of course I'm sure. We need to stick together. There's misery in company."

"Something like that. Okay, if you're sure you want to."

They walked up onto the cedar deck Ernie had built just off the remodeled kitchen, and Pete pulled open the patio doors.

Maxine took one look at them and screamed.

Ernie and Helmut, imagining some catastrophe, rushed from the living room to the kitchen. When he saw the cause of Maxine's fright, Ernie covered his face with his hands. "Help," he moaned. Helmut, however, took action. He shoved his pipe to one corner of his mouth and demanded, "You there, what are you doing in here! Get out right now or I'll call the police."

At that, Maxine burst into hysterical giggles.

Pete bit his lip, trying to keep from laughing, but it was no good. Will's broad face dimpled into a grin, and as the laughter rose, even Ernie dropped his hands and joined in. "It's Pete, Dad," he gasped. "Pete and Will."

"What?" The pipe dangled from Helmut's open mouth as a look of astonishment crossed his face.

"Hi, Grandpa." Pete came forward to give him a hug, but Helmut stopped him with a traffic cop's gesture. "What's the meaning of this!"

"It's my new image. Will helped me out in the wardrobe department."

"Hi, Grandpa," said Will.

When he also tried to give Helmut a hug, Helmut said, "Get away from me." Then he turned to Ernie. "Ernest, I demand an explanation. What is going on here?"

"I'd tell you if I knew, believe me," Ernie said. "Thanks a lot, Pete."

"Sorry, Dad. He looked like this when I went out to get him, so there didn't seem to be much point in toning my own hair down."

"This is great. Instead of one punk, I've got two."

Will's gray hair, thin as it was, was pasted up into a row of spikes. It was an odd shade of green. He was wearing an old T-shirt and an ancient pair of pants that had a hole in one knee.

"Ernie, explain!" demanded Helmut again.

"Life was getting boring, Dad. Pete and Will decided to liven it up a bit."

"I don't find this amusing."

"Neither do I," said Maxine. "The whole day's been a disaster."

"Well, as long as it's ruined anyway, I might as well make my announcement," said Ernie.

Pete knew immediately what was coming. He held his breath as Ernie continued.

"I was going to tell everybody later on, after I'd talked it over with you, Maxine, but now's as good a time as any. I'm going to quit working for Anderson Builders. I'm going into business with Carl Gregory. Heffelfinger and Gregory, Fine Homes."

"Go for it, Dad," Pete murmured.

"Bravo!" Will added. "And don't let that woman, whoever she is, talk you out of it."

At that, Maxine burst into tears.

It was Helmut who restored order. Putting his pipe in the pocket of his suitcoat, he asked Maxine if she required assistance in getting the food to the table. When she stared at him without comprehension, he said calmly, "After all, it is Sunday, and dinner is one of the reasons I drove all the way from Stillwater. And may I suggest that we avoid any topic that might create a renewal of hysteria during that time?"

His words worked magic. Maxine wiped her tears away and handed Helmut the dish of lasagna, Will the plate of garlic toast, Pete the salad bowl, and Ernie the pitcher of water. Sunday dinner progressed as usual.

At the conclusion of the meal, Helmut did not leave immediately, as was his custom. Instead, he called them all to join him in the living room, where he sat down in the wingback chair. Then he looked at Pete.

Here it comes, Pete thought, but Helmet had something else in mind.

"I will assume for the moment that this ridiculousness is just a passing phase," he said. "The issue I want to discuss is that of Ernie's proposed building company. Tell me about it, Ernie. In detail."

Ernie repeated everything he had told Pete, but in a more complete fashion. At the conclusion of his recital, Helmut said, "I believe that it could be a good move for you, son. I've always been of the opinion that you were wasting a good deal of talent pounding boards together."

"I do a lot more than that."

"And I've been told by someone in real estate that high-ticket homes are an especially good market."

"That's the clientele we're hoping to woo," said Ernie, warming to his subject again. "We want to do strictly custom stuff, starting at a quarter of a million."

"What is your opinion, Maxine?" asked Helmut.

"I don't know," she said in a subdued voice. "It sounds good, but . . . Too much is happening right now. First, there's Will. Then Pete goes off the deep end, and now you, Ernie. I can't give an opinion. I have to have more time to think."

Long after Helmut had left (having forgone his assessment of the world, America, and Minnesota), and long after Will had been sent to his barn and he himself to his room, Pete lay awake. He could hear muffled snatches of the conversation going on in his parents' bedroom, but he couldn't tell what was being said, and he couldn't guess, either.

He didn't understand his parents any more than they understood him. They were so different from each other that sometimes he wondered what had brought them together in the first place. His mother, who needed everything to be just right, had often accused his father of not caring where he lived or what he wore. Those things simply weren't important to him.

They did have some things in common, however. They shared a commitment to the Church, though Pete guessed that their ideas about what that commitment entailed were quite different. They also liked working in the garden, going for walks, and eating out. Those things made their differences seem less important, especially if things looked okay on the surface—which meant, if things were done Maxine's way. But now he, his father, and Will all seemed set on doing their own thing. No wonder she was getting strung out.

Everything's a mess, he thought. Had been a mess ever since his grandfather's accident and the move to Plymouth Road. Not that life had been idyllic in their old house on a shady street in South Minneapolis, but at least there he had felt comfortable. Being ordinary wasn't out of the ordinary in his old school. He had moved easily among the racially mixed, lower-middle-class student body.

Then Will had appeared, they had moved, and Pete had been dropped into the predominantly white, middle-class Wayzata North. It was like taking a bath in homogenized milk. No, considering that most of the student body came from the burgeoning developments of "executive homes" in Plymouth, it was more like drowning in cream.

He sighed, wondering what was going to happen next. Even as he wondered, he remembered that the next day was Monday, and that Knuckles Price would be waiting for him. His eyes, which had been drifting shut, popped wide open. It was all too easy to imagine what might happen next, and none of the possibilities were pleasant.

6

The next morning Pete came downstairs to the smell of pancakes cooking. Maxine, who had stopped fixing breakfast the day she began eating fruit until noon, was standing over the stove.

"What's the occasion?" he asked.

"Nothing special. It's been a long time since I fixed you a hot breakfast and I thought . . . "

"That's nice. Thanks," he said, giving her a quick hug.

"Sit down, and I'll bring your plate. Ernie! The pancakes are ready."

Pete sat down, and Maxine put his food before him. Hot breakfast! It was enough to make him wonder what was going on.

"Go ahead," she said. "Your dad's probably still in the shower."

He started eating, stopping only to mumble, "Good pancakes." Maxine fixed Ernie's plate and poured juice for all of them. Then she sat down at the table.

"You know, Pete, I don't want this punk business to come between us. It's just . . . " She shook her head. "I don't understand. I admit it. I don't understand any of you."

"Guess Dad's announcement threw you for a loop, didn't it."

"It's only that it was so unexpected. He hadn't said a word to me about it until that very moment. Did he ever say anything to you?"

"Hmm," Pete mumbled.

"I think it would be a great thing for your father," she said slowly. "It's just that change is hard for me to deal with."

Unless you're the one making the changes, Pete added to himself. But he knew his mother was trying to be understanding, if not sympathetic. The pancakes were proof of that. He finished up the last of them and gulped down his milk. "Thanks for the breakfast," he said, giving her a peck on the cheek before heading out.

"Have a good day," Maxine called after him.

He slung his book bag over his shoulder and hurried down the drive. He got to the end of the drive just as Bradley pulled up.

"I wasn't sure you'd be coming this morning," he said, climbing in.

"Why? I always pick you up for seminary."

"I thought, after the way your mom reacted at church, she'd forbid you to be seen with me."

"*Au contraire,*" replied Bradley. "She told me I needed to find out what's going on with you and try to get you back on track."

"That's just wonderful. I can see it now. I'll be the goal for the month in priests quorum: Rehabilitate Peter Heffelfinger." Pete sighed and looked out the window, feeling as bleak as the gray September morning.

"Is this what you figured would happen when you dyed your hair?"

"No," said Pete, thinking about Knuckles Price and the unavoidable confrontation that awaited him.

He managed to avoid Knuckles until the beginning of his lunch period. Then, on his way to the cafeteria, he turned a corner, and there Knuckles stood. Pete felt his insides clutch, but he tried to remain cool. It was not easy, considering the fact that Knuckles, who was leaning up against the wall, looked like a villain in a bad 1950s gang movie.

"Well, well, well," said Knuckles. "I heard you were still playing punk."

He's getting his lines from a bad movie too, Pete thought. He ignored Knuckles and took a step toward the cafeteria door. Knuckles blocked his way.

"We have some business, Heffelfinger. Or did you forget?"

"No."

"That's good. Come on, then."

"Where?"

"To the parking lot."

"I don't want to go to the parking lot. I want to eat."

"There are a lot more interesting things to do than eat," Knuckles said, his voice heavy with meaning.

"Yeah, I can just imagine. I don't go in for that stuff, okay?"

"What'sa matter? You chicken?" Knuckles pulled a lip balm tube from his pocket and waved it slowly back and forth in front of Pete.

"No, I'm not chicken," said Pete, guessing that the lip balm had been replaced with a different substance. "I'm hungry."

Knuckles shrugged and put the container away. "So eat in the parking lot. That's where I go."

"Maybe tomorrow," said Pete, hoping to avoid trouble. "I didn't bring my lunch."

He started toward the cafeteria, but Knuckles's grip on his collar brought him up short. "Just where do you think you're going?" he hissed into Pete's face.

Pete's insides turned to water, but he tried to pull away. "Let loose!"

"Try and make me." Knuckles pushed him into the wall, a malicious grin on his face.

"Let go of him, jerk!"

The voice—which was female—brought both their heads around at the same time. There stood a wisp of a girl with wild platinum hair, red lips, and kohl-smudged eyes, dressed all in black.

"Butt out, Ren," growled Knuckles.

"Let go of him. Right now."

"Why should I?"

"Because I can make a bigger scene than you can, Price. Do you want to spend the rest of your life in in-school suspension?"

Knuckles grinned.

"Let *go* of him!" she shrieked. The din from the cafeteria dropped abruptly. When Knuckles still made no move, she kicked him in the shins.

"Owww!" Shouting a string of vile epithets, Knuckles let go of Pete and grabbed his leg, hopping around on one foot.

Pete, totally surprised by this turn of events, burst out laughing at the sight. Then the girl grabbed him by the arm. "Come on, stupid. Let's get out of here!" she commanded, dragging him down the hall to the stares of other students.

"Where're we going?"

"How dense can you get? Anywhere Price isn't."

She was practically running, but she hadn't let go of his sleeve. Pete shuffled beside her, feeling silly. He was relieved when she turned into a short, dead-end hall unused except as a locker bank.

"Thanks, uh . . . What's your name?" he asked.

"Ren."

"Ren? That's odd."

"Yeah? Well, my parents are odd. They were going to have me at home, but they chickened out. It was too late by the time they started for the hospital, and I was born in the car two blocks from the emergency entrance. They happened to be driving a Renault, so that's what they named me: Renault Dykstra. I'm just lucky they weren't driving a Ford."

Pete grinned. "Ren Dykstra. It doesn't sound too bad. I'm Pete Heffelfinger."

"I know," she said, rolling her eyes. She opened her black bag and rummaged in it, finally drawing out a pack of cigarettes. She pulled one out with her lips, then held the pack out to him.

He shook his head. "You're not supposed to smoke in the hall," he said.

"That's why I do it." She lit the cigarette and dragged on it once, awkwardly and without enjoyment. "I want the jerks in this dump to remember I'm here, so I give them reasons to remember," she said. Then she dropped the cigarette on the floor and ground it out with the toe of her boot. "It drives them nuts when they find these. They know I'm the one who does it, but they've never caught me at it."

"Oh." Pete was astonished at such open contempt for authority. He shuffled uncomfortably. Finally he said, "Thanks for rescuing me, but I didn't need it."

"Really? You would have let Price walk all over you."

"Maybe."

"He was giving you all that garbage about being The Grand High Pooba of Punks, wasn't he?"

"He's not?"

She gave an exasperated sigh. "Shows what you know about it. In the first place, there aren't any real punks in this school, Heffelfinger, only kids who dress like they are. In the second place, the only reason some of us hang out together is because the rest of you stiffs are too goody-goody to have anything to do with us. Nobody tells us what to do, especially not Knuckles Price. He's nuts."

Pete leaned against the wall and stared up at the ceiling, wondering where he got his ability to make a fool of himself. Now, on top of everything else, half the school had seen a girl who barely weighed a hundred pounds do his fighting for him. Being invisible wasn't half-bad when you considered the alternatives.

"What's the matter now?" Ren asked, resting her hand with its flaming nails on her hip.

"You said it. I'm not a punk. I'm a nothing. Only now I'll be the most laughed at nothing in the whole school. Everybody's going to hear about it."

"So?"

"I think I'll jump off a bridge."

"You're not that desperate. Not yet."

"How do you know?"

Before she could answer, the bell rang. She grabbed her bag and slung it over her shoulder. "What are you doing after school?"

"Nothing. Going home."

"Meet me at the west doors. I'll drive you." Without waiting for a reply, she started running down the hall.

As he went to his next class, stomach growling for lack of lunch, Pete wondered if she always ran.

She did.

After school, he met her by the west doors, then followed her out into the parking lot. She moved half-bent over with her head stretched out in front, arms and feet moving double-time. Yet she didn't go as fast as the effort would seem to indicate. She was like a Yorkshire terrier, facing the world on prancing feet, her clenched teeth belligerently showing.

He almost ran into her when she stopped in front of a black 1987 Fiero.

"This is your car?" he asked.

"No. I'm breaking in someone else's," she said, shaking her head as if he were a lost cause. "Of course it's my car. Get in."

She backed out of her slot and pulled up to the stop sign. "Rockford Road, did you say?"

"Yeah. How did you get a car like this anyway? Did your parents buy it for you?"

"No. It belonged to my brother, Chris. They wanted to sell it or give it away after he OD'd, but I took it."

He stared at her, unsure if he had heard right. "He . . . "

"OD'd. You can say it, Heffelfinger. It's not a dirty word."

"I'm sorry," he said awkwardly.

"He wasn't."

"He did it on purpose?"

"Uh-huh."

"Are you sure? Couldn't it have been an accident?"

She looked into his questioning eyes for a moment before

turning back to the road. "No. He left a note, but I would have known anyway. I can tell things about people. It's a gift—it's in my stars."

Pete snorted. "How do you know it's not just in your head?"

"It *is* in my head," she said, beaming at him as if he had said something brilliant. "That's where everything is, don't you know that yet? You carry your own reality around with you."

"This is weird."

"Yeah? Why do you think I picked up on you? Because you're such a hunk?" Her amused expression indicated otherwise, and Pete felt his face burning.

"Why did you?"

"Because you seemed like a nice guy. There aren't many of those around. At least not that I've met. I was working up the courage to introduce myself, but before I had a chance to, you turned punk, and Price tried out his act on you. It's a good thing I saw you and Price in the hall today, Heffelfinger. You definitely need my help."

He needed help, all right, but he wasn't sure he needed the kind Ren Dykstra offered. If anything, Knuckles Price would be even more determined to get him now, and Pete knew that he could do real damage if he had the opportunity.

But to tell the truth, he was flattered by her attention, even though she was an odd girl. With her platinum hair, scarlet lipstick, and black clothes, she looked bloodless, as if she were cast as the victim in a vampire show. Yet there was something magnetic about her. It was her eyes, he decided. Eyes that were passionate, electric, Van Gogh blue.

7

"You're not listening, Pete!"

The sound of Maxine's voice brought him back to the present. "Oh, sorry. What were you saying?"

"I was trying to tell you what your father and I have decided about Heffelfinger and Gregory, Fine Homes."

"I'm with you now. What's the deal?"

But the minute Maxine began speaking, he was off in his own world again, one that had been immeasurably complicated by Knuckles Price and Ren Dykstra. He had spent the last two days trying to avoid Knuckles and at the same time trying to arrange casual encounters with Ren. He had been successful in the latter, but unsuccessful in the former. That worried him.

Ren had seemed to think it was no big deal. "Don't waste your time worrying about Price," she had said. "He won't hurt you, at least not permanently."

That assessment hadn't been exactly thrilling, but he was beginning to think she was right. In the last week, Knuckles had seemed more committed to general harassment than all-out confrontation. He never passed Pete without spewing some vile threat his way, pushing him, or elbowing him. It wasn't serious, but after days of it, Pete was in a state of constant tension. Whenever he walked down the hall his stomach was in a knot, and he had developed the nervous habit of clenching his teeth.

With all this on his mind, it was no wonder he was having a hard time paying close attention to what his mom and dad were saying. Maxine had been won over to the idea, he got that much. Then there was something complicated about investing some of his Grandfather Martin's money in Heffelfinger and Gregory. During the time he lay in a coma, legal steps had been taken to make Maxine her father's guardian and the custodian of his estate. The arrangement had been necessary at the time, and it had continued after Will appeared.

"Will was upset when I told him," Ernie was saying to Maxine. "He thinks he should have been consulted, and I agree."

"Maybe. It didn't even occur to me. I make decisions involving money all the time without asking him. He does think it's a good idea, doesn't he?"

"He's all for it. Only he would have appreciated being told what was going on beforehand instead of after the fact."

Maxine shrugged off the criticism, then asked Pete, "What do you think of the changes we'll be making?"

"Sounds good to me. Listen, I've got a lot of homework to do, and I want to get at it. May I be excused?"

"Don't you want to hear—"

But Pete was already halfway up the stairs. He knew he was being rude, but his own problems seemed so compelling that he couldn't sit still any longer. Once in his room, he turned on his stereo. The pulsing rhythms helped drive all thoughts from his head, and although he had been sure he wouldn't sleep, he did.

He slept fitfully, however, and when he woke up the next morning, his head aching and his jaws sore, he decided that he had two choices: He could either go running to Springer or challenge Knuckles and get it over with.

Springer will tell me to fight my own battles, he thought. *I don't have any choice.*

He was jumpy and distracted when he came down that morning. Maxine, who had continued to fix him a hot breakfast, had already set the table and poured his juice.

"Thanks, Mom, but I'm not hungry, he said, starting for the door.

"You're not sick, are you?"

"I'm okay. I'm just not in the mood for oatmeal."

"Are you sure? You look pale to me."

"I'm okay, all right?"

Bradley also picked up on his nervousness, noting how he kept wiping his sweaty palms on his jeans. "What's the matter with you?" he asked.

"Nothing you can help me with."

Bradley was silent for a while, keeping his eyes on the road. Then he said, "Listen, if there's anything I can do . . . "

"Thanks. I've got to do this on my own."

"You're going to take on Price, aren't you."

"You got it," Pete said with a conviction he didn't feel. Although he had decided to stand up for himself, he was hoping with all his heart that he wouldn't have to. At 5'11" and 150 pounds, he felt like a gnat compared to Knuckles, who had to be 6'2" and at least 230 pounds. Not only that, Pete had never been aggressive. The only fight he had ever been in was in fourth grade, and he hadn't started it. Knuckles was always looking for a fight. More often than not, he found one. There wasn't any doubt how it was going to turn out.

But by the time Pete saw Knuckles coming toward him between first and second hour, he didn't care. All he wanted to do was get it over with.

"Here comes the baby," Knuckles sneered. "Poor Heffelfinger has to have a girl protect him."

Pete's heart was hammering and his mouth was dry, but the time had come. "Oh yeah?" he said. "I can stand up for myself. If you're not too big a chicken to take me on."

"I could wipe up the floor with you."

Pete dropped his books and assumed what he hoped was a menacing stance. "Just try."

The punker's lips curled menacingly. He dropped his own books and began sidling to his left, his hands half-cocked. "Hey, we got a fight here!" someone yelled. The flow of students stopped, and several formed a circle around Pete and his adversary.

Pete's hands were shaking and his knees jelly as they parried. For a few seconds, nothing seemed to be happening. Then Knuckles jabbed at him. Pete flinched and put his hands over his head.

The blow never fell. Knuckles let out a high-pitched giggle. "Not very tough, are you!" he smirked. He loosed a string of short jabs, shuffling his booted feet as he did so. Pete heard a titter start among the onlookers. It grew into laughter. They were laughing at him! Fury sent its messages through his body, and his fist connected with Knuckles's stomach with a thwack. Heady feelings flooded through him. He had landed the first blow! And the onlookers were now cheering for him.

He smiled, acknowledging the applause, and dropped his fists. The smile was still on his face when Knuckles drove his fist onto Pete's nose. Pain exploded behind his eyes. The world turned red, and then it disappeared.

When he came to, Pete was lying on the nurse's couch. His head was tipped back, and a cold compress covered his nose.

"Take it easy, Pete," said the nurse, bending over him. "You've got a broken nose."

Pete tried to say something, but the sound that came out was blurred and thick.

"You've got a right angle where you shouldn't have one. You're going to have to see your doctor. Do you think your mom will be home?"

He nodded. Even that almost imperceptible movement was excruciating. He tried to give the nurse the phone number, but the sound was heavy, and he had to push it out of his mouth.

"That's all right. I can look it up."

He lay there, unable to move, listening to her punch in the number. He closed his eyes, wishing he had asked the nurse to call Ernie instead. Except he hadn't wanted to disturb his father, who, along with Carl, was meeting Heffelfinger and Gregory's first clients at a fancy restaurant.

Ten minutes later, Maxine arrived. She gasped when she saw how he looked. Then she grew indignant. And then downright furious.

"What happened?" she cried.

He couldn't talk fast enough to tell her, and the nurse's explanation was insufficient to satisfy her.

"I want to talk to the principal," she said to the nurse.

"Mr. Springer is the vice-principal in charge of discipline. I can tell him you'd like him to call."

"I don't want him to call. I want to talk to him right now."

"But Pete needs to get his nose straightened—"

"Now."

Pete struggled to an upright position. He felt as if he had no body. He was aware only of his head, which seemed as wide as the room and was pulsing painfully as if it were its own heart.

"Please, Mom . . . "

But the nurse was already paging Mr. Springer.

Mr. Springer was a short, wiry man in his thirties. When he had first come to the school, some of the kids thought he was a joke. But he had the strength and strategy of a street fighter, which he freely admitted to having been at one time in his life.

"Heffelfinger," he said when he came into the nurse's office. "The other half of the bruhaha. You look like—" Seeing Maxine, he stopped before finishing the sentence and started over. "You look terrible. Mrs. Heffelfinger? I'm Al Springer."

"Are you in charge of discipline?"

"Yes, I am."

"Then I want to know what you're going to do about this."

"I'm taking care of it. Mr. Price is already in my office—"

"That boy is a danger. He should be locked up!"

"I doubt if it will go that far, but in a case like this, we do call in the police, and Price will get suspended for a few days while we decide what to do with him."

"As far as I'm concerned, he should be expelled."

"That's also a possibility. A lot depends on what the administration decides, and that depends on what Price is willing to do. But he isn't the only one who'll get disciplined. Pete here will be spending some time in detention."

"And why is that?"

"I hear he hit Price first."

"Pete, is that true?"

"He's . . . been after . . . me . . . all week."

Mr. Springer nodded. "That's what Ren Dykstra told me. Rather vehemently."

"Who is this Ren?" asked Maxine.

"A rather unusual young lady, one who likes playing cat and mouse with me. But I'm inclined to believe her. Price has a history as a troublemaker."

Pete closed his eyes. The embarrassment, added to his pain, was making him sick.

"Now, I'll take care of things here, Mrs. Heffelfinger," Mr. Springer said soothingly. "Why don't you take care of your son."

Maxine took Pete to their doctor, who pushed his nose back into alignment, then home, where she settled him on the family-room couch with an ice pack. During all that time, she was protective and solicitous, but when she was certain he was going to be all right, she started in on him.

Pete only half listened. Once he got the jist of it (which was that none of this would have happened if he hadn't dyed his hair red), he tuned out. Besides, she really didn't expect or want any comments from him. Finally she ran down and, with a sigh, disappeared into the kitchen.

When Pete heard a car pulling into the driveway two hours later, he knew that it was Ren's black Fiero.

Ren and Maxine. The thought would have been enough to give him a headache if he hadn't already had one. He held his breath when his mother answered the door. The voice he heard had a distinctive huskiness that confirmed his suspicion. "Hi, I'm Ren. I've come to see Heffelfinger."

"You mean Pete?"

"Yeah. I heard he was dumb enough to take on Price and ended up with a broken nose. Can I come in?"

After a moment's hesitation, Maxine said, "Yes. I suppose so."

The last thing Pete wanted was for Ren to see him flat on his back with an ice pack on his face. He took it off and tried to sit up, but the pressure behind his cheekbones and nose was like a dagger. Color seemed to fade and spots danced in front of his eyes. With a groan, he lay back down. He heard her voice before he saw her, because it was too painful to move his head, and he wasn't even sure he could look out of the corner of his eyes without it hurting.

"Heffelfinger, you doorknob, you look terrible," Ren said, leaning over him and adding a word that made Maxine flinch.

"We don't use that kind of language in our home," Maxine said. "I'll have to insist that you refrain from swearing or using the Lord's name in vain around us."

"That's cool," Ren responded.

But Pete wasn't paying any attention to their exchange. He was too absorbed in Ren. Her voice held a mocking tone, but she smiled as she spoke, and her eyes were full of amusement—and something else that made his cheeks burn.

She likes me, he thought, full of wild, unreasonable joy. *She really likes me.*

"How did this happen?" she asked, touching his cheek tentatively.

"Knuckles . . . kept pushing me . . . so I decided to teach him . . . a lesson."

Ren's eyes gleamed. "You idiot," she said, but it seemed to Pete that she was pleased.

"Thanks for telling Springer."

"Somebody had to. It's about time they gave Price the boot."

"They suspended him?"

"Three days. He'll hate you for that, but to tell the truth, he really doesn't care whether he's in school or not."

"Great."

"It'll blow over."

"That's what you said last time."

"It will 'blow over' when Pete stops this foolishness," said Maxine, who had been standing silently by. "Nothing like this ever happened until he decided to go punk."

"It's not that easy, Mom."

"I don't suppose your parents approve of how you look," Maxine said to Ren, coming across the room to straighten the drapes.

Ren sat down on the arm of the couch and leaned against the back. The warmth of her body washed over Pete, making him uncomfortably aware of her nearness, but she didn't seem to notice. "Hardly," she replied to Maxine's comment. "They hate it."

"Then why don't you dress normally? You really could be a striking young woman."

Ren shrugged. "What's the point? The world's full of striking young women. They fit the mold. I don't."

"Maybe that's because you don't want to."

"Bingo. Well, Heffelfinger," Ren said, looking down at him, "what do you want to do? Watch TV? Listen to tapes? Or just lie there and watch me work on my report?"

"Whatever . . . "

Ren pulled a chair up by the side of the couch, sat down, and opened up her book bag. "I hate American History, but this report's kind of fun. It's on the hippies." Her eyes narrowed as she considered Maxine. "I don't suppose you were a flower child."

"Heavens, no! I was too busy doing what I was supposed to do. I didn't have time to rebel, even if I had wanted to. Which I didn't."

"Saving it up for the mid-life crisis, are you?"

Pete's groan caught Maxine before she had a chance to react to Ren's question. Assuming it was a groan of pain, she asked, "Do you need more aspirin? It's getting pretty close to time."

Pete shook his head, and instantly regretted it. "I'll just lie here . . . and watch Ren do her thing."

"Maybe Ren should go—"

"No."

"I won't bother him, Mrs. Heffelfinger. I'll just work on my report for a while." She looked at her watch. "I can only stay until five-thirty anyway. Sally has a fit if I'm late for supper."

"Sally?" questioned Maxine.

"Our cook. Mom never has been crazy about cooking, so when she got her new job, the first thing she did was hire Sally."

"What does your mother do?"

"She's vice-president of a company that specializes in out-placement services."

"Huh?" grunted Pete, for whom the phrase made no sense.

"Out-placement services. It's a nice way of saying they help people who've been fired to get back on their feet. You know, give them tests to pinpoint strengths and weaknesses, management styles, and learning modes, that sort of thing. And they help with resumes, interview techniques, and junk like that."

"How about your father?"

"He's got one of those time-sharing vacation condo companies. He's always dragging Mom off to some exotic place to check out a resort."

"It sounds like your parents are doing very well for themselves."

"If money is the criteria."

Maxine seemed surprised by the abruptness of Ren's reply. She hesitated for a moment, then said, "Well, I'd better get going on supper myself. If you need anything, Pete, just moan."

After Maxine was gone, Ren laid her hand on Pete's forehead. "Relax, Heffelfinger. If you don't, your mom will throw me out."

Pete took a deep breath and let it out slowly.

"That's right. Sleep if you want to. I won't mind."

Then she hunched over her book, flipping pages with typical intensity, wielding pencil against paper when she found something pertinent. After watching her for a while, he closed his eyes. As he drifted in and out of sleep, he could feel her presence close by, oddly comforting. Once, he felt the soft touch of her hand against his cheek.

And once, before sleep pulled him below the surface of awareness, he thought she kissed him.

8

On Friday Pete stayed home, so Maxine set him up on the family room couch again. She put juice and crackers on the end table next to him, in the hope that he would eat something. She put the remote control within arm's reach. "Is there anything else I can get you before I go?" she asked.

He could tell she was enjoying the chance to baby him now that she was over her initial shock and anger. It seemed to be easier for her to express affection when he was sick or hurt than at other times. The food she brought him, the comforter she tucked around him with murmurs of sympathy, and her gentle touch were her way of saying she loved him.

It was also easier for Pete to accept her affection under those circumstances. He reached up to give her a hug when she plumped the pillow behind him. "Thanks, Mom," he said, at the same time thinking how sad it was that it took a broken nose to give them a chance to show their most tender feelings.

The last thing she did before leaving for her day of multilevel machinations was to call Will and ask him to keep Pete company.

"Now, don't let Pete go anywhere or do anything. He's supposed to stay right on that couch," she instructed Will.

"You don't need to worry about that. I'm not going to move," said Pete. His head still hurt whenever he changed positions, and his eyes, surrounded by puffy flesh in shades ranging from blue to purple, were swollen almost shut.

So it was Will who answered the door when Ren stopped by after school. Always blunt, she asked right out, "Have you really lost your memory?"

Will nodded, adding, "But not my mind."

On Saturday, Pete stayed home from a scouting activity.

On Sunday, he stayed home from church.

On Monday, he slept in, missing seminary. He wanted to stay home from school as well, but Maxine wouldn't hear of it. "You're doing much better," she said firmly.

He couldn't argue with her. The discoloration had turned from black and blue to mustard and yellow-green, and the pain had withdrawn from his whole head to a point below the bridge of his nose.

"Okay, but I'm not riding the bus. I don't want to have to deal with any garbage."

"You'll have to ride the bus, because I can't drive you this morning. I've got a meeting in Duluth, and I won't make it on time if I don't leave right now."

"Then I'll ask Ren to take me."

Maxine looked doubtful, but there was no other alternative, since Ernie had left more than an hour earlier for a breakfast meeting with Carl Gregory.

It was the first time he had called her; it was, in fact, the first time he had ever called any girl. He was sixteen-and-a-half and had never called a girl, never gone on a date, and never been kissed. He couldn't count the kiss Ren had given him Thursday night as he lay on the couch, because afterward he wasn't even sure whether it had really happened or he had dreamed it.

Sally answered the Dykstra phone. Pete could hear her calling; then Ren was on the line.

"What's up?" she asked.

"I'm going back to school today. I just wondered if I could hitch a ride with you." He felt foolish even as he said the words, for Ren's house was west of the school building, his northeast. She didn't seem to think it was an unreasonable request, however. "I'll be there at ten to seven," she said before hanging up.

So he rode to school in the Fiero, thankful for the support and comfort of Ren's sideline glances and wry grins.

"Hang in there, Heffelfinger," she said. "It's only your life."

But it wasn't as bad as he had thought it would be. He actually got some grudging approval from other students, who acknowledged his guts, if questioning his sanity. Of his teachers, at least Ann Johnson was sympathetic. "Becoming can be a rather painful process, can't it?" she joked gently.

"I'm surviving," he answered. "At least, so far."

During lunch period, Ren shepherded him over to one of the cafeteria tables staked out by punkers. Pete found to his surprise that they weren't such a bad bunch, if you ignored their appearance and their colorful, crude language. That wasn't easy to do until it occurred to him how Will would react to them: "I'm a person, you're a person. Call me Will." It seemed to him that the old man knew something about getting along that most other people didn't know, or didn't want to know.

On Tuesday, Mr. Springer told him that Knuckles had decided to drop out of school and work with a special program designed to help troubled students get their GED, the equivalent of a high school diploma. Pete closed his eyes with relief. He hadn't wanted to admit even to himself how worried he had been about a possible rematch with Knuckles.

Then, on Wednesday, as they were eating lunch, Ren suggested they go to the *Rocky Horror Picture Show* together.

"You mean, like on a date?"

"If you want to call it that."

Pete flushed and tried to cover his confusion by taking a drink of his soda.

"Or don't call it a date. No big deal."

Still Pete floundered, not knowing what to say. His hesitation had nothing to do with the way he felt about her, or about the fact that she had asked him instead of the other way around. What held him back was knowing how his mother would react to the idea. In the first place, she didn't approve of Ren's looks or attitude. In the second, Ren was not a Mormon. "Never Date Nonmembers." He didn't know how many times he had heard that line. He himself thought it reflected a large dose of prejudice, but Maxine always went by the book. She had already asked him about Ren's church affiliation, and he had had to tell her what Ren told him: "I don't go to any church, but that doesn't mean I'm a nonbeliever."

"Don't fall all over yourself with enthusiasm, Heffelfinger," Ren said dryly, interrupting his thoughts.

"I do want to go," he said, making up his mind. "Which Rocky was it?"

"Not Rocky as in Sylvester Stallone. Rocky as in *Rocky Horror Picture Show*. It's a musical. It's a lot of fun, like nothing you've ever been to before. I can't explain it. You'll just have to see for yourself."

"Fine. Good. Let's do it."

"It starts late. Maybe we could mess around first."

"How late is late?"

"Midnight."

"Oh . . . Okay."

Another thing Maxine would object to. Well, maybe he could win her over on that point, too. "Where's it playing?"

"The Uptown."

Now Pete didn't even try to hide his distress. Hennepin Avenue meant only one thing to his parents—sleaze. They had formed this opinion on the basis of the footage they had seen on TV and the one short stretch they had driven down. It had been reinforced by what Will had to tell after he innocently wandered into an adult bookstore on one of his downtown forays. Hennepin Avenue was the first stop on the road to hell.

Pete started to explain to Ren how his parents would feel, but she interrupted.

"The Uptown isn't on the part of Hennepin Avenue they're thinking about," she said. "It's close to the corner of Hennepin and Lake, not far from Calhoun Square. There's a lot of renovated buildings in the area. There's even a McDonald's. And Atelier Lack."

"What's that?"

"Richard Lack's art school. He teaches art the way the old masters did. It's called the New Realism. I want to go there after I graduate if I'm good enough to get in. Anyway, you can tell your folks that the Uptown is in a respectable area."

"Doesn't matter. Hennepin Avenue is Hennepin Avenue to them."

"If it will make them feel better, tell them that everybody who goes into the theater is searched for alcohol."

"That's supposed to make them feel better? Ren, I don't think this will work. Besides, what's so big about *Rocky Horror Picture Show?*"

"It's fun. It's sort of a cult thing. Some guys I know have seen it dozens of times. Tell your folks it's Participatory Theater."

"What's that supposed to mean?"

"You bring props along: rice, toast, playing cards, TP, newspaper, a squirt gun. Ask your folks. It won't hurt to ask, will it?"

"I guess not."

"If you don't want to ask, sneak out."

Pete held his breath. He had never done anything behind his parents' backs before, and his recent experiences had taught him how hard it was to turn back once you have started something.

"Well?"

"No. I can't do that. I've never sneaked out before, and I don't want to start now."

She fiddled with her lunch sack for a moment, then said, "You really do like your folks, don't you."

"Yeah. They tick me off sometimes, but they're all right."

"I wish . . . "

"What?"

Ren dismissed her wistful comment with a wave of her hand. "Nothing."

"I'd like to go. I'll ask my folks, okay?"

* * * * *

Pete was right in his assessment of what his mother's reaction would be when he asked her. She hit every point he thought she would.

"Why not let him go, if he wants to," Ernie said. "It's his first date."

"All the more reason why he shouldn't. I don't want him starting out doing something questionable."

"Maxine, listen. If they just go to the show and come right back, it won't be too bad."

"The whole idea is bad."

"Mom, why is it the minute I want to do something that doesn't quite fit your image of a good little Mormon boy, you think I'm going to jump off the deep end? Why can't you trust me?"

"I did—until you turned into a punk."

"I didn't turn into a punk!" Pete yelled. Frustration was building inside him like an electrical storm, but he knew he had to keep his cool, or there would be no chance of getting permission. In a calmer voice he added, "I just changed the way I look."

"And got your nose broken. And took up with that Ren person. You should see her, Ernie. She has bleached hair and make-up caked as thick as Tammy Bakker's, and she smells like smoke—"

"She doesn't really smoke, she—"

"And she's impertinent."

"Don't put her down, Mom," pleaded Pete. "She's the nicest girl I know."

"How can you say that, with all the nice girls in our ward?"

"Easy. She's the only girl I know who cares if I'm dead or alive."

"I'm sure there are lots of girls who would like getting to know you."

"Only because you're my mother."

"I think your mother's right, son," commented Ernie.

"Only because you're my father."

"This isn't getting us anywhere," said Maxine, shaking her

head. "We're not going to solve this before supper, so you might as well go get your grandfather."

The minute Will opened the door, he picked up on Pete's sour expression. One question was all he needed to ask, and Pete told him the whole story. Will perked up at the mention of the show, Hennepin Avenue, and the props Ren had indicated as mandatory.

"I'd like to go," he said.

"What?"

"I would like to go. Take me with you."

"Not this time, Will."

"Why not?"

"It's a date. Nobody takes their grandfather along on a date."

Will set his jaw. "I'm not your grandfather. And anyway, Ren would. She likes me."

"Just because she likes you doesn't mean she wants to have you peering over our shoulders."

"You ask her. I'll bet she says yes."

"That won't make any difference, if Mom says no. And you going along won't change her mind. She doesn't think of you as an adult, so you don't qualify as a chaperon."

"Maybe not, but with two against one, the odds are better."

As Pete considered Will's suggestion, the tingling, aggravating points of energy began to dissipate, and in their place, an impudent delight began to grow. "You may be right."

"Call Ren. Ask her," instructed Will.

"Now?"

"Yes, now."

Ren's response was, "Cool."

"You're sure?"

"Why not?"

Pete hung up the phone and grinned at Will. "It's a go!" he said, giving Will a high five. "Let's tell Mom."

Maxine's eyebrows lifted with surprise as she listened to Will and Pete's proposal. "Having Will with you is supposed to be a selling point?" she asked with mild sarcasm.

"Sure. What kind of trouble can we get into with Grandpa along?"

"You can ask?"

"I don't think it's such a bad idea," said Ernie, scratching his ear. "You have to admit that in spite of all your worries, nothing has ever happened on one of Will's downtown excursions. If Ren's willing to have him go along, why not say yes? It sounds pretty harmless to me."

"I really object to this," Maxine said, her gaze going from Pete to Will to Ernie. "It's the craziest idea I ever heard of." When nobody moved from their position, she shrugged. "Okay. But just for the record, I think all three of you are nuts. And Pete, if you don't come directly home, you're grounded. Again."

They collected Ren, who had sprayed her hair red for the occasion, at eleven Friday night. Pete was driving Ernie's Ford pickup. While Maxine had finally agreed to let them go, she wouldn't budge on the idea of letting Pete drive the Cadillac. He felt silly pulling up the long, sweeping driveway to the Dykstras' multistory house. He knew it must have cost a half a million at least, and here he was in a 1979 pickup.

Ren was waiting for them on the front steps. She started down the walk as Pete brought the pickup to a halt and got out.

"Hi!" she said, giving him a quick hug. "Did you remember to bring your props?"

"Sure."

"Then let's go." She ran down the walk and got into the pickup before he could open his door.

"Aren't I supposed to come up to the house and meet your parents?"

"They went to the Ordway tonight. Some violinist was playing, very uppity. Besides, they don't care where I go or who I go with."

"Doesn't that bother you? I mean, parents are supposed to care."

"Tell them that."

"I can't believe they don't."

Ren twisted the loose button on the old men's overcoat she wore. "They do, I guess, in their own fashion."

"Maybe you should try to meet them halfway."

"I've tried. Only every time I make a move in that direction, they think it means I'm ready to have everything be the way it was before. They can't accept me for who I am, and I'm not willing to be who they want me to be. So we're stuck. But I don't want to talk about that. I want to have fun. Okay?"

"Okay," said Pete.

A half hour later, they had found a parking spot off Hennepin and were walking toward the theater. Suddenly Ren stopped. "I just thought of something," she said, and she began fishing in the black bag. When she found what she was looking for, she motioned to Pete. "Come here."

"What's up?"

"You'll see. Now bend over." She pulled a can of hair paint from her bag, and before he knew what she was doing, the tips of his spikes matched the red streaks in her hair.

The line already extended from the box office around the corner by the time they reached the Uptown. Although most of those waiting for the show had some odd feature of dress or grooming, the three of them got plenty of looks as they took their place at the end of the line, thanks to Will.

"Hey, Gramps. What's the deal?" asked one punker.

"Just want to check it out," said Will mildly. Then he asked Ren, "What smells so good?"

"The Croissant Express. Want one?"

"Uh-huh."

"A sandwich croissant or one with filling?"

"What kind of filling?"

"Cream. Blueberry. Strawberry."

"Give me one with cream."

"How about you, Pete?"

"Strawberry," said Pete, handing her a bill.

While they waited for her to come back, a vendor selling

roses walked along the line. Will bought a rose for Ren. Then he turned his attention to the groups of people he saw walking on the streets, the shops they stood in front of, and the others in line.

While Will was taking in everything around them, Pete was watching him. He couldn't help admiring the alertness, the inquisitiveness, and willingness to be delighted that was part of Will Martin. Somehow, it made him feel as if he were the old one and Will the kid.

Just then Ren came back with the croissants. "Here, take 'em while they're hot," she said.

Will took a bite of his and moaned with pleasure. "How often have you come down here?" he asked, his mouth full.

"Four or five times, maybe."

"Are there always this many people lined up?"

"Usually."

A good percentage of those in line were punkers. deep into black clothes, studs, combat boots, and shaved, spiked, or colored hair. But while some of them had a hard, almost vicious look, others seemed to be punk more for the style than the persuasion. Fashion Punks, Ren called them. The differences were subtle but discernible.

"Hey," Pete said as his eyes fell on a different group, "I have to remember to tell Mom that there were even some Yuppies. That might make her feel better."

"Think so?" Ren giggled.

"What's that smell?" Will asked, sniffing the air.

"Shhh!" Ren hissed. "It's marijuana."

"Mari . . . You mean people are—"

"Using? Yeah. I'd say half of the people in line are 'altered' one way or another, if you know what I mean."

Finally the line began to move. As Ren had warned them, they and their sacks were searched for hidden bottles. Then they found their seats and waited for the show to begin.

Pete was a morass of conflicting emotions on the drive home afterward. He had just experienced something totally unlike anything he had ever experienced before. There had been an electricity, an excitement in the audience, and he had joined in their enthusiasm. He had thrown rice when the actors threw rice after the wedding that began the show. He had thrown cards into the air when an actor said portentously, "The cards have been dealt." He had tossed his roll of toilet paper into the air after the line "Great scot!"

And he felt guilty about having enjoyed himself. Just how was he going to tell his mother that he and Will had seen a musical about transvestites?

"What's the matter?" Ren asked. "Didn't you like it?"

"I liked it. That's the problem."

"Why?"

"I dunno. It sets up a conflict, I guess. I liked something I know my folks wouldn't like, and I don't know what to do about it."

"Sooner or later, you have to make some decisions on your own, Heffelfinger."

"Yeah, I know. It's just that my mom doesn't trust me as it is, and now I've done something she can use as ammunition against me."

Ren shifted so that she could put her arm around Will, who was already asleep and was leaning heavily against her. "Tell you what. Next time you can decide where to go. Somewhere on your turf."

"How about church?" he asked, before thinking about what that might mean.

"Okay. This Sunday?"

"Uh . . . "

"Don't worry. I won't embarrass you."

"I didn't think you would. I was more worried about how the guys who go to my church might act."

"Whatever."

They rode the rest of the way in silence. When they arrived at Ren's home, Pete opened the door on his side and got out. Ren gently edged Will over until he was leaning against the door on the opposite side, then slid out after Pete.

"Is he okay?" she asked anxiously.

"Uh-huh. He's just tired."

"I hope he enjoyed himself."

"Don't worry about that. Will always enjoys himself."

There was something Pete had been wanting to ask her all evening, and finally, as they stood at the imposing front door of her house, he blurted it out. "You . . . you don't use any of that . . . stuff, do you?"

"After seeing what it did to Chris? Are you kidding?"

"I just wondered."

"I only have two addictions. Diet Coke . . . "

"And?"

"And you."

9

The year Pete turned punk was the year that the ward's Young Men's and Young Women's presidencies came up with the "Pick a Daisy" plan. It was announced the Sunday after Pete had halfheartedly asked Ren to come to church with him. He hadn't followed through on the invitation, however. He felt the pressure of disapproval whenever he walked through the chapel doors, and he didn't want her to be subjected to it as well.

The purpose of the "Pick a Daisy" plan was to insure that no girl in the Maple Hills Ward would suffer the embarrassment of going unescorted to the upcoming stake dance. Its implementation was simple: the priests quorum leader was to put in his jacket pocket slips of paper bearing the names of all the girls fourteen and older. Each priest was to draw a name. He was to pick up the girl of that name and escort her to a predance dinner and then on to the dance. There, his obligation would end. He might, if he wished, talk to her, dance with her, perhaps even drive her home. But it wasn't obligatory.

It *was* obligatory to pick a daisy from Brother Markham's jacket pocket.

Pete refused.

"Brother Heffelfinger, this is not going to work unless every one of the Young Men draw a name."

"What if I don't want to go to the dance?"

"I'm asking all of you to make a commitment to go."

Pete groaned. There it was again, Brother Markham's favorite ploy. "I'm asking you to make a commitment never to drink . . . never to smoke . . . never to get turned-on by a girl."

Or, in the positive vein: "To go on a mission . . . to get married in the temple."

And now, "To go to the stake dance."

It wasn't that Pete was against any of those things. He knew that they were all supposed to lead to a long and happy life. In fact, he had thought about them more than once while sitting under the big oak tree in the backyard. In those moments, he was willing to make a commitment, if not to God (about whom he wasn't always sure), then at least to himself.

But Brother Markham always asked for commitments from the whole class—in front of the whole class. Whatever the issue was, he gave them thirty seconds to think about it, all the while grinding his gum with a bovine motion and gazing at them unblinkingly from his mild brown eyes.

Pete hated it. He knew that Bradley did too, because they had talked about it once. He suspected that they weren't the only ones who felt coerced and manipulated into making commitments just because they didn't want to look stupid. Talk about peer pressure. Adults always told you to resist peer pressure, then they turned around and used it against you.

Pete didn't know if he wanted to go on a mission, for instance. He had thought about it often enough, and he knew that his parents expected him to go, but he hadn't make up his mind yet. Two years! It was a big decision. But when Brother Markham asked, "How many of you will commit yourselves to going on a mission?" what could he do? If he didn't raise his hand, Brother Markham would ask for an explanation right in front of everybody.

There was one thing in the man's favor, though. At least he didn't say, "I'm committing you to . . . " Pete had often heard leaders use that phrasing, as if they had power to commit another human being to any course of action. He hated it, and he always finished the line "I'm committing you to . . . " with *the state mental hospital at Anoka.*

The stake dance wasn't an important commitment—make it a .5 on a scale of 1 to 10—but for some reason, he felt his whole brain resist the words, "I'm asking all of you to make a commitment . . . "

And Pete said, "No."

"Now, Brother Heffelfinger. You don't want one of our young ladies to feel left out just because of you."

Pete was silent.

"We've got this all worked out so that everyone will be taken care of, *if* there is full cooperation."

Pete felt his face turn red as everyone in the quorum focused on him, but still he was silent.

"What's the real issue here, Pete?" Brother Markham asked softly, leaning forward in his chair and taking the compassionate counselor approach.

"No issue. I just don't want to. Besides, they won't let me in looking like this. You know that as well as I do."

"You could tone it down a bit."

The words were spoken softly, without emphasis, but Pete felt them like an electric charge in his brain. *That's what it's all about. They want me to go back to being a good little boy.*

"I don't want to change and I don't want to go to the dance. Even if I did, there's someone else I would bring."

"Who?" sneered Drew Conzet, pushing his chair back to balance on two legs. "That creep Dykstra? They wouldn't let her into the parking lot."

"Listen, Conzet, if they knew what you were doing before and after the stake dances, they wouldn't let you in, either. Okay?"

Drew dropped his chair back down with a *whap,* his eyes cold and his mouth no longer smiling. "Just what are you talking about?"

"You know what I mean, and so does everyone else here. With the possible exception of our fearless leader."

"All right, men, that's enough of that," said Brother Markham. "I don't know what's going on here, but we've gone far afield. We've only got a few more minutes left to take care of the business at hand."

He stood up and drew a bunch of slips from his jacket pocket. "I have here pieces of paper with the names of each girl on them. You'll each draw one. No trading or complaining, understand? Let's get at it."

One by one, the priests walked up to Brother Markham and drew out a slip.

"Not bad. I can stand an evening with Heather Donovan," Ken Kelley said smugly.

Drew Conzet drew the name of his steady. "Hey, how'd you do that?" demanded Bradley. "This is fixed."

"Man, why am I always the one to get the dogs?" Jeff Newmark complained.

Soon, all except Pete had drawn a name.

"Well?" asked Brother Markham.

Pete shook his head.

"You seem to be making an issue out of all the wrong things, Pete," said the quorum leader, working his gum. His lower jaw seemed to go around in a complete circle when he chewed. "If you're not going to take one of our young women, ask this girl you're interested in."

"Why?"

"Because I'd like to see you at this function. It's important that you take part in all the activities. That's how you keep yourself strong in the Church. Will you make a commitment to be there?"

Pete felt all eyes turn to him. He sagged and sighed. "Okay, I'll be there. But I'm bringing my own date."

"Ren Dykstra? You're taking Ren to a church dance?" Maxine asked, as if she hadn't heard what she had heard.

"Yeah. For some reason, Brother Markham made a big issue about me going. I don't really want to go, but I said I would."

"But why take Ren, of all people. Why not one of the girls at church?"

"I don't want to," he said, leaving the "Pick a Daisy" plan out of the conversation. If he mentioned that, he knew his mother would make him draw a name, even after the fact, because she was firmly committed to the notion that you never said no when it came to the Church. Never. So, wisely, he omitted his determined lack of participation in that program, and instead wheedled his mother for approval of a date with Ren.

"Come on, Mom. Ren's a real sweet girl."

"If you say so, but there are some things about her that bother me."

"Such as?"

"She drives a car much too expensive for a young girl, and she's always dressed in black."

"Those aren't mortal sins."

"That's just for starters. She seems too cocky, if you ask me. She doesn't show the proper respect to adults."

"You decided that on the basis of five minutes' conversation? You haven't even given her a chance."

"All right, maybe I have judged her too harshly. You ask her to come home with you tonight, and I'll make sure I get done with business early. We can spend some time together."

"So you can give her the Maxine Heffelfinger once-over? Why bother? I can tell you now that she won't pass, but not because there's anything wrong with her."

"I won't have you taking her to the dance unless I've had a chance to talk to her a little more."

"Hey, that's okay with me," Pete said, raising his hands in acquiescence and beginning to walk from the room. "I just won't go, and you can tell Brother Markham why."

"Pete! I didn't say I don't want you to go to the dance. All I said was I wanted to visit with Ren. Is that okay?"

Pete eyed his mother warily. He felt protective of Ren, although he didn't know why. She always seemed so strong, so sure of herself, in spite of the fact she seemed to be left pretty much on her own.

"Ask her over. I won't bite," Maxine said in a conciliatory tone.

"Okay. Tomorrow after school."

"Fine. I'll bake a batch of cookies."

"You don't have to do that."

"I know. I want to."

Yeah, thought Pete, *so you'll come off looking like Mother of the Year.* Although he knew that Maxine's invitation was a real effort at conciliation, he harbored a secret hope that Ren would say no.

Ren seemed delighted.

"Are you sure?" he asked. "Mom's convinced you're a bad influence on me."

"Why? I didn't talk you into going punk."

"No, but she probably thinks I would go back to being The Invisible Man if it weren't for the fact that you and I . . . hang out together."

"Would you?" Ren asked, eyeing him.

"I don't think so."

"So, no problem, right?"

"If you say so."

The minute they got out of the Fiero in the Heffelfinger driveway the following afternoon, the smell of cookies assailed his nostrils. His mother had been at it.

"What smells so good?" asked Ren, drawing in deeply.

"Chocolate chip cookies. Mom has a special recipe. She says hers are different from everybody else's. By that, she means better."

"Does she bake a lot?"

"She goes in spurts."

Maxine was at the door before Pete had the time to open it.

"There you are, just in time," she said brightly, showing her teeth. "The first batch is just out of the oven."

"They smell great," said Ren.

Maxine had them sit at the table, then brought over a plate of cookies and poured two tall glasses of milk.

Cookies and milk, groaned Pete. *You'd think we were seven years old.*

But Ren didn't see it that way. "I used to dream of coming

home to the smell of cookies baking," she said dreamily. "I thought if my mother baked cookies, that would be a sign that she loved me."

"Did she?"

"What? Love me or bake cookies?"

"Uh, bake cookies."

"The answer is no. And no."

Ren's matter-of-fact words flustered Maxine. "Oh, I'm sorry," she said. Then she added, disbelieving, "You don't really mean that. Do you?"

"My parents should have had dogs instead of kids," Ren said, licking melted chocolate from her red lips. "That way, they could have sent them to obedience school. Could have boarded them whenever they wanted to take one of their trips." She glanced at Maxine as if calculating the effect her next words would have. "They could have had them put down when they were tired of them."

Maxine stared at Ren, stunned. Pete was also shocked, but less so since he knew the circumstances of Chris's death. Ren's play on words had caught his attention. *Put down.* According to Ren, Chris had been verbally put down by his parents no matter what he had done. Until he had put himself down. Permanently.

Ren didn't seem to be aware of the tension; she was too busy eating. The first cookie disappeared with amazing rapidity, then the second. "May I have more milk, please?" she asked Maxine sweetly. She drank from her refilled glass, then sank her teeth into another chip-filled cookie, closing her eyes as she chewed. "Heavenly," she murmured.

"Yeah," Pete said awkwardly, filling the space left by his mother's continuing silence. "These are real great cookies, Mom."

Finally, Maxine cleared her throat. "Pete tells me he'd like to take you to a dance."

"Uh-huh."

"It's a church dance, you know."

"He told me all about it."

Maxine curled up the edge of her napkin. "Did he tell you about the dress standards?"

Ren stood up so Maxine could see her from head to foot. Her black skirt was almost to her ankles. "I won't have any problem with the length, will I?"

"No." Maxine chuckled in spite of herself.

"If it's my hair you're worried about, I won't dye it purple. By the way, this is my real color."

"It is?"

"Mom always expected it to turn mousy like hers, but it didn't."

"Doesn't your mother . . . I mean, she *tries* to have a good relationship with you, doesn't she?" asked Maxine, not willing to believe any mother could be as unfeeling as Ren had portrayed her own.

"I suppose. She comes up to my room once a week to see if I'm still alive. She buys me country-club clothes and leaves them on my bed as a hint."

"What do you do with them?" asked Pete. He was thinking of the new outfits Maxine had bought for him earlier in the week.

"I used to try to get her to take them back, but she wouldn't. I returned some of them for a refund, but going to the store all the time got old real fast. So now I stash them in the bottom of my closet. The pile's getting pretty big. One of these days I'll probably take them all down to the Salvation Army."

Maxine picked delicately at a cookie crumb. "Don't you ever consider wearing the things she picks out?"

"No. She only buys them for herself. I mean, she knows I hate looking too cute for words. She just wants me to stop embarrassing her."

"I think I can understand that," Maxine murmured. "I admit I've been embarrassed quite often the last few weeks."

"Can I give you some advice?" asked Ren.

Pete nearly choked on his milk. He tried to signal Ren, but she didn't pay any attention. Leaning forward, she focused her kohl-outlined eyes on Maxine. When she spoke, her voice was earnest.

"See, what you've got to do is stop thinking that the world's going to end just because Pete looks the way he does. You've got to stop caring what other people think when they find out you're his mother."

"That's pretty hard to do. Especially at church."

"Do it anyway. Listen, Pete here is one of the good guys. No matter what he looks like, he's as clean as Jimmy Stewart."

Pete flushed, pleased and embarrassed.

"I wouldn't have thought Jimmy Stewart interested your generation," Maxine said. Although she didn't mention Ren's assessment of Pete, it clearly pleased her. The stern lines around her mouth vanished and her lips curved softly.

"I love old movies. I rent them four at a time over the weekends. Anyway, don't worry about Heffelfinger here. He's okay."

Now Maxine's gaze met Pete's. "I know that," she said. "But sometimes I need reminding." She paused, then took a deep breath and said, "If you two would like to go to the stake dance together, it's all right with me."

10

"Why did you think this was going to be a disaster?" Ren asked Pete as he walked her out to the car. "Your mom's not so bad."

"She is kinda neat," he conceded. He stood at the passenger side of the car, his arms folded on the roof, his chin resting on them. "Ren, what was all that stuff about your parents and Chris? You make it sound like they were responsible for—"

"They were," she said bitterly, not needing him to finish the sentence. "He was supposed to be their Golden Boy, their monument to immortality, the perfect son. He couldn't do it."

Ren got into the Fiero, and Pete climbed in beside her. In the silence, he pulled thoughtfully at the hairs on his arm. "What happened, anyway?" he finally asked, not looking at her. "I mean, I've been riding around in his car for weeks now, and I don't even know . . . "

"How he did it? He took every downer he had and cleaned out the medicine cabinet for good measure. Then he got into his car and turned on the engine . . . "

She turned on the engine.

" . . . put the seat back . . . "

She lowered the driver's seat.

" . . . and he slept his way into eternity."

Uncomprehending, he stared at her for a second. Then the import of what she had said hit him. He jerked the door handle and scrambled out of the car.

Ren jumped out and came around to his side. "Are you all right, Heffelfinger?"

He was tingling with shock, and he hugged himself to keep from shaking. "I've been riding around in a . . . a *death-mobile!*" he said harshly. "Why didn't you tell me?"

"Wouldn't make a very good opening line. 'Hi. I'm Ren Dykstra. May I drive you home in the very car my brother committed suicide in? No extra charge.' "

"Don't ever ask me to ride in that thing again!"

"It's the only car I have."

"Then ask your parents to buy you a new one. They're rich enough."

"They could. They would. Actually, they hate the fact that I'm driving Chris's car. I drive it because I want to."

"You're crazy, you know that?"

"Maybe." Ren leaned back against the fender and looked up into the autumn sky. "But I don't want to ever forget what happens when people don't love each other."

Shocked into silence, he could only stare at her.

"See, he was never good enough for them. He wanted to please them. He was always trying to do something to make them proud. He was a tennis star at Edina. He was in National Honors Society. He even was a Merit Scholar." Ren shrugged. "It didn't do him any good. No matter how good you are, someone can always be better, you know? When he got beat in a match, they raked him over the coals. When he won, they bugged him if he didn't take it in straight sets. When his class ranking slipped a bit, they lit into him. When he went up a place or two, they asked him why there were still thirteen people in front of him.

"Dad always figured he'd go to Harvard and be a big-shot lawyer. Mom always figured he'd marry someone whose daddy had a big name and lots of money. Made me want to throw up."

Pete shook his head. "I don't know what to say . . . "

"What's to say? He got sick of it, finally. He started doing drugs, and things went from bad to worse. The night he died, he wrote me a note."

"What was in it?"

"Lots of things." She gazed at the scudding gray clouds for a moment, then continued. "He said he was doing what he wanted to do for the first time in his life. He said for me to fight them."

Pete's eyes widened with recognition. "So that's why you do it."

"You got it, Einstein. I'm everything they don't want. They can't show me off to their friends or brag about me." Her eyes met his. "I told you your reasons for going punk were different from mine. I think way deep down inside, you still believe in what your parents stand for. You still believe in your church. And there's one other thing . . . "

"Yeah?"

"You love your mom."

Pete blushed and turned away.

"See, you do." She grabbed his arm above the elbow and looked at him earnestly. "Don't be embarrassed, Heffelfinger. I think it's neat. If I had a mom like yours, I'd love her too."

"She's not so different from yours. She wants me to do things just so she'll look good."

"But there's an important difference. Your mom really thinks those things are in your best interest. It's like, she knows where the yellow brick road leads and she wants to make sure you're on it, because she cares."

Pete felt his heart warming to her words. His mom was a royal pain, there were no two ways about it, but she did love him and he loved her. That was something he couldn't question.

"The thing is," he said slowly, "loving me doesn't keep her from making mistakes."

"Bingo."

He sighed. "What a mess."

"You'll live through it."

"You think so?"

"Why do you think I keep hanging around you? I'm going to make sure that you do."

Pete drove them to the dance in his dad's pickup. They had no trouble getting in the stake center, although they didn't come anywhere close to the clean-cut image preferred by the leaders of the young men's and women's organizations. Pete had combed his hair flat and was wearing one of his own dress shirts and ties. Ren had ratted her hair up on one side as usual, but she had forgone spray-painting it. She had also used considerably less mascara and eye liner. Although she still looked strange with her white hair and long black skirt and black boots, she was acceptable.

Bon Jovi was playing when they walked into the decorated cultural hall.

"I thought you weren't supposed to listen to music like this, Heffelfinger," Ren said.

"Just wait a minute," he said, grinning. And almost immediately, the music stopped. The next tones they heard were less strident.

"Do you want to dance?" he asked, hoping she would say no. He was afraid of looking foolish on the dance floor.

"Sure. That's why we came, isn't it?"

No. That's not why I came, he thought. Still, he took her hand and led her to the edge of the dance floor. Very few couples were dancing, and only the extremely confident were out in the middle of the floor, Drew Conzet and his girl among them. The rest hung on the fringes, and the fringes were definitely where Pete wanted to be.

They began moving to the music. Pete did his usual shuffle, which he hoped would pass for dancing, but Ren *danced.* Every part of her moved in a jointless frenzy, as if compelled by the beat of the music.

It didn't take long before everyone in their quadrant of the floor was watching Ren. And watching Ren, they watched him. He gritted his teeth, wishing that he was anywhere but where he was. Siberia seemed quite attractive, especially given the fact that he felt as if he were burning up. Sweat popped out on his forehead, and he loosened his tie.

"Go, Pete!" somebody yelled. It sounded like Bradley.

Out of the corner of his eyes, he noticed that the dancers in the middle of the floor were becoming aware that the center of attention had shifted. Drew was looking his way, and their eyes met. Suddenly Pete grinned. This wasn't half bad. He started moving his legs a little, then his torso, and finally his arms and hands.

When the music finally stopped, some of those watching them clapped.

"You can really dance," he said to Ren as he led her to the refreshment table.

"You're not so bad yourself, once you loosen up."

"Thanks, but I'm not the one who had an audience. That was you."

Ren smiled shyly. "Did that embarrass you? I wouldn't want to embarrass you, you know."

"Are you kidding? You were great! Here, have some punch."

They were still standing there when Bradley walked up. "You really came," he said to Pete. "I wasn't sure you would."

"I told Markham I would. Where's your date? Or should I say 'Daisy'? "

"I don't know." Bradley shrugged. "I dumped her the minute I got here. Why don't you introduce me?"

"Sorry. Ren, this is a friend of mine, Bradley McEntyre."

"Hi," she said.

"Nice to meet you. I see you in school sometimes."

"Really?"

"I mean, who can miss you? But you look different tonight. Prettier."

"Thanks," said Ren dryly.

Bradley hit himself on the head. "Boy, that was really stupid."

"It's okay. I know what you mean. I toned things down a bit so I could pass inspection."

"I don't know why they care so much about how we dress," Bradley complained. "It's like, if we look virtuous, they think we are."

Before either Pete or Ren had a chance to reply, Drew Conzet approached them. "Enjoy your moment of glory, Peetie?" he asked.

"I didn't notice anybody watching you dance."

"They weren't watching you, either. They were watching Dykstra here. Nice going, Dykstra."

"Thanks."

"You go to North, don't you? Maybe we could eat lunch together sometime."

Pete felt the same hot rush that had preceded his blow to Knuckles's solar plexus, but Ren's hand on his arm and her reply helped him hold it in check.

"Thanks," she said coolly. "But I don't think so."

That night, he got up the nerve to kiss her at her front door. His hands were sweating and his heart thumping as he brought his dry, carefully closed lips in flat contact with her warm, moist lips. Once he had achieved that, he wasn't sure what to do next. Tentatively he moved his lips against hers, hoping he was doing what he was supposed to be doing.

To his chagrin, she drew back after a few seconds. "Relax, Heffelfinger," she said, chuckling softly. "You're doing great."

Later, walking back to the pickup, Pete had occasion to reflect on how far a little praise can go toward improved performance.

11

Six weeks into the first trimester, Pete already knew he wasn't going to get the grades he wanted to get. It wasn't a question of whether he was turning in good work or not. It was a question of how his teachers had reacted to his change of appearance and whether or not the class was highly subjective.

He was still getting a good grade in American history, but he expected that. For one thing, he had turned in some good papers. For another, Ann Johnson didn't take his punkhood personally.

Advanced algebra and chemistry were tough, but he was holding his own. And a right answer in those classes was a right answer. There was no debating it. The teachers had to give him the grade he deserved.

It was a different story in humanities and journalism. Right from the first day that Pete had appeared with his red spikes and shaved head, the battle lines had been drawn. He hadn't caused Mr. Longfellow or Mrs. Martingale any trouble, and he had turned in most of his assignments on time, but that didn't seem to make any difference. There was bad karma between them and him, and nothing he did could change that fact. When he wrote an essay test for humanities or an article for journalism, he got docked for the minutest of reasons.

He began to feel increasingly helpless and frustrated. In an effort to turn things around, he tried brown-nosing. He tried doing extra-credit work. Finally, he decided to talk to each of the teachers after school, hoping that the direct approach might help.

"There's no problem, Heffelfinger," Mr. Longfellow replied, making a great show of casual reasonableness. "I judge your work the same as anybody else's. I don't know where you get this idea that I'm against you just because you look so weird. Personally, I think you have a persecution complex."

Strike one, he thought as he made his way to Mrs. Martingale's room. Finding her alone, he said his piece.

"What's the matter with you people?" she asked tartly, fussing with the papers on her desk. "Why do you think you deserve some sort of special treatment?"

"I'm not asking for special treatment. I'm asking for fair treatment. I think I've been doing better work than B-minus and C-plus."

"Are you saying I'm not grading you fairly?"

Pete nodded.

"On what do you base that assessment?"

He pulled out his most recent article and indicated the lost points he thought were debatable.

They weren't debatable, according to her.

"Hey, I can show you other guys' papers with the same kinds of mistakes. You didn't dock them this many points."

"Listen, young man," she said, waving her index finger at him, "it is not possible to take errors out of context and ask that they be judged the same. If you want a better grade, do better work."

He was furious when he left her room. He started down the hall to the principal's office, but he stopped before he got there. He knew the principal would say, "Bring it in front of a committee, if you think you have a case. Otherwise, there's nothing I can do for you."

He was sure he had a case, but he wasn't sure he wanted the hassle that would go with presenting it. Muttering to himself, he went out to wait for the late bus. That was where Ren found him.

"What's the matter, Heffelfinger?" she asked, scrutinizing him.

"Nothing. Everything. I'm getting a couple of lousy grades this tri."

"Tell me about it while I drive you home."

Pete had declined to ride with Ren ever since he had learned the history of the car, but now his need for her company was stronger than his aversion to it.

"So what's the deal?" she asked as they got in.

"It's really sick," he said, swearing and smacking the dashboard. "My grade-point average is getting mucked up just because a couple of teachers don't like the way I look."

"Is that all? Welcome to the real world. Guilty by reason of orange hair. I told you it would happen."

"Yeah? Well, I didn't believe you."

"I know what I'm talking about. The minute you start dressing punk, you're sending a message to the rest of the world. You're telling them, go . . . uh, go take a hike."

"Maybe that's what you're telling them, and somebody like Price, but not me."

"You think anybody cares if there's a difference between how you feel about our safe, white, upwardly mobile corner of yuppiedom and the way Price feels? I love you, Heffelfinger, but you're so naive. Nobody cares. We've given them an easy way to categorize us. And once we're in a category, we're not real to them anymore. If we're not real, it doesn't matter what they do to us. Nobody's going to listen when we complain."

"They better. I'm thinking about taking Mrs. Martingale to the principal with this one. It'll end up front page in the school paper."

"Really? Good luck."

"I've got a case. I'm doing good work in her class. I get my articles in on time, and they've been good. The only thing is, she can always find some reason to knock my grade down a point or two."

"Is there any chance she might be right?"

"No way. When I ask her why she's taken off certain points,

she just says, 'It's not well-written.' How subjective can you get? Besides, Shawn Winston told me he wanted to put a couple of my articles in the school paper, but the old lady jerked them."

"What about your test grades?"

"A, A-minus."

"Then she can't give you too bad a grade."

"Oh yeah? The tests are only half the grade points."

"What do you think you'll get?"

"If I'm lucky, a B."

Ren burst out laughing. "A *B?* All this fuss because you're getting a B?"

"Getting good grades is important to me."

"I know." She was sober as she considered her crimson nails. "There's an easy way to fix things."

"How?"

"Go home and take your costume off. Go back to being your old self."

"What does that have to do with anything?"

"You still don't get it, do you. Listen good this time, because I won't say it again. I dress like this to get back at everybody who could have helped Chris but didn't. I don't care how tough it gets. I don't care if they laugh at me, or give me lousy grades, or pretend I don't even exist. Got it? I don't care. And it's me not caring that drives them crazy. They'll do anything to make me care, to make me play their game, but I won't. Not after what they did to Chris!" Her voice rose to the husky shriek that was her trademark, then dropped as she added softly, "That's the difference between you and me. You do care."

Pete lifted his hand in protest, but she waved it away.

"You do. You want to know how I know? I know because you're worried about your B. It's not good enough. You want an A so you can go to some uptight private college like Saint Olaf."

"I'm a Mormon. I'll probably go to BYU."

She shrugged. "Same difference. They're all stuck on their

own short-haired, earnest, bright-eyed, clean-cut image. Phase two is graduating with a good enough GPA that you can get a nice job with a big company and make lots of money. In phase three, you'll get married, buy a house, and have a bunch of kids. Right?"

"Isn't that what people do?"

"Not all people, but it's what you'll end up doing. It's a power struggle, Heffelfinger, and you don't groove on it. I do. I love every minute of it. I'll never let them twist me into thinking the way they do. But you?" Ren grinned, a little, sad turning-up of her blood-red lips. "Heffelfinger, you *do* think the way they do. There's no issue. You're getting the lousy grades for nothing."

Pete's sigh was heavy with unshed tears. "What if . . . what if I go back like I was before?" he asked, dreading the answer.

"You mean, will I still drive you home?"

"Don't make a joke out of it, Ren," he said thickly. There was something else he wanted to say, but it was so hard. Guys weren't supposed to get all mushy and personal. Finally he blurted out, "I don't want to lose you."

She laughed softly, putting her arms around his neck. Her breath was sweet and warm. "You're not going to lose me. It might be easier for you if you did."

"I don't think so. I don't know what I'd do without you."

"That's something you don't have to worry about." She kissed him lightly before settling back into her seat. "But giving it up isn't going to be easy. As far as everyone else is concerned, you'll still be punk, even if you change your hair and the way you dress. No matter how you look, punk is what they'll see first. Hanging out with me won't help that any."

"Are you telling me I'm stuck like this even if I do change my image?"

"Not forever, but it's going to take a while. You might not shake it until you get out of here and go where nobody knows you. Then you can start over with any image you want."

He stared out the window a long time. When he didn't say anything more, she finally started up the car and pulled out onto the road. At the intersection, she said, "How about coming out to my place for a change? Sally's been dying to meet you."

"Sure. Why not?"

Pete had never seen the Dykstra house except at night, and then only the illuminated front side. That was imposing enough, but now as Ren drove down the lane marked "Private," he saw for the first time the back side.

While the north-facing front hugged the hillside, the south-facing back dropped down four stories, each extending out farther than the other. The wooden decks, which on each successive level were larger, held potted trees whose leaves had turned color and planters full of autumn flowers, as well as differing assortments of casual furniture. The flagstone patio on the lowest level extended around the pool and out to the tennis court.

"Is that an indoor swimming pool on the bottom level?" he asked, catching a glint of blue.

"Yeah. There's a Jacuzzi down there too, and a sauna. The game room and media room are on the floor above."

"What's a media room?"

"You know, video, large-screen TV, stereo components. Et cetera and et cetera. Disgusting, isn't it? All that room, and only the three of us, not counting Sally."

He tried to keep from gawking as Ren led the way through the labyrinthine house. It was like nothing he had ever seen before. At the end of the entry hall, a four-story atrium formed the center of the house. The living spaces that opened onto it were defined more by level and color scheme than by walls. The decor was obviously expensive, but spare and cool, uninviting in its museum-like atmosphere.

"Does anyone ever sit down in there?" he asked when Ren showed him the living room.

"Only when my parents have a big party. This house was built for entertaining, not for living."

"What are those things on the coffee table? They look like fancy kaleidoscopes."

Ren laughed. "That's what they are. Try one."

The collection of kaleidoscopes was like nothing he had ever seen before. They were beautifully constructed, some of metal, some of wood. The smallest one was round and only five inches long, while the largest was triangular and almost fourteen inches long. He put them to his eye, one after another. "Wow, these are really something."

"The design on this one is square instead of round. It's supposed to be pretty unusual," she said, handing him a kaleidoscope. "And this one has oil in it. It flows from one design to another."

"Some toys."

"They're conversation pieces, actually. When a party hits a dull spot, Dad can always count on the kaleidoscopes to get things going again." She took the one he held and put it back on the table. "Come on, let's go see Sally."

When they walked into the kitchen, it was as if they had stepped through a space warp. A comfortable clutter reigned, and in the middle of it was Sally, plain-faced and dumpling-round.

"There's my sweetie," she crowed. "And you've finally brought Pete home with you. Oh, you do look a sight, young man." She shook her head disapprovingly, but her smile was genuine. "Come, sit. Are you hungry?"

"Starving," said Ren.

"How about an omelet? Or a sandwich?"

"We want something sweet, don't we, Heffelfinger?"

"Whatever you say."

"Something sweet it is," said Sally. "How about Belgian waffles with whipped cream and strawberries?"

Without waiting for an answer, Sally went to work, talking nonstop. Before long, delicious aromas filled the air, and she set a plate with a golden-brown waffle in front of each of them. She served the whipped cream and sugared strawberries in separate bowls.

"Eat up, now. Young people need food to grow on."

Pete didn't realize until halfway through his waffle that the tension he had felt after his unsuccessful talks with Mr. Longfellow and Mrs. Martingale was ebbing. He felt his shoulders drop as he relaxed. He ate the rest of his waffle more slowly, savoring its crunchy lightness and the sweet mixture of strawberries and cream.

"Heffelfinger here is worried about his grades," said Ren, licking her fork.

"Why, what's the problem, honey?" asked Sally.

"I've got a couple of teachers who don't like me."

"How could anybody not like you?"

"They don't seem to have any trouble."

"Oh, my. It's the way you look, I expect."

"I think he's about ready to give it up," Ren said. "Only we have to figure out how he can do it without it looking like he's crumbling under pressure."

"A new haircut wouldn't hurt," said Sally, eyeing him frankly. "Your roots are showing."

"Probably, but I haven't made up my mind about what to do yet."

"You're a nice boy, Pete. Don't you worry too much about it. And if you ever need somebody to talk to, Sally's always here."

Suddenly, he found himself pulled into her embrace for a breathless second. He blushed furiously while she went on to Ren, who got the same treatment. "How many is that for today?" she asked Ren.

"Four, I think."

"You've got eight to go. My goodness! I guess you'll have to give each other a few hugs. Only not too many." Sally's eyes twinkled. "And not too long, mind."

With that, Sally shooed them out of her kitchen. In the hallway, Ren explained the cook's countdown. Sally had once read that a person needed four hugs a day to survive, eight to grow on, and twelve to thrive. She was determined that Ren would get twelve hugs a day, even if she had to administer every one of them herself.

"Guess we'd better add to the total," he joked, trying to sound casual.

"Guess we'd better."

He was taller than she by a head-and-a-half, so when she came into his arms, the brush of her maroon hair tickled his chin. He bent down to kiss her, a strawberry kiss that warmed him so much that he backed away, embarrassed.

"You're getting good at that, Heffelfinger," she breathed.

He smiled with pleasure, but he didn't kiss her again, although he could tell she wanted him to.

"Okay," she said wryly. "On with the tour. Do you want to see the media room?"

"Sure."

He followed her to the open staircase, then hooted in surprise when he saw a teddy bear on the steps. "Whose is that?" he snickered, picking it up. The bear was old and obviously well-loved. Its fur was worn thin in places, and a black button had replaced one glittery plastic eye.

"It's mine. Can I have it back?" Ren asked, reaching for the bear. Perversely, he snatched it from her and started backing away.

"You mean the tough Ren Dykstra has a teddy bear?" he asked, smirking. "I wonder if she sleeps with it."

"Please give it back."

"Come and get it."

"Give it back, creep!" she screeched.

He carried the bear like a football, dodging and weaving through the living room. He turned his back to her while he opened the patio door, fending off with his shoulders and elbows her attempts to retrieve the bear. Then he was on the deck and running, holding the bear in the air as he crossed an imaginary goal line.

Suddenly he stopped short, his eye caught by something he saw through the trees. Ren took advantage of his lapse and grabbed the bear from his hand, at the same time delivering a kick to his shin.

"Hey!" he cried, feeling some sympathy for Knuckles Price.

"If you ever do that again, I swear I'll never speak to you the rest of my life," she threatened.

"I'm sorry. I didn't think it was any big deal."

"Now that you know, don't forget it."

"All right." He gave his shin a rub, then straightened. "Whose lot is that over there?" he asked, pointing westward.

"Why do you want to know?" she asked petulantly from behind her bear, which she had held up to her face as if needing to smell and taste it.

"Because that's my dad's pickup."

She looked in the direction he pointed. "Didn't you say your dad's a builder?"

Pete nodded. "He just went into it. That must be the Trembrells' lot. Their house is the first job for him and his partner."

"Oh-oh."

"What's the matter?"

"Your dad's in deep trouble."

"Why? What are you talking about?"

"The Trembrells are friends of my mom and dad. Nick and Keri," she said, articulating their names in a bright, artificially sweet tone. "They're almost as bad as my folks. When their last house was being built, they had a whole section of an oak floor torn up and replaced because of one scratch. The overrun on that place was so high, the builders lost their shirt on it."

"Oh, boy," breathed Pete. "I wonder if Dad knows." He squinted and scanned what he could see of the building lot. "There he is. Look, would you mind telling him what you just told me? It's important."

"I don't know if I want to," she said.

"Are you still mad about the bear?"

"I never thought you would make fun of me."

Regret flooded through him. "I'm sorry. I really am. I didn't mean to make you feel bad."

She looked at him warily. Tentatively, he reached out and ran his fingers over the bear's short fur. "He's cute. What do you call him?"

"Little Bear. You know, from the kids' book."

"I guess that's one I missed. Are we still friends?"

She lowered the bear from its protective position to reveal a brilliant smile.

"Will you tell my dad about the Trembrells?"

"I'll think about it."

"Start thinking about it now," he said. Taking her by the hand, he led the way down the deck stairs.

ERNIE'S GO-ROUND

12

Ernie squatted at the edge of the excavation, looking at the footings of the Trembrell house. He sucked air between his teeth as he did so, unaware that he had taken on a habit his first construction boss had had. His focus on the job at hand was so complete that he didn't immediately notice the car slowly making its way over the ruts and bumps of the construction road. Turning, he was surprised to see it was the black Fiero that had become so familiar in his own driveway.

What's Ren doing here? he wondered. When he saw Pete in the car beside her, he was even more bemused. He had ambivalent feelings about Pete's involvement with a girl who kept changing the color of her hair. The last time he had seen her, she had shaved off a section over one ear and had checkerboarded it yellow and black. Today the whole mop looked sort of reddish-purple.

When the car pulled to a stop beside the pickup, Pete opened the passenger door and bounded out. "Hi, Dad!"

"Hi yourself. What are you two doing here? How did you find me?"

"I was over at Ren's." Pete pointed toward the Dykstras' house, half-hidden by trees. "We were out on the deck and I saw your pickup. We thought it would be fun to see how the house is coming."

Ernie smiled, pleased that Pete had taken the time to visit the site. He loved talking about how wonderful the house was going to be and all the intricate steps that would raise it up to its final majestic presence.

Ren walked over to the edge of the excavation and peered over the edge.

"Quite a hole, isn't it?" he asked, joining her.

"It looks like it's going to be a monster of a house."

"That's one way of putting it." Ernie pointed out where the two-story entryway would be and the layout of the 25-foot living room, the formal dining room, and the spacious family room. "It's going to have a river-rock fireplace and pine built-ins," he explained. "This is going to be a real impressive house."

He still couldn't believe the good fortune that had come to Heffelfinger and Gregory. It would have been beyond his imagination to even guess that they would start out on a project like this. But both he and Carl Gregory were well-known in the industry for their craftsmanship—why else would they have been contacted by the Trembrells, who just happened to have heard that they were going out on their own?

"That sounds like Nick and Keri," said Ren. "Everything has to be big."

"Do you know them?"

"Sort of. They're friends of my parents." She paused for a moment, then asked, "What do you think of them?"

"Oh, boy. That's a loaded question if I ever heard one. They're my clients. They've given me the opportunity to work on the kind of place I've always dreamed about working on. They'll put a nice profit in my checkbook come spring . . . "

"But?"

He ran his fingers through his hair. "They're not the kind of people I feel very comfortable dealing with. Carl and I have worked it out so that he'll do most of the talking. Lucky for me. Keri's been calling him a lot, always wanting to know why or when."

"That sounds like her."

"Carl doesn't mind. Actually, I think he kind of likes it. Me, I feel more comfortable getting bids and lining up subcontractors. I didn't even mind being the one who had to come up with a dollar figure that made everybody happy."

"You're pretty happy about building this house, aren't you?" she asked.

"Who wouldn't be? I can't wait to get started on the framing." He wished he could explain to her and Pete what it meant to him, but he was too embarrassed to admit how he felt about seeing a design take tangible shape. To him it was a mystery, a sacrament of sorts. He often felt more spiritual while building a house than he did in church.

Ren shot a strange look at Pete and shook her head slightly. Ernie intercepted the gesture. "What is it?" he asked. "What's going on?"

"Nothing," said Ren. "It isn't important."

"It is too," argued Pete. "It could be very important."

"What?" asked Ernie again, feeling the tension between the two.

"Just something I told Pete," Ren said, trying to dismiss it.

"Not 'just something.' This could be very important to Dad. Come on, Ren. Tell him what you told me."

Ren swore. "Look, I don't really want to get into this . . . "

"You'd rather have him go bankrupt like the Eglers? Real nice." He kicked at a clod and walked to the far side of the site.

With the sound of the word *bankrupt* ringing in his ears, Ernie fastened his eyes on Ren's. "All right. What's this all about?"

Ren's jaw jutted forward and she held his gaze. Then she shrugged. "How did you get suckered into this, anyway?"

"Suckered? That's not how I'd put it. This is a honey of a house. Half-a-million plus on the bottom line. That means a nice profit for us."

"That may sound good, but I'm not sure the money's worth it. Nick and Keri Trembrell are real trouble. I'll bet there's not another builder in town that would touch them with a ten-foot pole."

"Really," said Ernie, unaware that his right eyebrow had raised in a skeptical expression reminiscent of Helmut's. "What makes you say that?"

"They've been friends of my mom and dad for a long time. I heard them talking about what happened on their last house . . . "

When she hesitated, Ernie made a "come on" gesture with both hands.

"I guess there were a lot of problems," she said finally. "They said it was all the fault of the builders, but knowing them, I don't think so. Anyway, it added up to a lot of overruns that the builders got stuck with. They went bankrupt—"

"Who?"

"Egler Brothers."

Ernie rubbed his stubble. "I did hear something about them going under, but I don't know any of the details."

"They went under because of Nick and Keri. You've got to watch out for them, especially her. She's a ditz-brain. She can't visualize how things are going to look. No spatial concepts, you know? She had them build full-size plywood mock-ups of the whole kitchen—"

"Are you kidding?" Ernie laughed. "They actually did that?"

"Not once, but three times. The last time, they even had to paint them to look like the real cabinets and appliances would look."

"I can't believe the Eglers let them get away with that kind of thing."

"Ren says they did," said Pete, who had returned. "You've got a good contract, don't you, Dad?"

"Sure, but it's probably not that much different from the one the Eglers had with the Trembrells. It should have been enough to protect them. They must've made some big mistakes to get into that much trouble."

"Aren't you worried?"

"Not really, son." Ernie clapped Pete on the back and continued, "This may be the first house Carl and I have done on our own, but we have a lot of experience between the two of us. We know what to watch out for."

"Oh."

Noting Pete's deflated expression, Ernie added, "I'm glad you told me about it, though. I'll keep my eyes open, but I really don't think there's anything to worry about, okay?"

That didn't satisfy Ren. Ernie could tell she was disgusted by the fact he wasn't taking her warning seriously. *What can you expect when you have purple hair,* Ernie thought. He, for one, would never take anyone with purple hair seriously. Besides, he wasn't about to let anything ruin his elation over being on this job.

"You'll excuse me, won't you? I have to finish checking the footings."

He hopped into the excavation and walked along the outer footings, then the inner, sucking air with satisfaction. The subcontractors had done a good job. There was no reason why the crew scheduled to lay the cinder blocks couldn't get started the next day, exactly as he had planned it. He felt good, knowing that. The more they got done according to schedule now, the less critical later delays would be. And there would be delays. It was the nature of things.

When Ernie scrambled back out, Pete was still talking to Ren, so he leaned against the fender of his pickup enjoying the beauty of the late afternoon. The setting sun glowed through the October haze, touching the grove of sugar maples and oak west of the site with fire and gold. In the distance crows cawed, and overhead a line of Canada geese flew in formation, their outstretched necks black against the sky.

He sighed with contentment. He was where he wanted to be, doing what he wanted to do. The sheer size and complexity of the house, coupled with the Trembrells' exacting tastes, would mean problems along the way, but he was confident he and Carl would be able to work them out. *It's worth the risk,* he thought. *No matter what happens, it's worth it.*

He hadn't felt that positive the Sunday evening after he had made his announcement to the family. He chuckled, remembering the disastrous moment in the kitchen when Helmut saw Pete and Will in their spiked glory, and the way he had blurted out his plans at the worst possible time. Only Helmut's calm insistence on going ahead with Sunday dinner had restored a semblance of normalcy.

He was still surprised at how easy it had been to win Helmut over. But then, Helmut had always thought he had made a mistake by dropping out of law school. He considered Heffelfinger and Gregory a step in getting Ernie back on track.

An even greater surprise had been Maxine's eventual acquiescence and (he could still hardly believe it) financial support. But that came after the inevitable staging of her martyr act, which had filled up what was left of that Sunday after Helmut left. It was a drama he knew forward and backward, having been treated to it all too often since his defection from the ranks of professionals. She was good at it. To his annoyance, she could use the same logic on him to make him feel lousy about going into the building business that she had used when he quit law school to become a craftsman. She made him feel that he was doing something terrible, that he had put the family in jeopardy, and that if it weren't for her influence and sacrifice, everything would be completely lost.

However, by the time he walked out to Will's the following morning, she had already softened somewhat. It was as if the drama was something she had to get out of her system before she could begin to look at his proposition rationally. That gave him the beginning of hope. Also, Carl was on the way over, and if anybody could tip the scales in their favor, Carl could do it. Still, Ernie needed the extra encouragement he knew Will could give him. Maxine's arguments had made him uncomfortably aware of the risks.

"I'm not being irresponsible, am I?" he asked Will. "It is possible we won't get this job that Carl's lining up, and even if we do, there's no guarantee we'll make a profit on it."

"Do you have to?"

"Everything depends on making a profit. Even you know that."

"Say you didn't. You wouldn't starve, would you?"

"No. Maxine would refuse to."

"Right on. She'd sell another million of her Vitamin Z tablets. And if worse came to worse, she could start drawing a salary for handling Bill's money."

"She probably would," Ernie chuckled, "but I don't want her to feel like she has to because she's got a dud for a husband."

"Would that threaten your masculinity?"

"Where did you get that idea?"

Will grinned slyly. "Television. You'd be surprised how much I learn watching Phil Donahue."

"I wouldn't tell Maxine that, if I were you. She's convinced he's ruining the moral fiber of the nation singlehandedly."

"Well, would it?" asked Will, refusing to be deflected from his target.

"It probably would have once, but I've gotten used to the fact that she's more of a go-getter than I am. She's been out beating the bushes ever since I quit law school."

Will's eyes brightened. "You? In law school?"

"Didn't you know that? Maybe I never mentioned it before. Yep, good old Ernie was following in Dad's footsteps when Maxine came along. She thought she was marrying the future partner in Heffelfinger and Heffelfinger."

"I bet she nearly croaked when you dropped out," Will chortled.

"I don't think she's ever gotten over it. Sometimes I think she feels I married her under false pretenses."

"She should have been a writer. That way she could make things turn out the way she'd like them to."

"Not being a writer hasn't stopped her from trying to make things turn out her way."

"Don't give in to her. Hold your own, boy."

"That can be pretty hard to do against Maxine."

"You think I don't know that?"

Ernie nodded. "You more than anyone," he said, remembering how it had been for Will after he woke up from his coma. He had had no idea who he was; all he knew was who he wasn't: Bill Martin. It had taken great courage and determination to resist Maxine's efforts to mold him into her father's image. That determination was one of the reasons Ernie loved him. "You're a good man, Will," he said, standing. "Thanks for the encouragement."

"Remember, Possibility Thinking!" called Will as Ernie walked out the door.

He was almost back to the house when Carl Gregory pulled into the driveway. Carl was short and muscular, and he had what he liked to call a "tenor's chest." "I've got good lungs," he would add, and he proved it daily, singing snatches of operatic arias as he wielded his pneumatic hammer. No amount of teasing had ever been sufficient to convince him to quit.

"*Bonjourno,*" he now said, striding toward Ernie. "Are you ready to do battle?"

"Let's just hope there's not too much blood."

Carl's tenor filled the air. "*Sangue, sangue,*" he sang with a dramatic gesture.

"And what was that?"

" 'Blood, blood!' " he sang again.

"At least it's appropriate," said Ernie dryly.

"I take it Maxine's upset?"

"She's calmed down a lot since last night. My dad talked to her. He thinks it's a good idea."

"Great."

"To quote him exactly, 'It's about time you stopped playing around and used your talents for something besides making sawdust.' "

"Nice guy, your dad."

"At least Pete and Will are behind me."

"Maxine will be too, after I talk to her," Carl said, impatiently shifting his briefcase from one hand to another. "Let's get this ball rolling. The Trembrells are serious."

"They are?"

"Uh-huh. We're starting out in the big leagues."

Carl's confidence was catching. Not only did it fire Ernie up again, it swayed Maxine. As he explained their plan in his persuasive, melodic voice, Heffelfinger and Gregory became irresistible. *It must be the tenor in him,* Ernie thought wryly. *Maxine always has had a thing for tenors.*

After he finished talking, Carl sat back, folded his arms, and waited for Maxine's reaction.

"Who's going to do your books?" was her first question.

"My wife," replied Carl. "She's done that sort of thing for years, so she knows all the ins and outs."

"Keeping it in the family, are you?"

He nodded. "Would you like to come on board? I'm sure we could find something for you to do."

"Would you want me?" she asked, smiling faintly.

"Are you kidding? We need all the help we can get."

Her next question seemed to be a non sequitur, for Ernie had no idea how it connected with their present comments.

"How much is it going to take to incorporate? And what sorts of bonds and insurance are you going to have to take out?"

"Sounds like you know a lot about business," Carl said.

"My father owned Martin Development Corporation."

"You mean that old guy out in the barn?"

"No," her voice was even, but Ernie could feel her disapproval.

"I told you about the accident, Carl," Ernie said. "Remember?"

"Oh. Sorry, Maxine. I forgot."

"That's all right. The fact is, I learned a lot from my father, and I know something about the start-up costs you two are facing. How are you going to handle it?"

"We'll have to get a loan. Ernie and I've been writing up a business plan. It's almost ready to present to the bank."

"Present it to me and Ernie's father first, will you?"

Carl looked questioningly at Ernie, who suddenly felt light-headed as he realized what she was going to say next.

"Helmut helps me administer my father's estate. There are funds available that might be appropriately invested in the company of Heffelfinger and Gregory. If your business plan is in order, that is. And if Helmut agrees."

"All *right!*" cried Carl.

Ernie found he couldn't speak, he was so overwhelmed. He hugged Maxine with one arm, while with the other he shook Carl's hand. He knew it was a moment that would be painted into his memory like a fresco into wet cement, a moment that would endure as long as he did.

Now, as he surveyed the building site from which would soon rise a monument to the Trembrells' economic prosperity and impeccable taste, the same swelling of gratitude he had experienced that evening came over him again. "Thank you, Dad," he whispered. "Thank you, Maxine."

13

Pete decided to ride home with Ernie, so he got his book bag from the Fiero, then kissed Ren good-bye. It was a simple, quick kiss, but one that disturbed Ernie nonetheless. Pete reminded him of himself at this age – uncertain, inexperienced, full of longing. Who knew where that longing would take him, how far he would go in Ren's direction to please her?

"Life was a whole lot easier when Pete was younger," he murmured to himself, climbing into the pickup. He and Maxine had set up expectations, which Pete had (more or less) fulfilled: Bedroom kept clean. Daily chores done. Homework in on time. Progress made toward an Eagle scout award. One hundred percent church attendance.

Pete had accepted the structure they provided for him as a given. Although he had balked at times, he hadn't questioned. Until lately. Now it seemed that he questioned everything. It was as if he had suddenly realized he could make up his own mind about things. This was all well and good except for the fact that he wasn't coming to the conclusions they wanted him to.

Free agency, the power to choose. It was the greatest gift of God to man. Too bad exercising it wasn't as simple as it was sometimes made to sound. You were supposed to study, pray, and come to your own conclusions – but if your conclusions didn't agree with the counsel of church leaders, you were wrong.

Pete had arrived at the age where he was making his own choices, and they didn't always agree with the counsel of the church leaders or his parents. So he was wrong.

Right?

I don't know, Ernie mused. *I really don't know. I just try to keep my nose clean, do what I'm asked to do, and pay my bills.*

Pete broke into Ernie's thoughts as he climbed in the pickup and shut his door. "Let's go," he said.

"Are you two getting serious?" asked Ernie, turning the key.

"I dunno."

"Would you like to get serious?"

Pete grinned. "Yeah. Maybe."

"Which is it, yeah or maybe?"

"Do we have to talk about this? It's embarrassing."

"You didn't seem too embarrassed when you kissed her."

"That wasn't much of a kiss," Pete protested, but he flushed anyway. "Don't say anything about it in front of Mom, okay?"

"I won't. She's not going to be home anyway. She's got one of those planning meetings. We have to fend for ourselves tonight. Again."

"Why did she agree to be the chairman of that Woman's Day, or whatever it is? She knew it was scheduled for the week after her Pure Organics whoopla."

"She didn't want to turn down the stake Relief Society presidency, for one thing. And she thought she could handle it."

"She probably can, only I'm tired of having tuna fish casserole for supper."

Ernie chuckled. "You're not the only one. We just have to hang in there until the first weekend in November, and then it'll all be over. In the meantime, what would you rather do, go home and eat tuna fish casserole, or go to the Cattle Company for a big steak?"

"No contest, man. Steak."

"Will you have any problems getting in?" Ernie asked, eyeing Pete's ragged jeans and his wild hair.

"Not as long as I have on a shirt and shoes."

"Okay. The Cattle Company it is."

Ernie was glad Pete agreed to eating out. He had been wanting to talk to his son for quite a while, but finding the right time wasn't easy. Almost every night after supper, Pete disappeared into his bedroom and turned on that wretched music of his. A couple of times, Ernie had gone upstairs intending to knock on the door, but he didn't. There was something about that metallic dissonance that defied interruption. This is my world, it proclaimed, and my world is not your world.

Talking to Pete wasn't entirely his own idea. Maxine was concerned about him too. According to her, Pete had made a series of decisions that were leading him down a dangerous path. First, he dyed his hair. That led to spending time with Ren, which in turn led to a drop in his seminary attendance. The year before, he had gone 88 percent of the time. At the rate he was going this year, he would be lucky to hit 70 percent.

Maxine had tried to talk to Pete about it, but her approach had led to disastrous results. "If it weren't for Ren Dykstra, you'd be going to seminary every day," she said to Pete. "Get your attendance back up, or I'll forbid you to have anything to do with her."

"How would you like it if I didn't go at all?" he countered, starting off another of the arguments that were becoming so frequent.

Afterward, Ernie had tried to suggest that she not make everything into a life-and-death issue. She had accused him of not taking anything seriously enough.

He wondered if she was right, as he threaded the pickup through rush hour traffic toward the Cattle Company. The truth was, he didn't think missing a few days of seminary was critical, as long as Pete kept going with some regularity. He didn't think Pete's casual attitude about attending Mutual was that much of a problem either. Since Pete had gotten his Eagle award at age fourteen, there didn't seem much for him to do on Wednesday evenings. "We just mess around," was the way he put it.

Ernie was more concerned about the fact that while Pete still went to church with them, he was spending more and more time out in the parking lot. He was also concerned that simple conversation between them had virtually ceased. That was what he wanted, really, a good conversation with his son. He made a tentative beginning while they waited for their steaks by asking, "How are things going?"

"Okay."

"You're getting along all right in school?"

Pete shrugged. "Not the best, but not the worst either."

"What's the problem? Aren't you studying enough?"

"I'm studying. I just have a personality conflict with a couple of teachers. No big deal."

"Oh. Well . . . " Ernie sipped his ice water and let his eyes wander over the heavy beams and rustic finishing of the restaurant. After a while, he tried again, aware even as he spoke that the topic he was introducing would hardly be conducive to simple conversation. "You haven't been going to seminary as much this year. Any particular reason why not?"

"It's not fun anymore. All we get is lecture, lecture, lecture. You'd think we were in a graduate class."

"The point of seminary isn't to have fun. You're supposed to be learning something."

"Hitting us over the head doesn't help us learn. Besides, knowing something doesn't necessarily mean we believe it."

"Oh?"

"We can be the best scripture-chasers in the stake, and that doesn't mean we have the strongest testimonies."

"Are you saying you don't have a testimony?"

Pete tipped his chair back on two legs and looked at Ernie with a wry grin. "So that's the point of this father-son discussion. I was wondering what you were leading up to."

"I wasn't leading up to anything. I was just asking."

Instead of answering his question, Pete posed one. "Do you have a testimony, Dad?"

"I think I do. I must. The bishop gave me a temple recommend the last time I went in for an interview."

"That could just mean you know how to answer the questions right."

Ernie's voice was reproachful. "I answered them truthfully."

"Sorry, Dad. I didn't mean anything by that."

"I'm not much of a scriptorian, you know that. Intellectual discussions don't do much for me. What I am is a pragmatist. I'm interested in what works, and for me, the gospel works. It's just too bad . . . "

"What?"

Ernie drew a breath and paused before finally answering. "I just wish I felt more comfortable in our ward, that's all."

"Yeah?"

"It makes it hard for me sometimes . . . " He sighed. "But the problem is me as much as them. I admit it."

"Them?"

"The pin-striped yuppies."

"Oh, *them.*"

"Let's change the subject. The ward I'm in shouldn't affect my commitment to the gospel, and most of the time it doesn't. At least, I don't think it does."

At that point, the waitress arrived with their food. She set before Ernie a plate laden with an opened baked potato steaming fragrantly and a steak broiled to slightly pink perfection. "This looks great. I'm starving," he said. He put three pats of butter on his baked potato and glopped sour cream on top of that. Pete followed suit, and for the next few minutes, both of them concentrated on their food.

Then Pete asked, "Why didn't you listen to what Ren was saying, Dad?"

Ernie swallowed a piece of steak before answering. "I did listen."

"You didn't seem to think it was anything important."

"I can't spend too much time worrying about what went on with the Trembrells' last house. Each job is different, Pete. Maybe the Trembrells and the Egler Brothers had problems communicating. Maybe the Eglers didn't cover themselves. I don't know. But so far, we're doing fine."

"You don't like Ren. That's why you're not taking it seriously."

"I do like Ren."

"No, you don't."

Ernie laid down his fork and knife. "I don't dislike her, I just don't feel comfortable around her. Her hair . . . "

"Pretty wild, isn't it?"

"She changes hair color like some people change shoes. I wouldn't be a bit surprised if it all fell out one of these days."

"What else?"

"She doesn't do it often around us, and I appreciate that, but she can talk pretty rough for a young lady."

"Everybody talks like that, Dad. You probably hear it as much on the job as I do at school."

"Probably," conceded Ernie, "but I'm not used to hearing those sorts of words coming out of the mouth of a girl."

"That's reality. That's the way things are now."

"I'm still not comfortable around it." Ernie scraped the last of his baked potato from the skin and ate it before adding, "Your mother says Ren doesn't get along with her parents."

"That's a nice way to put it," Pete said sarcastically. "The truth is, she might as well not have parents, for all they care about her."

"You might hear a different story if you talked to them about it."

"Good old Dad. Always taking the other guy's side."

"I'm just saying you don't know the whole story. All you know is what Ren's told you. Kids can be pretty rough on their parents, Pete. You probably think your mother's coming down hard right now, but she's really worried about you."

"She's more worried about her reputation."

"That's exactly what I'm talking about. You're not giving her half a chance. She only wants the best for you. She wants you to be happy."

"Then why doesn't she leave me alone? That would make me happy."

"Would it? You just got through condemning Ren's parents for not caring about her, and now you want your mother to act like she doesn't care about you."

"I don't want her to stop caring about me!" Pete's voice was exasperated. "I just want her to stop trying to manipulate me. She can't make me do what she wants me to do anymore, Dad. I'm not five years old."

"That's not easy for her—"

"Tough."

"We do have some legitimate concerns."

"Such as?"

"Such as your grades this trimester. Your attendance at seminary. The fact that you're skipping out during Sunday School. The fact that you're spending an awful lot of time with a young lady who seems to have some serious problems. And—"

"Look, can't you trust me just a little? I've never done drugs. I haven't wrecked your pickup. The police haven't called you in the middle of the night. What more do you want?"

"Good question," Ernie said, looking across the table into his son's eyes. They were open, clear, guileless. In spite of the way he looked and the things he was doing, he was still Pete. Still Ernie's little boy.

Only he wondered how long it would be before that changed too.

14

Ernie didn't totally ignore Ren's warning. That evening he called Carl and told him what she had said. They decided that the best way to avoid problems down the line was good communication. "We can't make any assumptions about what the Trembrells want or are agreeing to. We have to have everything black and white," Carl said. Then he sang full-voiced, "*Che cosa faccio? Scrivo.*"

Ernie held the receiver away from his ear. "Forget the translation," he started to say, but he was too late. "My business? Writing," Carl sang again, adding, "If I have to, I'll make them write a change order on everything, no matter how picayune it is."

"I don't know. I agree with you about the communication part, but we don't want to push them. I can't think of anything worse than building a house for someone I'm not getting along with."

"That's for sure."

"Besides, we might not have any problems. We haven't so far. It doesn't make sense to cause some, just because of something my son's girlfriend overheard. She may have it all wrong."

"I'm with you. We take it easy for a while, only we keep track of everything that happens. The minute it starts looking like we're getting shafted, we get mean."

"Right."

"Is the crew coming in to lay the blocks tomorrow?"

"Uh-huh. So far, we're on time. We should be framing by the end of the week."

They started on Friday. Ernie was exhilarated. He loved the smell of wood, the sound of hammer connecting with nail. But a layer of unease marred the clarity of his enjoyment, the way a fall haze fuzzes crisp lines. Although he didn't like feeling suspicious of the Trembrells, he knew it would be hard not to interpret everything differently now that Ren had planted the seed of distrust.

Why can't life be simple? he thought as he measured and cut and pounded. *All anybody wants is to be happy.*

He was thinking of himself and Pete at the moment. He had no idea he could have added another Heffelfinger to the list of those trying to find a way to be happy, his father, Helmut. He got the first hint when Helmut called Saturday evening.

"You get it, it's probably your dad anyway," Maxine called from the kitchen when the phone rang. "Tell him we're expecting him for dinner as usual."

It was Helmut, but he wasn't calling about the standing dinner engagement. "I'm thinking of driving over early," he said. "Maybe I'll get there in time to go to church with you."

"What?"

"You don't mind, do you?"

"N . . . no. I was just surprised, that's all."

"Why?"

Ernie laughed shortly. "I've been a Mormon for seventeen years and not once have you ever wanted to come to church with us. Not even when something special was happening, like Pete's blessing and baptism."

"I would have come if you'd asked me to be his godfather."

"Dad, we don't have godfathers in our church, you know that."

There was a pause, and Ernie could imagine his father's right eyebrow raising in an expression of disbelief.

"Ah, well," Helmut said, accompanied (Ernie imagined) by a forgiving shrug of the shoulder, as if he had indeed forgiven Ernie for joining the church and the church itself for its anomalies. "And what time does your service begin?"

"Nine. And we won't be done until noon."

"Noon! What can you possibly do that takes three hours?"

"We have all our meetings back-to-back, remember? It's easier for the ones who have a long way to drive."

"Hummph."

"You could come to sacrament meeting and then drive back to our place . . . "

"I'll stay for the duration. If I arrive at your place at eight-thirty, will that give us enough time to get there punctually?"

"Plenty."

"Eight-thirty, then."

Feeling strangely disoriented, Ernie hung up. He stood by the phone, wondering if he had really heard what he thought he had heard. His father, Helmut Heffelfinger, coming to the Maple Hills First Ward! He couldn't believe it.

Neither could Maxine. "Are you sure that's what he said?"

"Yes."

"How odd. He made it perfectly clear when you got baptized that he wanted nothing to do with the Church. He's stuck with that decision all these years. Why change now?"

"I have no idea."

"Unless . . . "

"Unless what?"

"Unless he's lonesome. Bored. Feeling left out of things."

"My dad? Helmut H. Heffelfinger? Not likely."

"Why not? It happens when high-powered executives or professional men retire. After all those years of pushing themselves, they wake up one morning with nothing to do. It's like a diver getting the bends because he's coming up too fast."

"Maybe," said Ernie, whose own steady plodding offered no clue to what that might be like.

"Mom used to worry a lot about what would happen to Dad when he retired. He was always going full speed ahead . . . " Maxine's voice trailed off as she looked out the window at Will's place.

"Say you're right, and he *is* bored or lonesome. Why doesn't he do something with one of the clubs he belongs to?"

"I imagine even that isn't the same once a person's retired."

"I still don't get it," Ernie said, pacing.

Maxine leaned against the kitchen counter and looked at him through squinted eyes. "You don't want him to come, do you?"

Her insight caught him in midstride. He knew instantly that she was right.

"Why not?" she persisted.

"I guess I'm worried about how he might react to it. We don't have the quietest ward in the world, you know. At least it's not Fast Sunday."

"What's wrong with Fast Sunday?"

"Don't tell me you *like* hearing travelogues? And listening to half-a-dozen sniveling teenagers trade compliments and promises of undying friendship?"

"We do get that sometimes, but that's not what—"

"Or is it being called to repentance by some overachiever that you like?"

"Ernie! Your inadequacies are showing."

"Thank you, Maxine."

"You wouldn't be talking like this if you didn't feel so out of place."

"Whose fault is that?"

"Not mine, that's for sure. And not the ward members'."

They stared at each other across the room for a long moment; then Ernie said, "We've had this conversation before, haven't we?"

"About a thousand times."

"Then let's not have it again."

"That's fine with me." Maxine's expression softened. She put her arms around Ernie and rested her head on his shoulder. "Come on," she cajoled. "Let's not fight. There's been too much of that lately. Anyway, you're not mad at me—you're just upset about Helmut coming. Why?"

He found it hard to articulate what he was feeling. "Dad

won't . . . he's so smart, Maxine. He can make words say anything he wants them to. I'm afraid he'll think we're deluded—"

"If he does?"

"I won't be able to defend the Church against him."

"Maybe you won't have to."

"Fat chance of that happening."

Maxine sighed. "I don't supposed there's any chance of getting our son in his suit, either."

"About as much as the Twins winning the pennant."

Helmut was punctual that Sunday morning, having arrived seven minutes early and then parked on the side of Rockford Road to wait until the appointed time arrived. Ernie saw the car from the bedroom window. "Why doesn't he come in?" he asked, cracking his knuckles. "It makes me nervous knowing he's just sitting there, waiting for the exact moment."

"That's Helmut," said Maxine from the bathroom.

Ernie dressed quickly. He put on the pants of the charcoal gray suit Maxine had recently bought for him, a white shirt, over-the-calf socks (Maxine hated seeing the hair between the top of his socks and the cuff of his pants when he had one leg crossed over the other), dressy leather loafers, and a gray and silver tie that had a discreet but interesting line of pink. The uniform of a successful businessman. He looked good, he decided, looking in the full-length mirror on Maxine's closet door. He wished he felt as good as he looked.

At 8:29, Ernie went to the top of the stairs and waited until he heard his father's footsteps on the porch. He walked quickly down and opened the door just as Helmut raised his hand.

"Am I on time?" Helmut asked, flicking a bit of lint from his suit jacket.

"On the money." Ernie automatically straightened his shoulders as he took in his father's spit-polished image. Helmut had a neat, elegant air about him that Ernie had never been able to achieve, no matter what he did. No matter what Maxine bought him.

He motioned his father in. "Sit down while I get everybody together."

Maxine appeared first, putting on an earring as she came down the stairs. "Good morning," she said, offering her cheek to Helmut.

Then Pete thundered down. He had taken scissors and clippers to his hair that morning. The now-brown hair at the back and sides of his head was cut short, and the two-tone hair on the top looked as if it had had a run in with an egg beater. He was wearing a dark blue, narrow-collared shirt of ancient vintage, a narrow black tie, and pleated pants of indeterminate age.

"Are you going like that?" Helmut asked Pete.

Pete nodded.

"Your bishop allows you to?"

"Yeah. He's a good guy. Hey, Mom! Did I tell you he's going to talk to Markham about me blessing the sacrament? He says it's okay by him. I'm going to make some toast. Want some, Grandpa?"

Helmut shook his head. Pete had his toast, Will arrived not long after, and they got on their way at fifteen to nine. Ernie kept pulling nervously at the collar of his shirt. He couldn't imagine what was going to happen, or how Helmut would react to a ward full of noisy little kids—and noisy adults.

He needn't have worried. There was something about Helmut's very presence that seemed to draw people to him. Ernie could see it happening from the moment they stepped into the corridor. Men who hardly ever paid any attention to him now stopped to shake Helmut's hand and inquire if he was going to move into the ward.

Helmut accepted their attention as if it were his due. He was gracious. He was witty. He completely captivated those he met in the foyer before and after the meetings. Ernie was stunned. Helmut's easy camaraderie made his own awkward participation in the Maple Hills First Ward even more painful. He felt as if he were the outsider, Helmut the member.

It hadn't always been that way. He had been happy in the Minneapolis ward they had attended prior to moving out on Rockford Road. He had felt at ease in the diverse mixture of members. There were professional men among them, a lawyer, a doctor or two, several executives, and a teacher. But there were also factory workers, a garbage collector, tradesmen, civil servants, and some welfare recipients. It was a small ward, one in which everyone depended upon everyone else for support and survival.

The move out to the place on Rockford Road put them in an entirely different type of ward. Maple Hills First Ward was full of professional men, mostly executives. There was even a retired corporate president among the lot. Control Data Corporation was represented, as were Honeywell, General Mills, Pillsbury, and Carlton Company. There were bankers, too, from the Federal Reserve Bank and Norwest. And those were just the big names. There were plenty of smaller companies represented as well.

Ernie came up with his description for the ward the first Sunday they attended. "Great," he muttered. "I belong to a ward full of middle-management Mormons."

Maxine, on the other hand, was thrilled by their new ward. "What a lovely group of people," she gushed on the way home. "Did you get a chance to meet some of them?"

"A couple of brethren talked to me for a while," he replied flatly. "Then they went back to exchanging tips on which hotels in New York are the best and which Broadway show is worth the price of a ticket."

She picked up on the tone of his voice. "Are you mad about something?"

"Yep, as a matter of fact, I am. I'm not going to fit into this ward, Maxine."

"How can you tell? You've only been once."

"I can tell."

"You'll feel better after a while. You'll get a calling soon, and we'll have some people over . . . "

When he was invited to join the Saturday-morning

basketball group, Maxine exulted, "See? I told you it was just a matter of time. You're a good shot. They'll be glad to have you play with them."

He hoped she was right. He was a good player, and he took pride in his ability. He played with the determined athletes of the Maple Hills First Ward only a few times, however. He had expected to have fun but found instead that the games were deadly serious. He was shoved, pushed, and elbowed by other players in pursuit of a point. The day he was tripped (deliberately, he thought) when he came in to make a lay-up, he decided he'd had enough. The fierce competitiveness and will to win that propelled the other players was foreign to him and far out of proportion to the importance of the game.

He was ready to give up then, but Maxine wasn't. She did everything she could think of to help him feel comfortable in their new ward. She bought him new clothes. She talked him into getting his hair cut by a stylist instead of a barber. She was unceasing in her efforts to prod him into a social life, inviting couples over for polite dinners that he hated.

"Stop trying," he finally said. "I'll never feel comfortable with any of them."

"See, that's the problem. You separate yourself from the other men in the ward."

"Maybe. But they separate themselves from me, too. They don't even talk about the things I can comment on. Let's face it, I'm just a cabinetmaker. I'll never be a Frequent Flyer."

"That shouldn't make any difference."

"Maybe it shouldn't, but it does."

"Okay, so find some other friends in the ward. Not all of the men are executives. George Mallory is an electrician. Bob Zeller is a repairman for Sears. Make friends with them."

"Working stiffs should stick together, eh?"

"Oh, what *do* you want?" cried Maxine.

He shook his head sadly. He didn't know what he wanted.

There had been times since their move when he wondered if his inability to fit in was the result of some defect in his own personality, or if it was more perceived than real. Then he would put out more effort, hoping that by extending himself, he might find a place that was warm, inviting, accepting.

It didn't happen. Every Sunday he dressed in the fancy clothes Maxine bought him. He looked like the other brethren when he was dressed that way, but he wasn't like them. And he never would be. They were confident of their ability, their righteousness, and their upward mobility (in this world and in the next), while Ernie wondered what it was all about, and if anything he did was of any value to himself or anyone else.

If Maxine had asked him why he hadn't gotten upset over Pete's sudden transformation, he might have told her that he understood what was going on in Pete's head. He felt as invisible in the Maple Hills First Ward as Pete felt in Wayzata North Senior High. He was appreciated as someone who would do what he was asked to do, but it was an impersonal appreciation, more for the function he filled than for himself as a person.

Which was why the sight of Helmut in animated conversation with men who rarely bothered to acknowledge his presence brought resentment so swift, it took Ernie's breath away.

15

"I'm glad I came," said Helmut as they drove home. "You have a fine group of men." His eyes twinkling, he added for Maxine's benefit, "And women, I assume, only I didn't get a chance to meet many of them."

Maxine, who was sitting in the back seat between Helmut and Will, began listing the luminaries of the Maple Hills First Ward, indicating their secular and social position as well as their church callings. Ernie turned his attention from that conversation to Pete, who was in the front seat with him.

"What was it you were saying this morning about the bishop letting you bless the sacrament?" he asked. "When did you talk to him?"

"On Wednesday at Mutual."

"He isn't worried about how you look?"

"I didn't say that. He'd like it better if I looked normal, but he doesn't think it's a criminal offense." Pete chuckled. "He said, 'I doubt very much if you're going to start a trend in our ward.' "

"I doubt it too."

"Anyway, punk is passé, did you know that?"

"It's what?"

"Out of it. Old. At least that's what an article in the *Star and Tribune* said. I guess that's what happens to us slow starters. By the time we decide to follow a trend, it isn't a trend anymore."

"What else did the bishop say?"

"That he'd rather offend some people in the ward than turn me off about the Church."

"Hmm. I wouldn't have expected that from him."

"He's not as hard as you might think, Dad. He had to tell me he didn't approve of what I was doing—that's the party line. But then he said he understood, and I think he did."

"Did you talk to him about Ren?"

Pete looked at him sharply. "Why should I talk to him about Ren?"

"You two are getting pretty involved."

"So what? It's none of his business if we are."

After that, there was silence in the front seat, while Maxine continued her Who's Who the rest of the way home.

The conversation was directed entirely toward church the rest of the afternoon. Maxine, delighted by Helmut's interest, answered most of his questions. Every so often she would look at Ernie first, giving him a chance to respond, but when he didn't, either she or Pete would fill in the empty space.

Helmut seemed most intrigued by the lay ministry of the Church, which offered everyone a chance to make a meaningful contribution. He was also impressed by the conservative views, which coincided with his own.

"I guess I didn't realize what your stand was on certain issues," he remarked. "Women in the home, for instance."

Oh, oh, thought Ernie. *Wrong topic to bring up in front of Maxine.* She had had a difficult time working through her feelings about the very clear message of the church leaders concerning the calling of women. It was a calling centered around home and family, with work outside the home being an option to be exercised only when need made it necessary.

But Maxine had never felt that her talents lay in the housewifely arts. She did everything that was necessary for the household to run smoothly, and not only that, she did it well, having been blessed with great organizational ability and energy. She applied the same vigor to the preparation necessary for her church callings and to her volunteer work. Her ability to perform won many hours of free time, however, and not for her were the arts and crafts, sewing, reading, or visiting that might have filled them. So she had ventured into the world of multi-level marketing.

Ernie understood the motivation behind her move, for he and Maxine had talked about it a lot during those early years. Beyond the financial considerations, he knew that she was much happier when she spent some time each week out among other people, making sales and building her organization. But he also knew that her recognition of that part of herself had made the Church's stance particularly painful. She felt as if there were something intrinsically wrong with her.

More than once she had prayed and agonized over what she should do, and in the end she had continued to pursue her career, but not without ambivalence. She felt the constant need to reevaluate and balance her life. It had been much easier for her to justify taking over the management of her father's business affairs. That had been done out of necessity.

Helmut seemed unaware that the light had gone out of Maxine's eyes when he had begun talking about the role of women. He stated his case, eloquent as always. "I have long held the opinion that half of the world's problems could be solved if women stayed home, insuring the perpetuation of the race, transmitting cultural values, and making it possible for men to take their place in the world."

Ernie groaned into his napkin, Pete choked on a mouthful of water, and Will grinned, as Helmut blithely continued.

"Consider the fact that there wouldn't be the current scramble for day care. There wouldn't be so many unemployed men or this bruhaha about comparable worth. Not only that—with women home during the day, the incidents of burglary would dramatically drop in some areas."

"Does that mean you think I should be staying home instead of working?" asked Maxine, too sweetly.

"My point is not that you specifically should stay home, my dear, but only that the world would be better off in general if women weren't competing so strongly with men in the marketplace."

"Oh. You're stating a principle, but leaving the door open for exceptions?"

"You could put it that way."

"Every woman who works has her reasons."

"No doubt. But are they justified?"

Maxine looked out the window without answering.

Helmut turned to Will. "What do you think about it? Do you go along with the stand of the Church?"

"I think everybody should do what they want to do," said Will, stirring his mashed potatoes and peas together.

"Obviously," murmured Maxine with a pained expression.

"That would lead to anarchy," commented Helmut.

"I don't think so." Will worked with obvious enjoyment on his mound of mashed potatoes as he added, "Most people have a sense of what's right and what's wrong. From there, it's up to them to decide what to do about it."

"You mean you don't think your church leaders should state their opinions about how the principles are to be translated into action?"

"I didn't say that," said Will. He forked some mashed potatoes and peas into his mouth, chewed once, and swallowed. "It's their job to state their conclusions."

He took another mouthful.

"Or opinions."

And yet another. Maxine looked back out the window, unable to bear the sight.

"Or counsel."

He laid down his fork, wiped a blob of potatoes from the corner of his mouth, and leaned back, replete. "It's the individual's job to discover the truth and then figure out how to make it work in his own life."

"It sounds like you think truth is relative," commented Pete.

"Nope," said Will, shaking his head. "Truth is truth. Life is relative. If there's one thing I've learned, it's that black and white don't exist except in the mind. As long as we're on the earth, we're smack dab in the middle of the gray."

"You've become quite the philosopher, haven't you," said Maxine, whose face wore an incredulous expression.

"I've had to. I woke to this world an old man. I don't have much time to figure out the whys and wherefores."

An uncomfortable silence followed Will's words. Authentic communication had never been part of the Sunday routine. Helmut's intellectualizing had precluded the expression of feelings and the discussion of real issues. Ernie realized at that moment why they had been willing to maintain the status quo. This conversation had become far too personal and definitely uncomfortable.

"Pie, anyone?" Maxine asked, rising. And it seemed to Ernie that they were all relieved by the bustle necessitated by the removal of the dinner plates and the serving of the pie.

They finished up the day according to the usual pattern. Then, as Helmut stood at the door, he said, "See you next Sunday at eight thirty."

Helmut arrived the next Sunday in time for church, and the Sunday after that as well. Although it was highly unusual, Ernie didn't attach any significance to this sudden interest in the Church. He was too absorbed by the Trembrell house to worry about what his father might be thinking. He and Carl had put together a crew of carpenters, and the work was progressing rapidly in spite of Carl's operatic interludes.

Often, Keri Trembrell stopped by in the late afternoon to check on the progress of her house. She was petite, vivacious, and tanned. Even on the days when she came directly from playing tennis, she was carefully made up, and gold twinkled on her ears, wrist, and fingers. She flirted with them and fed them, cookies one day, brownies the next. After a few such visits, her presence on the site was taken for granted, her treats looked forward to.

"Pete's girl had a bee in her bonnet," said Carl a week later. "Keri's okay. She's a little picky, but who isn't?"

"I hope that's all," murmured Ernie. Already, they had had

to absorb the cost for some extra excavation and a retaining wall, something Ernie thought the Trembrells should have paid for. They had disagreed.

"You didn't tell us you needed to build a retaining wall," Keri had said, smiling into Carl's eyes.

"Yeah, but it's a part of the site preparation," Ernie objected. "You wanted the house located here, and it couldn't be without the extra work. Unless you were willing to put up with water in your basement."

"Now Ernie, you led me to believe the costs were all figured in."

"Well, it was more complicated than I thought."

"I'm sorry about that, but figuring out everything that has to be done is your job, isn't it?"

"Right, but you're getting the benefit, so you ought to pay for the material at least."

"I don't know . . . "

When Keri left, Ernie persuaded Carl to call Nick Trembrell. Nick took the same logical, understanding, and immovable stance as his wife. Finally, Heffelfinger and Gregory agreed to eat the extra cost. The incident put Ernie on guard. Ren had called Keri Trembrell a ditz-brain, but Ernie was inclined to think that she knew exactly what she had to do to get what she wanted.

When the Trembrells decided that they wanted French doors where a window was indicated, Ernie made sure that Carl explained to them Heffelfinger and Gregory's policy not to make changes unless they received a change order, including a ball-park figure, within seventy-two hours of the time the work was to be done. The change order didn't appear, so Ernie insisted on proceeding according to the blueprint.

"It's no big deal. Let's go ahead and do it the way they want it," Carl encouraged.

"No go."

"They'll have a fit when they see we've framed for a window."

"Let them."

"Okay, buddy. You explain it to them when they come."

"That's all right with me."

They came early in the afternoon two days later. Keri, who held a bakery box, was casually dressed as usual. Nick, however, had come directly from his office. His precisely tailored dark suit skimmed his torso. The expensive watch on his wrist showed when he straightened the flap of his jacket pocket.

Ernie hated confrontation, but when he saw Nick, he was determined to hold his own. He couldn't have explained why standing up to the Trembrells was so important to him; he only knew that he had to.

He and Carl waited silently until the Trembrells noticed their change had not been made. It didn't take long.

"I thought we talked to you about the French doors," said Nick calmly.

"You did," replied Carl.

"Then why is this wall framed for a window?"

Ernie waited for Carl to go on, but he didn't. He stepped back, serious about having Ernie do the explaining. *Okay, if that's the way it's going to be,* Ernie thought. He hitched up his belt and said, "You didn't get the change order to us."

"Oh, I'm so sorry," apologized Keri. "I guess it slipped my mind. But a window won't work there. This vista just *calls* for a French door, don't you think?"

"I don't know what it calls for, but we'll do whatever you want—as soon as we have a change order."

"I'll get it to you right away," she assured him.

"Fine. Only now it's going to cost you more than we talked about."

"Why is that?" asked Nick.

"First you're going to have to pay for the work that was done on that wall, then you're going to have to pay for ripping it out."

Keri Trembrell turned away as if deeply offended. Nick took Ernie by the arm. He bent his head near Ernie's and said in a confidential tone, "Listen, Ernie, we're on the same side. We both want a great house at the end of this, right?"

Ernie nodded.

"We're not adversaries, are we?"

"No."

"Then why are we fighting?"

"We're not fighting. I'm just explaining how things are. We won't make a change without the order. Carl told you that."

"Right. I understand your position. But to make an issue out of a mistake . . . "

"The kind of mistakes that pulled the Eglers under?"

Nick straightened up and stepped back from Ernie. "The Eglers are responsible for their own problems. They are good builders but poor businessmen."

"That's not what I heard."

"Who have you been talking to?" asked Keri, who stood at her husband's side.

"Ren Dykstra. She's a friend of my son Pete."

"That little troublemaker," said Keri coldly. "If she were my daughter, I'd turn her over my knee and paddle her behind. Then I'd lock her in her room until she came to her senses."

"For telling me about the Eglers?"

Keri gave him a pitying look. "You don't know, do you? I didn't think so. Ren would hardly tell her boyfriend's father that she's breaking her parents' hearts. It was hard enough on them when Chris committed suicide, but when Ren accused them of driving him to it, it was simply too much."

"I didn't know—"

"Of course not. They tried to handle it on their own—they do have some pride left—but when Ren flipped out with this punk stuff, they sent her to a psychiatrist. They paid thousands of dollars for nothing."

"It didn't help?"

"Quite the opposite. Ren took him in hook, line, and sinker. By the time she was through with him, he was spouting some psycho-babble to her parents about Ren being the 'presenting problem' and them all needing therapy."

"Did they go?"

"You must be joking. It was ridiculous of him even to suggest it. Ren's the one with the purple hair, after all."

Why is she telling me all this? Ernie wondered, and suddenly he realized that she had been hoping it would divert him from the point he had been wanting to make. *It's time to get back on track,* he told himself. Again he hitched up his tool belt. "All this is beside the point, isn't it?" he said firmly. "The issue is how we're going to work together from now on. It's clear to me that the only way for us all to get what we want out of this is to make sure everything's covered. That means in writing."

Having said his piece, he held his breath, wondering what her reply would be. But to his amazement, her expression completely cleared. With a bright smile, she said, "Of course, you're right. We'll get the paperwork to you first thing in the morning. And we'll pay for the work you did wrong."

She smiled sweetly as she emphasized the last word. Then she opened the bakery box and began passing out donuts.

16

Ernie took off his carpenter's belt the moment the Trembrells left. "I'm going home early," he said, brushing aside Carl's congratulations on a successful outcome. "I can't work on this house anymore today."

He was angry, angrier than he had ever been in his life, and his white-knuckled grip on the steering wheel while he drove home showed it. Although he had managed to win his point with the Trembrells, Keri's last words had made him look stubborn and uncooperative. That stuck in his craw. He was also disturbed by Keri's revelations about Ren, but not in the way Keri had intended he should be. He was less horrified by what she had told him than he was by her attitude of cold disregard for the girl.

"I should have stuck up for her," he muttered. "She's such a little thing. And she was right about the Trembrells."

The feeling of protectiveness that welled up within him was something new. He had never felt protective toward Maxine. Someone as able and determined to take care of herself as she was didn't inspire that kind of emotion. Nor had he felt that way about Pete. Pete was a boy, and boys were supposed to tough it out.

His previous assessment of Ren underwent a metamorphosis under the influence of his changed feelings. While he had seen her before as harsh and belligerent, he now saw her as fragile and childlike. And he was glad that she had someone as solid and reliable as Pete to look out for her.

Maxine was at Martin Development Company when he got home, so he walked over to Will's and told him the whole story.

"Why do you suppose she hates Ren so much?" he asked as he finished.

"You did say that the Trembrells are friends of Ren's parents?"

"Uh-huh."

"I guess they hear a lot of war stories from Ren's mom and dad. Keri probably has picked up on some negative vibes."

Ernie smiled at Will's word usage. "She was sending out some negative vibes of her own this afternoon." Then he turned sober. "I wish I had said something in Ren's defense. I should have."

"Maybe. But it sounds to me like you did all right for yourself. You didn't back down from your position."

"No, I didn't." Ernie plopped into an overstuffed chair, his hands dangling over the sides limply. His adrenalin surge had dropped off, leaving him feeling washed out. "It's the hardest thing I've ever done. Where do you get it?"

"Get what?"

"Strength. Assertiveness. The guts to say what you want to say and to be who you want to be, regardless of everybody else."

"You think I've got that?" Will smiled, a rueful yet sweet smile. "Don't forget, I didn't choose the battle. I've had to dig in to convince everybody I don't like asparagus, *La Traviata,* or Impressionists." He laughed and shrugged. "Bill may have liked those things, but me, I've got simpler tastes."

"Don't try to fool me, Will. You're a lot more complicated than you like to let on."

"Maybe. But I don't understand what you're complaining about. You won the battle."

"I may have won the battle today, but the outcome of the war is up in the air. Man, I don't like that kind of people, I really don't. And you know what's funny? I have a wife who does. She wants the good life, Will, and I don't care one way or the other."

Will nodded.

"You talk about your tastes being simple—well, I'd be happy living in a box. I'd be happy wearing the clothes I bought when I was in college. I don't care what I wear, or how I look, or what I eat. Do you know what Maxine says?"

"No."

"She says I'd eat dried beet pulp if it had sugar and milk on it. Maybe she's right. Maybe I would."

"Sounds to me like you're having an identity crisis."

Ernie smiled as he felt some of his tension ease. "Is that something else you learned from Phil Donahue?"

"Uh-huh."

"Could be I am. All I know is, I'm tired of being apologetic about who I am and what I think. I'm going to start doing what I want to do."

"Seems to me you made a big step in the right direction with Heffelfinger and Gregory."

"I suppose so, but Maxine figured out how to get her oar in, didn't she? She wasn't all that thrilled until she realized she could make the success of our business dependent on her, with that loan and all."

"I never thought of it that way."

"And you know what else? I think she has the idea that I'm joining the ranks of the upwardly mobile. You just wait. One of these days she'll suggest we get a membership in a racquetball club."

"So stand up for yourself."

"That's hard to do when you're wearing Italian loafers that your wife picked out."

"Then don't wear them. Or anything else she's picked out for you."

Ernie laughed. "That will leave me with just my work clothes. Maxine bought all the rest."

She had taken over the management of his wardrobe right from the first. She had even picked out the suit he was to wear at their wedding, a dark blue worsted. Conservative. Correct.

He had hated it, but Helmut, who was in on the shopping

trip, approved. Ernie saw a look pass between them and knew they had become co-conspirators. Between them, they would get Ernie Heffelfinger shaped up.

At first, Maxine made some attempts at subtlety, but it didn't disguise what was happening. As her choices went into the closet, his old things began disappearing. He would put into the wash a favorite shirt, one worn into softness of fabric and color, never to see it again. Or he would come home from work to find a pair of pants missing. The first time it happened, he had asked Maxine about it. "Oh, those old things," she had said. "I took them over to the Salvation Army along with some other things we won't be needing anymore."

So it went. Ernie and Maxine had now been married almost nineteen years, and aside from his work clothes, there had not been a single item in his closet that Ernie had picked out for himself in the last seventeen.

Ernie raised his eyes. Will was looking at him in that speculative manner of his. "How about if we go shopping?" he asked.

"Naw. Things are a little tight right now. Besides, I don't know what I like anymore."

"Then it's time you found out."

"How?"

"The same way I do. I try things on."

"I know," chuckled Ernie. Will had not only tried on clothes, he had tried on different personalities and accents, from Tom Brokaw to David Letterman, from Balke to President Reagan.

"How about it? Shall we go on a shopping trip?"

Ernie felt a flush of excitement, but it was followed by swift denial. "It's not a good idea. I've got to save all the money I can in case something goes wrong."

"With that kind of attitude, it probably will. Think positive!"

"You've been watching Robert Schuller again."

"Probably. But a little positive thinking does go a long way. Now, getting back to the clothes, I've got some money saved—"

"I'm not letting you spend it on me. If I decide to get some new clothes, I'll pay for them myself."

Will looked at his watch. "We've got some time before rush hour. Let's go downtown."

"To one of your haunts? Do you think that's a good idea?"

"Sure. My friend Hank'll give you a good deal. And Maxine won't be able to get mad at me for going downtown, because you took me."

"What a bargain," murmured Ernie.

He had his doubts about this shopping trip, doubts that were reinforced when he pulled into a parking space next to an old brick building north of Hennepin Avenue. Only a few blocks from Butler Square and other renovated buildings in the old warehouse district, the building was as yet untouched by any positive effect. The sidewalk was strewn with litter and empty liquor bottles. There were no large display windows on the street level, only small windows either painted an institutional grey-green or boarded over, giving the building an abandoned look. The sign on the door announcing the second-floor location of Hank's Suits and Such did nothing to dispel the impression.

"How did you find this place?" asked Ernie, getting out of the pickup.

"I like to snoop around when I come downtown. I went up the stairs one day, and I met Hank himself."

"Will—"

"It's all right. He's not a fence."

"How do you know?"

"I asked him if he was, and he said no."

Ernie shook his head incredulously. "Of course. What else would he say?" He was about to get back in the pickup, but Will was already at the door to the building, holding it open for him. With a sigh of resignation, he walked through it, up the stairs, and into Hank's.

The second-floor store was clean and bright. Sunshine streamed through rows of spotless windows and glinted off racks that held row after row of suits and jackets. Ernie was relieved to see that he and Will were not the only ones in the place. There were several well-dressed shoppers, as well as salesmen. A short, round man with a shiny bald pate hurried toward them, hand outstretched.

"Will! You haven't been down for a long time, my friend. Too long."

Will shook the man's hand, then gestured toward Ernie. "Hank, I want you to meet my son-in-law, Ernie. He's in the market for some new duds."

Hank looked at Ernie appraisingly, his gaze taking in the plaid flannel shirt, the faded jeans, the leather work boots. "What exactly did you have in mind?" he asked.

"Uh . . . a suit, I guess. I really don't know what I want."

"Ah," said Hank, nodding. "But you know what you *don't* want, I would venture to say."

"Pinstripes." Ernie said it so vehemently that Hank smiled.

The round man's frank gaze took him in again, this time so thoroughly that Ernie had the uncomfortable notion that Hank knew everything about him. "Yes, I can see that pinstripes are out."

"What do you suggest?" Ernie asked, willing to be directed so long as he wasn't forced.

"Perhaps something in separates. A sports jacket, for instance. A Harris tweed in gray with touches of mauve and blue would be nice."

"I hate gray—always have," said Ernie.

"That's it!" crowed Will. "You're getting the idea."

"I like brown . . . "

"Brown is good," said Hank, "although charcoal and navy are more authoritative."

"Forget charcoal and navy."

"Brown Harris tweed it is, then. Come with me."

Hank led them to a rack of sports coats. "I'm guessing size 42 regular," he said, pulling a coat off the rack. "Why don't you try this one on."

Ernie was already reaching for the jacket. The moment he saw the slightly rough texture of the fabric and the suede patches on the elbows, he knew this was the jacket he had been longing for without even knowing it. He slid his arms into the sleeves, and the jacket settled on his shoulders. It felt good, yet years of disapproval and denial of his taste in almost everything had left him hesitant and without confidence. Instead of looking into the mirror, he waited to hear what Will and Hank had to say.

"Nice fit," murmured Hank, running his hand across Ernie's shoulders. "You have the kind of build suit jackets are made for. No alteration necessary. Now, button the top button and move your arms a bit. Do you have enough room?"

"Feels great. What do you think, Will?"

"Sorry," said Will. "I'm not going to make your decision for you. Look in the mirror."

But instead of doing that, Ernie looked at the price tag. He gulped at what he saw and started to take the jacket off.

"Don't you like it?" asked Hank.

"I like everything about it but the price." He held the jacket out to Hank, but Hank refused to take it.

"Don't pay any attention to the tag, Ernie. I've been in the business twenty-five years now, and I've never once sold anything for the suggested retail price. For you and my friend Will, I'll make it even better." He quoted a price less than half of that on the tag and added, "And I'll throw in a couple of pairs of pants at no additional cost."

"I don't know . . . "

"Ernie." Will's voice was stern. "Think now. What do you *want?*"

Ernie ran his hand over the fabric. This was a real piece of material. It was sturdy, yet beautiful. And thanks in part to the suede patches on the elbows, it would hold up to years of wear. The color reached out to him, a rich, deep brown that seemed real and earthy. But he didn't need it. He already had two suits and a sportcoat hanging in his closet.

"I'll take it," he said.

By the time he walked down the stairs from Hank's, he had also chosen two pairs of pants, one brown and one tan, a new brown leather belt and wallet, two shirts, and several pairs of socks. "I've got plenty of socks, but they're all charcoal or gray," he explained with a grin. "They may be authoritative, but they won't match."

And on the way home, Ernie Heffelfinger stopped at a shoe store and bought the kind of shoes he had always wanted: brown, thick-soled Hush Puppies.

17

Ernie hung his new jacket and pants in the back of his closet. He felt silly doing it, as if he were a boy hiding something from his mother, but he wasn't sure how Maxine would react. He wanted to wait for the right moment to appear in them.

Whenever that would be.

Maxine was under a lot of strain lately, and it had made her snappy and irritable. She was finishing up on the preparations for the Minneapolis Stake Woman's Day and, at the same time, arranging for the big evening Pure Organics meeting that was the high point of her year's activity. As if that weren't enough, there was always something that needed to be taken care of at Martin Development Corporation. The clothes would have to wait, but that was all right. Just having bought them made Ernie feel stronger and more decisive.

His feeling of strength was heightened the next time the Trembrells came out to the building site. He had been uncertain as to what their response to his stubbornness might be, especially considering the fact that Keri had stopped dropping by with treats. They were pleasant and cooperative, however. Both Keri and her husband seemed to view him with more respect.

He viewed them with less respect, however. He had no idea what might have passed between them and Ren, but he couldn't get out of his mind Keri's cold dismissal of her. He had spent some time with Pete and Ren since then, and to his protectiveness was being added a genuine fondness. She was still everything he had thought she was—somewhat crude, impertinent, and abrasive. But now he began looking past that for the little girl he thought was also Ren. Looking for her, he found her. And having found her, he began to like her.

He still didn't know how much of what Keri Trembrell had said about Ren's family life was true. He had tried asking Pete about it, but Pete had only shrugged, saying, "She has her troubles, we have ours." Then something happened that gave him a level of understanding he would never have thought possible before. Ren invited him to join her and Pete in Sally's kitchen on his afternoon break, and that led to his meeting her mother, D. Dykstra.

Ren and Pete picked him up at the site a little before three. "I'm a mess," he said apologetically as he got into the car. "You'll have to bring me in through the back door."

Ren laughed, a sound of pure delight. "No friend of mine goes in the back way."

So Ernie walked through the imposing front door, feeling like an interloper in the grandly pristine Dykstra home. He relaxed measurably when they entered Sally's domain. The warm, casual clutter presided over by the marshmallow figure of Sally herself was welcoming in a way the rest of the house could never be.

Sally greeted them enthusiastically, hugging both Ren and Pete. Ernie half-expected to get a hug himself, and was somewhat disappointed when she contented herself with shaking his hand instead.

"Make yourself comfortable," she said, motioning to a stool. "Ren tells me I can't compete with Maxine's chocolate chip cookies, so I made fudge brownies instead."

"They smell great," he said. "This is a real treat. Keri was in the habit of coming over with goodies for us in the afternoon, but she hasn't been by lately."

"How is the house coming?" Ren asked.

"We've had our problems. We've been working at getting

the brick laid around the entryway before it gets too cold, right? And I'm not about to have the yard send out just any pallets of Chicago brick. No sir. I ask Nick to come down and pick them out himself. That way everything will go smoothly. So he comes down with me and picks out five pallets. I have the guys mark them, and when they get delivered, I check to make sure they're the right pallets. So far, so good.

"The bricklayers come a few days later, and I get them right on the job. We're making real good progress, and I go home feeling great. But the next morning when I drive out to the house, what do you think I see?"

They looked at him expectantly, and he grinned. He was making what had happened into a good story, but inside he still felt like strangling Nick Trembrell whenever he thought about it.

"What I see is every fourth brick X'ed out with red spray paint. First I think it's a vandal at work. Then who should drive up but Nicko himself. Seems he didn't want any white bricks in his mixture. He had picked out the pallets by looking at the bricks on the outside, not thinking that the mixture on the inside might be different. I figured he knew what he was doing, so I went with what he chose. What else was I supposed to do?"

"Goodness' sakes, I couldn't begin to guess," murmured Sally, who was cutting huge slabs of brownies and laying them in large bowls.

"The upshot was, we had to tear all the bricks down and start over. Only this time, I had Mr. Nick Trembrell take the pallets apart and choose what he wanted, brick by brick."

"And who pays for the ruined brick and the time lost?" asked Ren.

"We split down the middle. Nick is paying the extra it'll cost in wages to the bricklayers, and we're forking over for the new brick. It worked out all right."

"But Keri doesn't bring treats anymore."

"Now, Ren. Don't you go adding up two plus two," said Sally. "You might end up with five."

"And I might come up with four, right, Ernie?"

Ernie grinned, taking a bite of the huge fudge bar Sally had topped first with ice cream, then chocolate sauce and chopped nuts. "This is great, Sally. Aren't you going to have some too?"

"I've never been able to break the habit of tasting while I cook. I've probably had that much or more already—a nibble at a time," Sally confessed. "If I don't watch it, I'll start looking way too much like Ren's caricature of me."

She pointed to a framed pen-and-ink caricature that hung on the wall above the kitchen desk.

"It's you!" exclaimed Pete.

"Thanks very much," said Sally dryly.

"But it is. It's great. I didn't know you could do that, Ren."

Ernie had to agree. Ren's Sally was an almost too-rich concoction of curves and dimples. Her arms were open in an invitation to rest in her cushioned embrace.

"You're a real artist," said Ernie. "You've got Sally to a T. How do you do it?"

"It's easy. You pick out the most interesting characteristic of a person and exaggerate it."

"What do you do with someone who isn't interesting?"

"Like who?"

"Like me."

"There's always something. Sometimes I just have to look harder."

"What would you pick on if you drew one of me?" asked Ernie.

"I *have* drawn one."

"You have?"

Ren nodded shyly.

"May I see it?"

"Sure. Why not?"

Ernie waited uneasily while she fetched her work, suddenly unsure of wanting to see how she had presented him. He hesitated before looking at the picture she withdrew from her portfolio. Then he flushed as his thoughts caught up with the initial impression.

She had drawn him in the challenging attitude of a gunslinger, tool belt hung low on one hip. Everything had a subtly unfinished look—except his hands. They were outsized, the proportion of finger to palm exaggerated even beyond the ridiculous disproportion foisted upon him by genetic lottery. He held a hammer in one hand at a tilt that conveyed an almost imperceptible hint of menace, as if he were saying, "This is who I am. Want to make something of it?"

He was silent so long that Ren finally asked in a timid voice, "You're not mad, are you?"

"No. I just didn't expect to see . . . " His voice trailed off as he gazed at the caricature. With stunning accuracy, she had tapped into his deepest feelings. "Why did you pick my hands?"

"No reason. I just had a feeling. Do you want to see yours, Pete?"

Pete shifted uneasily. "I don't know. Yeah, might as well."

Ren's Pete was a slight figure, dwarfed by heavy leather, studs, and an outlandish mohawk that looked like nothing so much as the brush on the top of a Roman helmet. A waif of a figure, lost in the trappings of an assumed identity.

"Is that the way I look to you?"

"Sometimes. Not always."

"I really look stupid, if that's how other people see me."

"That's just how I saw you one day. If I did you today, it would come out entirely different."

Pete's grim expression softened a little, especially when she ran her hand playfully over his brushy topknot and kissed him lightly on the lips.

"Who else have you done?" asked Ernie.

"She's done some real good ones of her parents," volunteered Sally.

"Would you mind showing them to me?"

She considered for a moment, then laid her father's caricature before them with a flourish. "My dad, Curtis Dykstra."

Curtis Dykstra was a handsome man, thought Ernie, but probably not a very likeable one. He was all smile, only it wasn't an engaging smile. It was, rather, the brilliant smile of a perpetual promoter: easy, real enough, but meaningless, since it didn't seem to be a response to authentic feeling.

"And my mother, Doreen Dykstra, known as Dee Dee to her friends and capital D, period, to her business associates."

"Which one is this?" asked Pete.

"This one is D."

D. Dykstra was simply *too*. Her figure was too thin; her sculptured nails too long; her hair too carefully arranged; her ears, fingers, and neck too gilded.

Ernie was about to say something when the front door opened and a voice echoed down the hall. "Ren? Sally?"

"It's her!" Ren gasped, turning white. Quickly she squared her papers and slipped them back into her portfolio, which she stashed in the kitchen closet.

"Ren." Sally's voice was quiet and authoritative. "Slow down. Take a deep breath. And give your mother a chance."

Ren's eyes glistened. "I don't know how to act around her anymore."

"Act like a girl who needs and loves her mother."

There was no time for Ren to reply, for suddenly D. Dykstra stood in the doorway.

The caricature still fresh in his mind, Ernie found himself seeing Ren's mother as Ren herself did. He had to blink twice before she came into focus—a fashionable, forceful woman, who at this moment hesitated in surprise at the presence of guests in Sally's kitchen.

She was also a lady. Smiling warmly, she said, "Ren, I didn't know you had company. Hello, Pete. How are you?"

"Fine, thanks," mumbled Pete.

"And this must be your father. I've been waiting to meet you and Maxine for some time, Ernie," D. said, extending her hand. Then she turned to Ren and chided gently, "You could have told me you had invited him, Ren."

"Sorry," Ren said. Then she thrust her jaw forward. "But what difference would it have made if I did? You're never home this early."

"I am today."

Ernie caught the look that passed between mother and daughter, the flash of yearning quickly dampened. The moment stretched uncomfortably until Sally said, "I made some fudge brownies. Would you like one?"

"No, thanks. I have a dinner meeting later on."

"Ah, if only I had your self-control. Ernie, one more round?"

"If I took you up on that offer, I wouldn't be able to move." He stood, adding, "Besides, I need to get back on the job."

"I'll drive you," Ren offered quickly.

"That's okay. It's not far, and I don't mind walking."

"Nick and Keri are very pleased with your work," said D.

"Are they really?"

"They've been talking about nothing but the house for weeks now. They can't wait to move in."

"That's a long way off yet," he replied, finding it hard to believe that the Trembrells would say anything nice about him to D. "Thanks for the brownie, Sally. And thanks for inviting me, Ren."

Ren nodded.

D. accompanied Ernie to the door, asking all the right questions, keeping the conversation at precisely the correct level of interest, pleasant but detached. Then, as she stood with her hand on the doorknob, he found himself the uncomfortable object of her scrutiny. She seemed to come to a decision about him, for her next question was forthright and open.

"How much time do you spend with Ren, Ernie?"

"Not a lot."

"You may not know this, but she is quite a troubled young lady. It has to do with . . . "

Ernie came to her rescue, knowing as he did that she had no need to be rescued. "I know what happened to your son."

She was visibly relieved at not having to explain. "It's been unbearable since then. Neither Curtis nor I can reach her.

We've tried to get her help, but she seems to revel in this rebellion. I suspect you can sympathize with that."

He smiled wryly, but didn't express his thought that Ren's and Pete's acts of rebellion were not to be equated.

"For some reason, Ren seems to be drawn to your family. Perhaps you may be able to do for her what Curtis and I can't."

"I don't think—"

"I'm not asking for anything particular. And I'm certainly not abdicating my own responsibility. I just would like to know there's someone looking out for Ren. Besides Sally, of course. This is important to me. I do love her—she's my daughter."

"I think she'd like to hear that from you."

There was a hint of asperity in her voice as she replied, "No doubt. But the truth is, there is a huge barrier between us that we can't seem to get over."

"Chris, again."

Her eyes widened in response to an emotion that momentarily refused to retreat. "I hate it. Everything goes back to Chris, and that hurts too much to even think about, much less talk about." She reasserted her command and continued in calmer tones. "He made a choice. She has to understand that. He made it in a moment of supreme selfishness and left us to deal with the effects. In a very real way, we've lost both our children, because Ren has effectively cut herself off from us, as well. But we can't put our own lives on hold while we wait for her to come around. I know she thinks we're cold and unfeeling, that we put more value on work than on relationships, but it is a way of surviving. Is that something you can understand?"

"Yes. I'll keep an eye on her, if you'd like me to."

"Thank you," the gracious D. Dykstra said, her voice once more impersonal as her cloaking devices clicked back into place. "I'm glad I came home early today. Tell Maxine I hope to have the pleasure of meeting her in the near future."

What a meeting that would be, Ernie thought, as he walked

back to the site. *If it ever happens, which I doubt.* The only thing he could see they had in common was an interest in Renault, and that would not be enough to sustain more than fifteen minutes of carefully couched conversation.

Having said he would keep an eye on Ren, Ernie was glad when the miracle of the Minnesota Twins gave him an opportunity to spend more time with her and Pete. He liked baseball, but he had given up on the Twins years ago, so he wasn't very excited about their prospects as the regular season came to a close. He figured the Detroit Tigers would win the American League pennant with a sweep.

Ren disagreed. "They're going to go all the way," she said.

He smiled indulgently.

"They are," she insisted, and Pete added, "You better listen to her, Dad. She has a way of knowing things."

"If you say so."

When the Twins won the first two games against the Tigers, Ernie wrote it off as a function of the Dome. "Wait until they get to Detroit."

Ren just smiled.

Then the Twins clinched the pennant in Detroit, and he began to wonder if she might be right. He couldn't resist teasing her about it, though. "No way," he said, playing the devil's advocate. "Especially when Puckett's not hitting."

"Don't you say anything bad about Kirby. He's my favorite. I love the way they rub his fuzzy head for good luck."

"Won't do them any good."

"What do you want to bet?"

The upshot of their banter was that Ren watched every game of the World Series in the Heffelfinger family room. When the games were played in the evening, Ren, Pete, Will, and Ernie took up their places on the couch and floor. Ernie had stocked up on pop, corn chips and dips, and chocolate-covered peanuts, and Ren always had something in hand from Sally's kitchen. Once it was caramel corn, once fudge brownies. And it was Ren who arrived with a Homer Hankie for each of them. So they made a celebration out of it, especially during the first two games in the Homer Dome.

Ernie's chief delight wasn't the game itself, however. It was watching Ren. She was a real Twins fan. She knew all the players by sight and seemed to have a soft spot for each of them. Depending upon what was happening, she screeched, moaned, jumped up and down, or hid her face in her hands.

"Well, that's it," he said when the Twins left for St. Louis. "They can never beat the Cardinals in their own ballpark."

He was just trying to rile Ren up, and he felt bad about it afterwards when he saw her despair over the Twins' losses. "Don't give up," he encouraged her. "Remember, the last two games will be played in the Dome."

"Who's giving up?"

But Ren wasn't with them when they watched the sixth game one Sunday evening late in October.

"Where is she?" Ernie asked Pete.

"I don't know. She said she had something to do."

"She should be here," Will complained. "It's not half as much fun without her, even if we are winning."

"I think you guys are getting to like her," Pete said.

"I think you're right," said Maxine, who had left the kitchen table, where her work was spread out.

Ernie scooted over on the couch to make a place for her. "Come here. Sit down for a while. You can't spend all your time working."

She did—for a very short while. And all during that time, she kept fidgeting. Finally she stood up. "I don't understand how you can stand watching baseball. There's so much wasted time."

"This isn't baseball, this is history," protested Ernie.

At that moment, the doorbell rang.

"I bet that's Ren!" said Pete, galloping to answer it. "You're late," he remonstrated as she entered, flushed with excitement.

"Where have you been?" asked Will. "We needed you here. They're playing Cardinal ball this time around."

"I know. I've been listening on the radio. Come on, Twins!" she urged, settling herself on the floor beside Pete. But soon she was up and pacing. "Go, Kirby!" she called when her favorite was up to bat, and she exulted when he connected. "See, he's hitting again!" She had worked herself into a fine frenzy by the last out. And even Maxine, who had been unable to resist the mounting excitement, joined in their jubilation when the Twins won.

"They're going to take it all! Didn't I tell you?" cried Ren.

"I'm beginning to be a believer," said Ernie.

"Boy, I wish I could be there for the final game," added Will.

A secretive smile crossed Ren's face. "Really?"

"It would be a once-in-a-lifetime experience."

She put her hand in her skirt pocket and asked, "Guess what I've got?"

"You don't . . . ," began Pete.

She drew out some tickets and tossed them in the air. "Tickets to the seventh game!"

Ernie picked one up and looked at it in amazement. It was exactly what she had said it was. "How did you get these!"

"I figured there would be some unbelievers who would want to sell their tickets after what happened in St. Louis, so I went down to the Dome and hung around until I found them. I couldn't get four in the same spot, so we'll have to split up." She hesitated. "I didn't think you'd want to come, Maxine. You're not mad, are you?"

"No. Don't worry about it. Baseball's not my thing."

"I can't believe it! Tickets to the seventh game!" Ernie said, putting his arm around her. "We'll need to leave early. It's going to be a madhouse downtown tomorrow."

They were on their way by five the next day.

Listening to Ren's chatter as he drove the Cadillac downtown, Ernie was amazed at how natural, how comfortable it seemed to have her around. She seemed like part of the family. That could create another set of problems, he realized, but it was something he would worry about when the time came. If the time came.

So they watched the Minnesota Twins win the World Series in the Homer Dome, under the Teflon ceiling and near the blue Hefty Bag right field. They screamed their throats raw and waved their Homer Hankies. They hollered and waved more once they were back out on the street. They hugged each other. They hugged strangers. Ren danced with Will. Pete high-fived a grinning cop. And by the time they had worked their way through the press of celebrating fans to the parking lot, a bond had been formed between the four of them.

It was something Maxine didn't understand. "I don't see why you're encouraging Pete's relationship with Ren," she complained.

"I'm not exactly encouraging it."

"What do you think you're doing? The three of you with your heads huddled together, whispering. All that laughing—"

"I'm just trying to get to know her. And my own son. He's growing up, Maxine. I don't want to have him walk out the door one day without my even noticing it."

Maxine didn't respond immediately. She sifted through the stack of mail on the kitchen desk, threw some in the trash can, and put the rest in the letter holder. Then she said, "I suppose you're right. One of us needs to keep in touch with what's going on, and I'm snowed under. I don't think I would have the patience for it, anyway."

"I know you're busy, but don't you think you might be using that as an excuse so you won't have to deal with them?"

"Maybe." Then she threw up her hands and said, "Yes. You're right, and I hate it when you're right."

He smiled. "Good thing it doesn't happen that often."

She had to smile too. "See, that's why you can deal with Pete and Ren better than I. You don't get uptight about them. Every time I look at Pete, I want to shake him! If he were littler, I swear I'd put him over my knee and blister his behind. I can't stand the fact that I can't make him do what I want him to do anymore."

Ernie, glad that he hadn't displayed his new clothes, put his arm around her comfortingly. "That's what we have kids for, I guess. So we learn to let go."

"I can't let go."

"I don't think you have a choice. We can't control him like we did when he was a kid."

"No kidding. Every time I threaten to take away a privilege, he threatens to do something worse. He escalates the conflict to the point where I don't know what to do."

"Drop it. See the good things about him. He resents the fact that we don't appreciate what he's doing right." She leaned against him, and he could feel the tension in her body. "Relax, why don't you. Everything's going to be okay."

"I hope so. I can't take any more surprises right now."

18

But they both got a surprise on Sunday, thanks to Helmut. He delivered it after they had gone to church and enjoyed Maxine's coc au vin (without the *vin*). When Ernie shoved his chair back, saying, "Anybody want to watch the football game with me?" Helmut asked, "Can that wait a minute?"

"Sure," said Ernie, sitting back down. "What's up?"

"We need to talk about something."

Ernie waited.

"I wish to gain admittance into your church."

Ernie's mouth dropped.

"Good deal," said Pete, clapping his grandfather on the shoulder and shaking his hand.

"Oh, that's wonderful news!" cried Maxine.

"Why?" asked Ernie.

Helmut smiled slightly. "That's not the reaction I would have predicted. Aren't you pleased?"

"Y . . . yes," stammered Ernie, "but I don't understand."

"What's so difficult to understand?" asked Maxine.

"You're the last person I would have expected to join the Church, Dad. Not just my church—any church. Aren't you the one who always said churches cater to the ignorance of the masses?"

Helmut pulled out his pipe and put it, still unlit, between his teeth. "I still think that is basically a true statement."

"Then why join?"

"Ernie," warned Maxine.

"It's a valid question. Why do you want to join?"

Helmut considered, making little chewing motions on the stem of his pipe. "I like going," he said finally. "I like the people I meet there."

"They are a wonderful group of people," concurred Maxine. "Just the sort that you would enjoy spending—"

Ernie interrupted. "You don't join a church because you like the people, for heaven's sake."

"Indeed? That's one of the functions of religion, is it not? Providing a positive context in which to interact?"

"I suppose so, but . . . "

"I happen to feel quite at home in your church."

"My ward, you mean. You wouldn't be joining my ward, Dad. You'd be joining the Mormon church. Then you'd go to your own ward in Saint Paul."

"I don't want to go to a ward in Saint Paul. I like yours."

"That's not the way it works."

"They wouldn't forbid me, would they?"

"Of course not," Ernie said with a sigh.

"Then?"

"The Church isn't like the Rotary Club or Jaycees. Baptism isn't an initiation rite. Really, you don't know what you're saying. Before you got baptized, you'd have to have an interview with the bishop. He'd ask you all sorts of questions."

"Such as?"

"Such as, Do you believe in Joseph Smith as a prophet? Do you believe that the Book of Mormon is the word of God? You haven't even read the Book of Mormon."

"That's easily taken care of. I generally read two or three books a week. I'll add it to the list."

Ernie moaned into his hands.

"What's the matter? I always thought you wanted to convert me."

"I did."

"Now I'm willing to be converted."

"Wonderful!" cried Maxine, before Ernie had a chance to

say anything else. "I'm so pleased. We'll need to set up some missionary discussions and an appointment with the bishop, of course. Then there's the date to set, and the baptism to plan . . . "

"While you're at it, make it a double," said Will.

She looked at Will as if she had to see his face to know what he had said. "What?"

"I said, make it a double."

"I don't understand . . . "

"I want to get drowned in the waters of baptism and come forth a new man. It shouldn't be too much different from being in a coma for three months and waking up as another person."

Hours later, sleep having eluded them, Ernie and Maxine lay wide awake in their king-sized bed. Ernie lay on the eastern shore, Maxine on the western, the Serengeti Plains in between.

The silence was broken when Ernie sighed. It was a long, heavy sigh, one he hoped would signal Maxine that he wasn't feeling too good and needed her to comfort him. She gave no indication she had heard.

Five minutes later from her position on the opposite shoreline, Maxine sighed. It was a deep, heavy sigh, one that, Ernie thought, carried the same message as his own. He gave no indication that he had heard. After all, he had sighed first. It wasn't fair for her to ignore his sigh and sigh herself.

Some time later, he sighed again, accompanying it with the delicate touch of his toe on the bottom of her foot. To his disappointment, she neither jerked nor twitched. She had finally fallen asleep.

He lay there a while longer, then quietly slipped out from under the covers and padded down the stairs to the kitchen for a cup of warm cocoa. He made it the way he had loved it as a boy, with lots of canned milk and sugar and a little bit of vanilla. He felt better as he sat at the table drinking it, but he couldn't stop thinking about what had happened that afternoon.

Helmut wanted to get baptized.

Will wanted to get baptized too, but Will was Maxine's problem. It was Helmut that Ernie was thinking about most. And as he considered Helmut's reasons for wanting to be baptized, he couldn't avoid considering what his own reasons had been.

It was hard to remember them, eighteen years after the fact. To be truthful, Ernie wasn't sure he had really understood what they were even then, so inextricably intertwined were they with the way he felt about Maxine—and Helmut.

He had first seen Maxine in a cafeteria line on the University of Minnesota campus. He had been intensely aware of her as he stood behind her, listening to the bright lilt of her voice as she talked to her companion. Her hair, which was ratted and sprayed into a bouffant, was strawberry blond, and her laughter was bubbly and full of infectious delight.

Ernie watched her in silence; glib words were beyond him. He knew that if he tried to get her attention, he would only end up making a fool of himself. So he walked behind her in the line, content to watch the motion of her hands giving spatial reality to her words.

When it was his turn to order, he said, "Sloppy joe." It didn't look that appetizing, but it would fill the hole.

To his surprise, she turned to face him. "You don't want that," she said, canceling his order with a wave of her hand. "Growing boys need *nutrition.*"

"What do you suggest?" he asked, too taken aback to object.

"The chef's salad. That way you'll get your greens."

"I need greens?"

She nodded, grinning impishly. "Otherwise you'll stink."

"I—"

"Not you personally. Everybody. If we don't eat enough green vegetables, we stink. I learned that in a class I'm taking."

He breathed a sigh of relief, having had momentary doubts about how well his deodorant was working. Then he took a step back and reached for a chef's salad. It didn't look as if it would fill even a corner of the cavern that was his stomach, but he took it anyway, hoping it would give him a reason to talk to the bright and teasingly bossy girl.

By the time he had the salad on his tray, she was at the end of the line, handing her money to the cashier. Quickly he grabbed some milk, a sandwich, and a brownie and put them on the tray with his salad. He paid for his lunch impatiently, one eye on her progress through the crowded lunchroom.

"May I?" he asked, approaching her table.

"Oh, you did get the salad after all. Good choice. My name's Maxine, and this is Barb."

"Glad to meet you," he said, pulling out a chair. "I'm Ernie."

He never remembered afterward whether Barb said a word during lunch—he was too taken with Maxine. He found out that she was a junior majoring in education, that she liked opera, and that she was a Mormon.

"I don't know anything about Mormons," he said truthfully. "There aren't many of them around here, are there?"

"Enough to have an institute."

"What's that?"

"Classes in religion. We're studying the Book of Mormon this quarter. That's where I'm going next," she added, checking her watch, "and if I don't hurry up, I'll be late."

Although he had never been interested in religion, Helmut's attitude toward churches having prejudiced him, he said, "I have an hour free. How about if I come with you?"

After that, lunch with Maxine on Tuesdays and Thursdays followed by the institute class became a regular part of his schedule. At first he had listened out of politeness only, but gradually he found himself genuinely interested in the discussions. One day he asked Maxine for a copy of the Book of Mormon so that he could do the reading assignments. "If I'm going to sit there anyway, I might as well know what you're talking about."

She gave him a copy, and he began to read it. Sometimes as he sat with feet propped up on his desk and Book of Mormon in hand, he wondered why he found it so intriguing. Was he interested in the book itself, or in Maxine?

Ernie swirled his cup as he reflected on the events that had led up to his joining the Church. A dark layer of cocoa had settled on the bottom of the cup, so he added more warm milk and stirred it absently.

He still didn't know the answer to the question about his motives that he had asked himself so many years before. Why had he joined the Church? Was it because he had a testimony? Because Maxine wanted him to, and he wanted Maxine? Or because it was something he could do that was his own idea, and not Helmut's? It was hard to untangle all that had influenced his decision, but he knew that at the time, he had felt good about it. And in the eighteen years since, he had never regretted it.

Be honest, he thought. *There have been some bad moments. Especially since we moved out here.*

And then he understood.

He resented Helmut's interest in the Church because it was the result of the acceptance he had found in the Maple Hills First Ward. Acceptance that Ernie had yet to find.

"Grow up, Heffelfinger," he said disgustedly. He walked to the sink, poured the rest of the chocolate down the drain, and rinsed his cup. "The gospel's true, no matter what ward you're in. You ought to be glad your dad's interested in it."

19

Ernie crept into bed as softly and quietly as he could, thinking that Maxine was asleep.

She wasn't. "Are you all right?" she asked, turning over to face him.

"Yes. I couldn't sleep, so I went downstairs for a while. I'm sorry if I woke you."

"You didn't. I haven't been sleeping very well myself."

"Were you thinking about Will?"

She nodded. "Were you thinking about Helmut?"

He nodded.

"And?"

"I'm going to call him in the morning and tell him I'm glad he's interested in the Church."

"But you're not."

"I'm trying to get over feeling that way. Only I can't help wondering if he really understands the level of commitment he'll be asked to make."

"If he doesn't, he'll find out soon enough."

"I suppose so. A double baptism. I can't imagine it."

"Don't bother trying, because it will never happen."

"Why? Don't you think Will was serious?"

"Oh, he was serious, all right. Only they'll never let him."

"Sure they will."

"No they won't. William H. Martin has already been baptized and confirmed. I have the certificates to prove it."

"Oh boy. I wonder how Will is going to react to that."

"The way he always does. He'll say, 'I'm not Bill Martin.' "

"I'm not Bill Martin," Will said.

He was sitting at the kitchen table opposite Maxine. Ernie, who at Maxine's request had stayed home to give her some support, leaned against a cabinet with folded arms.

"That's just a matter of semantics," Maxine said. "Look, here's the certificate. You were baptized when I was five, and you and Mom were sealed in the temple a year after that."

Will shook his head. "I don't remember any of that."

"I know," said Maxine, her voice thin and tight. "But look at it from a practical point of view. Your name is William H. Martin. Same as on this certificate. Your birthdate is the same. Your parents are the same. If you were to get baptized, it would be like doing the same ordinance twice for one man."

"Except it isn't."

"Okay. Be stubborn if you want to. Talk to the bishop if you want to. But don't drag me into it."

"What do you think, Ernie?" asked Will.

"It could be a problem. I guess the best thing is to ask the bishop about it."

"What do you think he'll say?"

"I haven't got the slightest idea."

Will pursed his lips thoughtfully. "Life do get complicated, don't it?"

"That it does," agreed Ernie.

"Are you going to set up some missionary lessons for Helmut?"

Ernie shifted uneasily. "Yeah. Why?"

"I thought I might sit in on them, if that's all right."

The missionaries agreed to come on Thursday nights. Now Helmut made the hour drive from Stillwater two times a week, on Sundays and Thursdays. Ernie had suggested that missionaries from Saint Paul Stake would be glad to teach him at his own home, but Helmut said he didn't mind the drive.

The lessons didn't go very well. Helmut, with his razor intellect and mocking wit, could always find some way to stymie the young men who were so eager to teach him.

Something positive did come from it, though. As Ernie listened to the lessons, he felt his heart (which he hadn't even realized had begun hardening) soften in the light of truth. He knew that however intermixed his own reasons for converting might have been at the time, he had made the right decision. He would still feel awkward and out of his element in his ward, he knew that, but having reaffirmed his primary reason for attending, it would be less of a problem.

It was during this time that Ernie chanced upon Ren one Saturday when he drove out to the house. She was walking alongside the road, lost in thought, her eyes on the ground ahead of her. He was busy with his own thoughts, so he almost drove past her. At the last minute he recognized her, slammed on the brakes, and rolled down the window. "Hey, Ren!" he hollered.

Her cheeks were red from the biting wind, but he knew instantly that the redness of her nose and eyes had to do with something else. Without waiting for her response, he reached over and opened the opposite door of the pickup. "Get in," he said.

She obeyed without meeting his glance.

"What's going on?"

"Nothing."

"Are you and Pete having problems?"

"No."

"Then what?"

She was silent so long that Ernie began to think she wasn't going to answer his question. Then she drew a shuddering breath. "I just wonder sometimes what it's all about."

"What what's all about?"

"Life. Right now, I can't think of any good reason for getting up in the morning, in spite of Sally's twelve hugs."

"It's that bad?"

"Yes."

"Do you want to talk about it?"

"No."

Ernie began to tap the steering wheel nervously. He wanted to do or say something to help her, but he felt tongue-tied. Suddenly he remembered the conversation he had had with D. Dykstra, and he said, "It's about Chris, isn't it?"

She nodded. "Maybe Chris was right."

"No. Don't ever think that, Ren. Chris knows things now that you don't, and if he could, he'd tell you to keep on. There is meaning to life."

"And that is?"

Thinking back to the beautiful progression of missionary lessons and the purpose they had endowed him with, he said, "Has Pete ever talked to you about our beliefs?"

"Not very much. I know more about what you can and can't do."

"I can tell you some things that would comfort you, if you want to listen."

"I could use a little comfort right now."

Speaking slowly and quietly, Ernie outlined the plan of salvation, beginning with the council in heaven, then told her about life after death and the continuation of the family unit. She began crying softly as he spoke.

"You loved Chris a lot, didn't you."

"I miss him every day."

"You'll get to see him again, I promise."

"You believe in this enough to make a promise like that?"

"Yes, I do," he said. And the strength of his belief gave him an unaccustomed eloquence as he continued. "Nothing is ever lost. Our efforts have eternal effects. Our decisions have eternal consequences. Our lives continue on past this earth."

She wiped the tears from her cheeks, and he noticed that her eyes no longer looked so flat and empty. "I'd like to believe that."

He chuckled a little.

"Did I say something funny?"

"I'm not laughing at you. I was just thinking of a prophet

in the Book of Mormon who says that wanting to believe is the beginning of belief."

"Oh."

He sat quietly for a while, waiting to see if there was anything else she wanted to say; then he asked, "Do you want me to drive you home?"

"No. I think I'll walk back. Thanks, Ernie. I'm glad you happened up the road when you did."

"So am I."

As Ernie watched her start back down the road, he couldn't help wishing that his father was as receptive to the gospel as Ren had appeared to be.

But that wasn't the case, Ernie was forced to admit the next Thursday. Helmut bated the missionaries all evening long. When they finally left and Ernie was in the living room alone with Will and Helmut, he said, "I don't understand, Dad. You say you want to join the Church, but you have a way of making everything the missionaries say look ridiculous. Why keep coming if you're going to do that?"

"I do put them on the skewer, don't I." Helmut chuckled. "I don't mean to, but they have such an innocent faith. They don't rely on logic or persuasion, yet they expect me to take what they say without question."

"Now, that's not true. They always challenge you to pray about what they've said."

"Yes."

"Do you?"

"Ernie, a person can talk himself into having a so-called spiritual experience. Then, when it suits his fancy, he can talk himself out of it as well. It seems to me that kind of convert is not very strong. On the other hand, one who has arrived at a conclusion by rigorous examination of the facts will be more solid and reliable."

"So you haven't been praying."

"I find religious fervor embarrassing, and I try to avoid it whenever possible."

"Then why are we having the missionaries teach you?" Ernie said in exasperation.

"Now, now. No need to raise your voice."

Ernie gritted his teeth. He had been afraid the lessons would take this turn.

From his corner of the sofa, Will said, "You'll have to give that up, you know." He was pointing at Helmut's pipe.

A look of regret passed over Helmut's face.

"It won't be easy, will it?"

"No." Helmut held out the pipe, cradling it in his palm. "You must understand—this is not just a pipe, it's a work of art. Look at the grain of the wood on the bowl and the curve of the stem."

"It is beautiful," agreed Will.

"Will has a point, Dad. Even though you don't light up when you come here, you've always got that pipe in your hand. How are you going to quit?"

Helmut didn't answer.

"I'm not sure he *is* going to quit," said Will. "Or that he's going to get baptized."

Ernie felt as much as heard Will's words. He knew Will was speaking the truth.

"Why do you say that?" asked Helmut, his face betraying only curiosity.

"Because I think you are honest, and when it comes down to the bottom line, your interest in the Church has less to do with a commitment to the gospel than with a need to be appreciated for the sophisticated and knowledgeable man you are."

"Maxine was right," Helmut said. "You're becoming a philosopher."

"Plus, you're bored, and these meetings have given you something amusing to do on Thursday nights."

"Very clever, Will. Have you examined your own motives for wanting to join the Church as well as you have examined mine?"

A benign smile lit up Will's face. "I don't want to join the Church."

"But you told us you wanted to get baptized," said Ernie, perplexed.

"I do."

Ernie held up his blocky hands. "Wait a minute. I'm missing something. You don't want to join the Church, but you do want to get baptized? That's just two different ways of saying the same thing, isn't it?"

"No. Joining the Church sounds to me like making a social contract. Like joining a service club. What I want to do is make a covenant with Jesus Christ."

Helmut's right eyebrow raised. Ernie could tell by the way Helmut's teeth clamped down on the stem of the pipe that his father was uncomfortable. Will's statement of intent obviously qualified as "religious fervor."

"You don't have to join a church to do that," Helmut said. "It's a personal matter."

"Perhaps, but I'd like to do something to make it official."

Helmut tapped his pipe against his palm, a gesture Ernie knew was the same as a cat twitching his tail. He had seen a break in Will's logic and was ready to spring. "You say joining the Church and making a commitment to Christ are two different things. But when you are baptized, you assume obligations to the organization as well, don't you?"

"Yes. I look at it this way: part of my covenant with Christ is to help other people, like he would if he were here. The Church is organized to help me fill that obligation."

"That sounds like hair-splitting to me," murmured Helmut.

"You're the lawyer."

"So I am. Tell me, why do you wish to make this commitment?"

"Because I want to believe that the world makes sense." Will paused a moment, then asked, "Do you know what existential emptiness is?"

"No. But I can see you're going to tell me."

"It's the space a Snickers bar can't fill."

Helmut laughed, softly and a little sadly. "And this covenant with Christ will fill it for you?"

Will nodded.

"Well, Ernie, have you been listening?" Helmut asked his son.

"Yes."

"Then you understand why Will is going to become a member of your church and I am not."

"But Dad, you don't have to—"

"Will has expressed my position with uncomfortable accuracy. I am a man without purpose for the first time in my life."

"The Church could give you purpose."

"I don't doubt it. But I can't make the type of commitment that Will has spoken of. I suspect you understood that all along, didn't you?"

Ernie nodded, unable to deny it. "I wish there was something I could say."

"There isn't. And don't worry about me. I'll find something to do. Tell Maxine we'll be going back to the old schedule of dinner every third Sunday of the month. And Will, you've let the cat out of the bag. You can stop playing the fool."

"Do I have to? It serves me well at times."

"No doubt."

Ernie said good-bye to Helmut at the front door, then walked with Will to the sliding glass door in the family room.

"Speaking of letting the cat out of the bag," said Will, "when are you going to let your new clothes out of the closet?"

"Oh, boy. I haven't even thought about them lately."

"Wear them this Sunday."

"I don't know. Maybe . . . "

"I'll make you a deal. You know those fancy suits Bill had? The ones I've never worn? If you put on your new jacket, I'll wear one of those."

"Why would you want to do that?"

"I like those suits. I always have. I only refused to wear them because Maxine wanted me to."

Ernie considered for a moment. "Okay. I will if you will."

Will shook his hand. "You're on," he said.

MAXINE'S GO-ROUND

20

Maxine Martin was born with a ribbon in her hair, Bill Martin had been fond of saying. However, her birth having taken place in the unenlightened forties when fathers were not allowed to be present (and when, in the days of knock-out gas, even the mothers were only partially present), his was not a reliable report.

The fact was, Helen Martin had brought the small pink bow to the hospital with her, and when the nurse presented Maxine to her the first time, she had affixed it to the head of her new daughter with a fold of transparent tape. From that point until, at age fourteen, she convinced her mother to let her get her hair cut, Maxine Martin always had a ribbon in her hair. And as a young married woman, she hoped for a daughter of her own, so that she could in turn dress the child in ribbons and ruffles.

Instead, Pete was born.

The trial of my life, thought Maxine, who was looking through the Woman's Day programs she had just picked up from the printer. *If I had had a little girl, she wouldn't have done what Pete's doing.*

A picture of Ren flashed before her mind's eye, and she amended her conclusion. *Then again, she might have turned out like Renault Dykstra.*

Maxine couldn't understand her son's fascination with that girl. She herself always felt uncomfortable around Ren. The girl emanated a restless energy, as if something seethed inside. She never took anything at face value, and she had a most disconcerting way of looking right into people. And her language! Although Maxine had told her right from the first she wouldn't tolerate swearing or taking the Lord's name in vain in her home, nasty words still slipped out of Ren's mouth now and then.

She was definitely not the kind of girl Maxine would have picked for Pete, and Ernie's growing affection for her was an added source of frustration.

The more Maxine thought about it, the more convinced she became that she should do whatever she could to break Pete and Ren up. She was even more convinced when the Fiero pulled into the driveway, and she saw Pete kiss Ren good-bye before getting out of it.

That's it, she thought. *This has gone on long enough.*

She knew it would be best to wait until later to talk to him, after he had had some time to relax and she had had time to think about what she wanted to say, but the minute he set foot inside the kitchen, the first salvo flew out of her mouth. "I want you to start riding the bus home after school, Pete."

He looked at her for a moment before replying, "My day was fine. How was yours?"

"Don't get smart with me. You're seeing way too much of Ren Dykstra, and I want it to stop."

"Can I put my books down and get something to eat before we have this discussion?"

"No. We're having it right now. That girl is not the sort of person you should be associating with."

Pete dropped his books on the counter and slouched into a chair. "I suppose the next thing you're going to say is that I should only date members of the Church."

"Well, you should. I wouldn't say a thing if you were taking out Jenny Daley or Lee Marksbury."

"Forget it. Jenny is a world-class snob, and Drew Conzet is putting the moves on Lee."

"What about Julianna?"

A pained look crossed Pete's face. With exaggerated patience, he said, "Mother, have you ever really looked at Julianna?"

"I know she's not pretty, but she's sweet."

"*Sweet* is not a real great recommendation."

"There must be someone . . . "

"Did it ever occur to you that they're not exactly holding their breath waiting for me to ask them out?"

"You could at least try."

"Why? I like Ren, and I don't like any of the girls at church."

Maxine felt herself stiffen, as if she were leaning against some unseen force, as if the area between them were alive with warring magnetic fields. She was heading down a path that would only cause more contention, yet she felt she was right. And if the church leaders said that young people should only date members, wasn't it up to her to make sure Pete dated members? On the other hand, he was sixteen, and as the issue of the hair had proved, he had a mind of his own that no amount of coercion, manipulation, or bribery could change.

But I am still his mother, and I have an obligation, she reminded herself. Taking a deep breath, she stepped into the fray. "If you don't start taking out someone from church, I won't allow you to go out with Ren."

"How are you going to stop me?"

She looked at him across the kitchen table. His eyes met hers unwaveringly. They were there again, at the all-too familiar impasse. Tears sprang to her eyes, and she had to bite her lower lip to keep her chin from quivering.

"Oh, right. Now you're going to cry. The next thing, you'll be telling me how you did all you could to bring me up right, and you just can't understand how come I'm not following in your footsteps."

"I did," she said in a quavery voice. "I've taught you all the principles of the gospel— "

"I don't know if I believe all that."

Maxine clapped her hand to her mouth to stifle a gasp.

"Do you think just because you say something, I should believe it? I don't know if the Church is true. I only go because you'd have a fit if I didn't."

"That's what comes of not going to seminary regularly!"

"You're really determined to hit all the bases, aren't you? Even if I were a one-hundred-percenter, I don't think it would make any difference in how I feel. I don't know what I believe."

How did I ever end up with a son like this? Maxine thought. *Why couldn't he have turned out like Drew Conzet?* Drew had looked so handsome and clean-cut as he stood before the congregation to bear his testimony the previous Sunday. *He* knew what he believed. And he had given his parents a wonderful tribute. It had been painful to hear, with her own son sitting beside her.

"Hey, Mom. Don't take it as a personal failure if I don't believe what you believe."

"But it is. If I had taught you right . . . "

Pete sighed. "Okay. Feel bad if you want to. I'm going upstairs."

What now? she wondered after he was gone, realizing she had no way of enforcing her demand. When she remembered Ernie's advice about letting go, she decided to pretend the conversation had never happened. Instead of confronting Pete when he brought Ren home the next day after school, she offered both of them cookies and milk and talked to them for a while before she went down the list of phone calls she had to make before the day was done.

Still, she couldn't get rid of the feeling that she was on a merry-go-round that was going too fast.

The merry-go-round was given a big shove that Sunday.

Maxine was busy getting a casserole ready to go into the oven before they left for church when Pete thundered down the stairs. His newly dyed hair was a sickly blond.

"Oh, no. I knew that was what you were doing in the bathroom last night, but I had no idea it was going to look so awful."

"It is disgusting, isn't it," he agreed cheerfully.

She hadn't completely registered the change in Pete's appearance when Ernie walked into the kitchen. One look at him, and she dropped the casserole lid.

"Where did you . . . ," she began, but couldn't finish.

"How do I look?" he asked, turning around so that she could get the full effect of his tweed jacket (cum patches), his brown pants, and his shoes.

"Are those . . . *Hush Puppies?*"

"Yup. I always did want a pair of these. They're real comfortable, nothing stiff about them."

"When did you . . . "

"Go shopping? The other day. Will took me to a place a friend of his has downtown. It looked pretty bad from the outside, but I got a real good deal on the coat."

"Oh."

"I've gotta tell you, I feel great in this jacket. It's what I've always wanted," he declared, giving her a smack on the cheek. "Here comes Will. We can go any time."

When she saw Will, she made a strange, gurgling sound in her throat.

He was wearing one of the expensive, beautifully cut business suits that had belonged to her father. The tip of the handkerchief that showed just the right amount above the jacket pocket echoed the color of the silk tie. He looked so much like Bill Martin that she grabbed onto the edge of the counter to support her sagging knees.

"Do I look all right? Does the tie go okay with this suit?" he asked Maxine.

Maxine didn't know how to answer. She felt as if she had lost her footing in reality.

No wonder.

There stood a boy who didn't look like her son but was, and a man who didn't look like her husband but was.

To say nothing of the man who did look like her father but wasn't.

21

At least she had her business, Maxine thought, on her way to a meeting hosted by one of her first-level coordinators, Christine Markham. While everything else was falling apart around her, her business was growing and getting stronger. She had a solid organization based on her five first-level people. Three were go-getters who really kept their down-line organizations working. The other two were less committed, but they kept plodding along, and their purchase orders added to her monthly check, which had recently jumped to an enviable figure.

Christine was one of her best people, a self-starter who appreciated rather than took for granted Maxine's help. As if to substantiate this assessment of her, Christine met the car in the driveway, ready to help carry in charts and easels. "Thanks for coming to this meeting," she said, taking the easel Maxine handed her.

"That's what Pure Organics is all about. If we support each other, we can all be successful together."

"Speaking of supporting, I've been meaning to ask you how Pete's getting along. You know Steve is leader of the priests quorum. He's been quite worried about what we can do to help."

"I wish I knew," sighed Maxine. "Then again, I sometimes wonder if we need to do anything at all. He's really a good kid. He doesn't smoke and he doesn't swear—at least, not much. He's willing to go to church. He does his homework. Things could be a lot worse. It's just his hair . . . "

"I bet you wish you could strangle him."

Maxine laughed self-consciously. "Every day."

"Is he still going out with that girl?"

"Ren Dykstra. Yes."

"I'd like to get him interested in some nice Mormon girl."

"You and me both. I told him he could drive the Cadillac if he asked one of them out."

"What did he say to that?" asked Christine.

"He said he would rather take Ren out in the pickup any day."

"Oh dear. Well, I want you to know that Steve and I are praying for him."

"While you're at it, put in a word or two for me. I'm not sure I'm going to survive this."

"By the way, Will sure looked dapper on Sunday, and Ernie, too. I can't remember when I've ever seen those two looking so sharp."

"I'll convey the message," said Maxine dryly. Then she put her three men out of her mind. She had work to do.

First she surveyed the table on which the company's products were displayed. On one end of the table Christine had placed the various vitamins and herbs, in the middle stood the personal care products, and at the other end was an array of cleaning products. "You've done a nice job of setting up," she said. "There's just one thing . . . "

"What?"

"It's really a minor change, but what do you think about putting the food supplements in the middle?" Maxine suggested. "They're the foundation for everything we do in Pure Organics, so we want to give them the most important position."

Christine agreed, so they made the change. Giving the new arrangement an appraising glance, Maxine felt a surge of pride in Pure Organics. She had found her niche when she discovered it. Before then, she had been involved with several multilevel organizations, selling everything from custom-fitted bras to dried algae. She had ridden the Cambridge diet crest. When it began to falter, she and her entire organization took up the Genesis banner, wooed by Monte Hall and a pay-out schedule next to none. But despite its slick packaging and jet-powered take-off, Genesis also skidded to an ignominious halt.

Disillusioned, she drifted for a time after that. She got numerous calls from other promoters offering her a chance to "get in on a big deal," but she wasn't in a hurry. Then another multilevel marketer told her about Pure Organics, a small company that had a solid base of committed people, people who wouldn't leave, taking their down-lines with them, for the sake of more money or a fancier bonus car. She tried the products and was impressed. When she signed up, she brought most of her organization with her. It had been uphill all the way since then.

The two women had just put the finishing touches on the display when the first of the expected guests arrived.

Christine started out the meeting, then turned it over to Maxine. Maxine rose with a smile and began her presentation: The Beneficial Effects of Pure Organics' Vitamin, Mineral and Herb Products, as Illustrated by the Miraculous Recovery of William H. Martin.

She told them about Will's accident, about the months he had spent in a coma, and then about his reeducation. She knew how to make a good story of it, and before long she had them in the palm of her hand, laughing and crying at the same time.

"We had to start right from the beginning with him," she said. "He didn't know any of us, didn't remember any of his life before the accident. He lost all his vocabulary—except every four-letter word he had ever heard. He'd open his mouth and they'd come flying out."

"I can't imagine what that would be like," murmured Roxanne, the woman Maxine had picked out as being the most likely to sign up that day.

"It was simply ghastly," said Maxine, rolling her eyes. "My father had never said a swear word in his whole life that I know of, and here he was . . . " She sighed dramatically.

"Did he ever get over that?" another woman asked.

"After a while. Actually, that sort of thing isn't unusual when someone's had a head injury, so the neurosurgeon said. Even after he stopped swearing, he still had a funny way of talking. He would mix things up. Like, he'd want to say 'Nip it in the bud,' and he'd come out with 'Nip it in the butt.' "

More laughter.

"The poor man had no sense of appropriateness. And it wasn't just what he said—it was when he said it. He would blurt out what he was thinking wherever he was. He's even done it in church. One time, our Sunday School teacher was giving a wonderful review of the Church structure and the aims of each organization, and Will blurted out, 'The proof's in the footing!' I nearly died."

She shook her head dolefully. She was "on." She was always "on" when she had an audience. Her eyes would light up. Her body would loosen up. Her normally dormant sense of humor would cavort into the open, accompanied by an unerring sense of comic timing. Her upbeat meetings were one of the reasons her business was so successful.

"Does he do it on purpose?" someone asked.

"He didn't at first, although I've got a suspicion he does it now just to make me mad. But otherwise, he's as healthy as can be, thanks to Pure Organics. I really believe he would never have come this far if it hadn't been for the food supplements I've been giving him ever since he came out of the coma."

Roxanne raised her hand. "Did his doctor okay that?"

"Knowing doctors, what do you think?"

There was a general murmur of agreement.

"He pooh-poohed the whole thing, so I sneaked the supplements in. I told Dad they were candy."

"That was mean," said the skeptic in the back.

"Maybe so, but he took them. Only you can guess how mad he was when he ate his first Snickers bar!"

"Weren't you worried about a possible interaction with other drugs he was taking?" asked the skeptic.

"No. Our products are 99 percent pure and 99 percent natural. They're specially formulated to work with the body, helping it to heal. We in Pure Organics don't believe in masking symptoms or artificially stimulating the body's systems. Healing our way sometimes takes longer, but it is better for the body in the long run. Christine can attest to that."

"Can I ever," said Christine, launching into her testimonial. She described her symptoms at length, as well as her harrowing round of doctor's visits. Then she told how Maxine had come to her rescue with a program of Pure Organics products.

"Let me tell you, it works. I felt better right away, even though it took months for me to get my body back in balance. And it wasn't the doctors who did it. It was Pure Organics!"

"Thanks, Christine. Now, Christine's story isn't isolated. I hear things like that over and over. We in Pure Organics can't prescribe our compounds the way a doctor prescribes pills, of course, but we have personal testimony after personal testimony about the way they work to bring people better health. The real proof, though, is how they will help you personally. Think about that while Christine shows you our basic nutrition package."

Maxine watched while Christine took over. It was going well, she thought. Except for the skeptic in the back row, there was good response to everything that was being said. She figured they would end up with over a hundred dollars in orders, and, judging by Roxanne's level of interest, a new member of the Maxine Heffelfinger organization.

Christine finished her presentation by passing out order sheets. While the women were filling out their orders, Maxine gave a short introduction to the Pure Organics marketing plan. "It's the only business I know of where a person can give himself a raise," she said. "You can see your company grow right before your eyes. You see the return for the time you put in. The Cadillac Seville parked out in front is mine, just because I am a Level One Master. I've earned trips to Hawaii and Hong Kong, and I've got a mink coat in my closet, all thanks to Pure Organics."

Maxine's eyes glowed. She spoke with the enthusiasm of the true believer that she was. Intuitively, she knew that here were women who were looking for something that would answer their questions and solve their problems, whether financial, physical, or personal. She was confident she had the answer. When a candidate Maxine had picked out as a likely recruit showed no interest in Pure Organics, it always came as a surprise to her. She could never understand how they could fail to see what she had seen.

Roxanne did see. "When can I sign up?" she asked excitedly.

"You can buy your starter kit right now," said Maxine, who believed in hitting them while they were hot.

"Good meeting!" Christine complimented her after all the women had left. "There's no doubt why you're the top Pure Organics Master in Minneapolis."

"You can come right up behind me. All it takes is determination."

Maxine was high on adrenalin as she started driving home. *Great!* she thought. *I know it'll be a little slow from November through the first of the year, but I'm going to reach my goal. Daddy would be proud of me.*

That thought was like a sudden blow-out. Deflated, she sagged back into the seat and slowed down. Her daddy would never know unless she could somehow find the key to unlock his memory. If only she knew how to work that miracle.

In the days after this awakening, Maxine had tried everything she could think of. She had told Will about the things they had done together, coming close to tears when she described those lovely days when he had taken her, as a child, to the park and pushed her on the merry-go-round. He listened with no sign of remembering.

At the doctor's suggestion, she and Ernie had taken him to his condominium in Edina. "We're going to show you where you used to lived," she said, unpacking the bag of clothing she had brought for him.

Will emerged from his bathroom tugging at the crisp collar of his dress shirt.

"What's the matter? Do you need some help with the top button?" she asked, reaching out to help him.

He slapped her hand away. "I don't want it buttoned. What kind of shirt is this anyway?"

Barely controlling her tears, Maxine answered, "It's the kind you always wear."

"I don't like it. I want a shirt like Ernie has."

Ernie was wearing a polo shirt with an open collar. No matter what Maxine hung in his closet, he always ended up looking like a K-Mart blue-light special.

"You don't really want a shirt like that," she said in a placating tone. "Why, I doubt if you've worn a polo shirt once in the last ten years."

Will looked at her, his gaze level and steady and totally without recognition. "I haven't ever worn a shirt like that," he said with finality.

He strode down the hall, Ernie falling in beside him. Disconsolately, Maxine trailed behind. She hoped, she prayed that this trip to the condo might give Will's memory a jolt, but it didn't seem likely.

"This is it. This is where you lived," she said when Ernie pulled the car into a lot before the Greenridge complex. "This is one of your own developments. You were really proud of it. It's very elegant."

"Why did I want to live where there are so many people?"

"Oh, you loved city life. You always wanted to be where the action is."

"Hummph."

Will walked toward the entrance, with Ernie and Maxine following. Ernie put his arm around her, and she leaned against him, grateful for his support. "I don't think this is going to turn out the way you want it to," he said. "His injury may have robbed him of his memory, but he certainly has definite ideas about what he likes and doesn't like. And I don't think he's going to like Dad's place."

"What are we going to do if he doesn't ?" she asked, trying to blink her tears away.

The thought made her particularly sad because she herself loved it. It was open and light, its spaciousness enhanced by the flat white walls against which her father's collection of Western art was displayed. He had chosen the decor himself, an eclectic mix of modern, Southwestern, and Early American. It was an odd combination, but it worked. A museum-quality Navajo bowl, her father's favorite find, sat comfortably on a pine quilt box next to a white leather loveseat heaped with pillows in the colors of desert sand and sky.

"Hummph," said Will.

"If you want to change a few things, go ahead," said Maxine. "It's yours. You can fix it any way you like when you come home."

Will poked his head into the master bedroom. "Let someone else change it. I'm not going to live here."

"But that's the whole point of what they're trying to do at the hospital. They're trying to get you ready so you can come home. The sooner the better."

Will said a nasty phrase that made it very clear he had absolutely no intention of moving into the condominium.

Maxine gasped. "Where did you hear such a thing!"

"From an orderly. He said I should use it to show I really mean something. He was right."

"Maybe, but that's not something you should say."

"You mean, that's not something *he* would have said."

Will opened the door to the walk-in closet. His eyes ran over the wardrobe picked out by William H. Martin, and he said without enthusiasm, "I can see where you got the shirt."

The only thing that caught his attention in a positive way was the bookcase in the family room. "Who was the reader—him or his wife?"

"Mother loved to read. You didn't have much time for that."

"Do you suppose there's a sack around here somewhere?"

Maxine nodded.

"Well, get one. I want to take some of these back with me."

By the time she got back with a grocery sack, Will had pulled a stack of books from the shelves.

"Going to do a little reading?" she asked, with a tinge of sarcasm, glancing at the titles as she put the books in the sack. Most of them were from Time-Life history and nature series. Maxine guessed that the ratio of pictures to words was one of the things that had attracted Will to them. Two were books her mother had ordered after seeing Public Television programs of the same name, *The Story of English* and *The Day the Universe Changed.* The biggest book Will kept in his hands. It was the immensely popular cocktail-table book, *A Day in the Life of America.*

"That will keep you busy for a while," commented Ernie.

"Don't get too involved in them," warned Maxine. "You'll need to take some time to go down to your office. I'm sure the people there would like to see you. They've been really worried."

"I won't have time."

"Why not? What are you intending to do, figure out the meaning of life?"

"Yes," said Will simply. "And I'm not coming back here. I don't like this place."

"But, Dad . . . "

"Call me Will."

"Where else would you go?" she asked, avoiding the issue of parentage all together.

"I'm rich, aren't I?"

"Yes . . . "

"Then I want to buy a new house, out in the country where there aren't so many people."

"I suppose you'll be wanting to buy a horse and a dog as well," said Maxine.

"That's an idea."

Several months later, with Will's approval, Maxine and Ernie bought the place on Rockford Road. The purchase was financed partly with their money, partly with the proceeds from the sale of those items Maxine didn't keep for herself. The selling point of the new property was the barn, which, with its solid stone foundation and interesting architecture, could be remodeled to serve as a home for Will. He would then be close enough for them to keep an eye on him, but he would have some autonomy.

Which Maxine translated to not having him underfoot. She couldn't stand to look at him, to see the beloved face devoid of reciprocated feelings.

Shortly after they moved into the new house and settled Will in his new surroundings, Maxine read an article in the *Reader's Digest.* It was about a man who had received a series of blows to the head. When he came to after the last blow, he didn't know who he was. He was taken in by a family living in a nearby town, and there he made a new life for himself, while not far away, his wife and children anxiously waited for news of their lost loved one. Fifteen years passed. The man worked as a mechanic and lived with the family of his boss. Then one day, he suffered another series of blows. Instantly his memory came back, and he went home to the wife and family he had left fifteen years earlier.

She set the magazine down, her lips pursed thoughtfully. She was trying to devise a way to hit Will on the head. Not so hard as to hurt him, certainly not. Just hard enough so that the plug that was loose would go back into the socket. It was a stupid idea, she knew, but she couldn't help wondering.

Perhaps a rolling pin wrapped in a nice, fluffy towel would render a hard enough—yet nonlethal—blow.

Or perhaps a door, pushed hard when Will was just beginning to walk through the doorway, would do the trick.

She was truly desperate when she tried the door idea. It didn't work, for there was nothing wrong with Will's reflexes. She tried to cover herself by apologizing. "Sorry. That was stupid of me," she said.

But Will accused her of attempted murder.

I can't think about that now, Maxine told herself as she turned into the Heffelfinger driveway. *I've spent a whole year planning for this year's Pure Organics gala and for Woman's Day. I don't want to blow it because I've got my mind on something I can't change.*

22

The rest of the week, Maxine focused on what needed to be done, narrowing her vision so that anything disturbing was excluded. She checked off lists. She phoned the caterers, the flower shop, and the musicians. She went over last-minute details with both her Pure Organics people and the Relief Society board. She bought a new dress that could be worn both to the Pure Organics meeting Friday night and the Woman's Day conference Saturday.

"Can I do anything to help?" asked Ernie.

"Except for loading my car Friday night and again on Saturday morning, no."

"Okay. Anything else?"

"Just stay out of my way."

It sounded harsher than she had intended, but she knew she could handle everything if she didn't have any interruptions.

Afterward, it seemed as if the events she had spent months planning had played on "fast forward." Everything was a blur of light, sound, and color, with a moment here and there clearly captured on "hold." But she knew from the compliments people gave her that all of her planning had paid off. Both the Pure Organics gala and the Woman's Day were a success.

On Sunday, she was still revved up, riding high on a second wave of compliments. On Monday, she woke up to a feeling of emptiness and the sounds of Ernie's happy splashing in the bathroom.

He was at it again. For the last month and a half, he had never failed to sing while in the bathroom, cheerfully mutilating his favorite Country Western songs. Country Western was bad enough, but by the time Ernie was through with it, it was even worse.

She turned on her stomach and put her pillow over her head. That shut out the sound, but it couldn't erase the picture of Ernie Heffelfinger in his tweed jacket and Hush Puppies. He had taken off on a course of his own—and not just in the clothes department—without any direction and guidance from her. That was bad enough, but worst of all was the fact that he was having so much *fun* doing it.

"We're putting in the living-room windows today," he said, emerging from the bathroom, freshly scrubbed and boyish-looking with his sandy hair still damp from his shower. "It's going to be tricky, but I can't wait to get at it. This is going to be a wonderful house, Maxie."

She rolled over and came to a half-sitting position. "What?"

"The house. It's going to be great. We'll get all the business we need just from the people who see it. Custom all the way. Boy, I'm sure glad I stood up to the Trembrells when I did. We've had some disagreements since then, but we've been able to work them out. There's only one thing I feel bad about—Keri doesn't bring us donuts anymore."

Maxine stared at him. His obvious delight in the house was not what had shocked her like the poke of a pin. It was the word "Maxie." He had never called her anything in the eighteen years of their marriage but Maxine. It was a good, solid, no-nonsense name, and she liked it.

Maxie? Yuck.

Maxie and *Ernie?* Totally disgusting.

With a groan, she lay back down and pulled the covers over her head.

"Not feeling well today?" Ernie asked solicitously, tweaking her toe. "Why don't you stay in bed for a while. Take it easy. After what you've done, you deserve it."

She pulled down the covers just long enough to say, "Don't patronize me."

"How could I possibly patronize you?" said Ernie good-naturedly. "I don't even know what the word means." And whistling, he left the room.

Two minutes after he had gone, the lingering intervals of his song registered, and Maxine realized what he had been whistling: "Heigh ho, heigh ho, it's off to work we go."

It was obscene to be that happy.

She lay in bed feeling oddly empty. For the last few months, all of her energy had been directed toward the first weekend in November. *What now?* she wondered. But she couldn't bring herself to think any further than getting out of bed and taking a long bath with bubbles up to her chin. *And I will get up,* she assured herself. *Any minute now.*

She was still under the covers when Pete stuck his head inside her room. "Hey, Mom, is it all right if I ask Ren to come over here for Thanksgiving dinner?"

"Thanksgiving's a family holiday, Pete. Won't her folks want her to be at home?"

"They're not even going to be there. They're going to Cancun for the week."

"You mean, they're leaving that child to her own devices?"

"If you're asking whether they're leaving her alone, no. Sally's going to be there most of the time. Only the Dykstras promised her the day off weeks ago, and that leaves Ren by herself on Thanksgiving."

Maxine fleetingly considered telling Pete that what Ren Dykstra did on Thanksgiving Day was no worry of his, but it seemed as if it would take too much energy. "Ask her," she said. "It's all right with me."

And another Heffelfinger went whistling down the stairs.

So we'll have Ren on Thanksgiving Day, thought Maxine idly. Then she sat bolt upright. "Thanksgiving Day!" she said aloud. It was two and a half weeks before Thanksgiving, and she hadn't even put up her Indian corn decoration or set out the little wooden pilgrims to welcome people into her home from their station on the hall table.

She bounded out of bed and started for the bathroom, but

she had taken only two steps in that direction when she grabbed onto the dresser. "Oh!" she gasped. She had the oddest sensation of not knowing where to step. Although she could feel her right leg, it was oddly heavy and tingled as if it were asleep, and she couldn't tell where it was without looking down at it.

How strange, she thought, for she felt no pain, only an oppressive sense of wrongness. She took a few more steps in the direction of the bathroom, then stopped as the room seemed to split in half diagonally. One half slid downward, as if it were on a fault line, as if she were looking at that half through water. When the nausea and pain hit, she clapped her hand over her mouth and slowly sank to the bedroom floor.

She felt—and heard—the pounding of her heart in her head. *I'm dying,* she thought. *Please help me, I'm dying.*

But both Pete and Ernie were gone.

What am I going to do? she wondered, her brain scrambling in a panic that her body couldn't react to. Then she thought of Will. Will was right next door—she could ask him for help. Slowly she began to crawl to the phone. It was still out of her reach when she collapsed in agony. She lay there, not trying to stop the tears that streamed down her face.

When she heard the sound of the patio door sliding open, she knew it could only be Will, who sometimes came to the house in search of company.

"Will," she mewed. "Oh, Will . . . "

First there was only silence.

"*Will . . .* "

Then the sound of his footsteps coming up the stairs. He was moving with a vigor and speed she hadn't expected from him. In an instant, he was at her side.

"What is it? What's wrong?"

"Get me . . . to the hospital . . . ," she managed, never once thinking what that directive implied.

Ever so carefully, with a strong yet gentle touch, Will helped Maxine to her feet and down the stairs. She couldn't help emitting a little gasp with each step, the pain was so great.

"Hang on," he said, giving her shoulder a little squeeze. "We'll get there."

"My purse. We'll need it. The insurance. The keys . . . "

Will leaned her against the wall by the door, then grabbed her purse. They progressed slowly out the door and down the sidewalk.

"Back or front?" he asked once they were at the car.

"Front. I can . . . tell you where . . . to go . . . "

"You've already been doing that."

In her mind, she smiled a little.

"All right. In you go. Careful, now."

As if he were accustomed to driving the dark blue Seville, Will slipped behind the wheel and started the engine. He backed onto the road smoothly and then turned east. When he came to the first stop sign, he asked, "Where?"

She tried to open her eyes, but couldn't. "Where . . . are . . . we?"

He told her. She said, "Straight."

So they went, Will pausing at each major intersection to tell Maxine where they were, then following her one-word instructions. "Right. Left. Straight."

It didn't occur to her to wonder at his driving ability, at the sure calmness with which he took over. All her efforts were directed to surviving until he pulled up to the emergency entrance of North Memorial. Attendants were at her door immediately, easing her from the car and helping her into the hospital.

She was only vaguely aware of what happened after that. She was in such pain that she thought death was preferable. She clung desperately to the hand that had such dear, familiar contours. Her father's hand. As she went in and out of the pain, it almost seemed to her that Bill was at her side, taking care of her, like he always had.

After what seemed like hours, the doctor stepped up to her bedside. She could hear him talking to her, but the sounds didn't make any sense. She could feel him as he bent over her, trying to ascertain what the problem was, but she couldn't help him.

"Mrs. Heffelfinger," he said slowly—and suddenly, the words meant something—"I want you to open your eyes and tell me what you see."

"I can't."

"Please try."

She opened her eyes the barest slit, and there it was, the out-of-focus world, where nothing fit as it was supposed to.

She spoke the words with great difficulty, trying to make clear to him what she saw. Finally he put his hand on her shoulder. "That's fine. You're doing great. I know what the problem is now. You're having a migraine crisis, Mrs. Heffelfinger. I'm going to admit you to the hospital. You'll be feeling much better tomorrow, I guarantee it."

When the shot they gave her began working, she felt as if she were suspended in a place of heavy darkness. But the darkness wasn't total. Nebulae swam across the screen of her closed lids. Galaxies turned and kept turning. Then she felt herself turning, as if she were standing in the middle of a merry-go-round. Then, suddenly, she was. She was little, and she was laughing at her father, who was making a great show of huffing and puffing as he pushed her around.

She didn't stay little, however. Like Alice in Wonderland, she began to grow. There were others on the merry-go-round now, and she was giving them orders. They did what she told them to, and the ride was smooth, just the way she liked it.

Until one of them refused to obey. "Do as I say," she demanded.

He stood before her, his spiked hair flaming, a sardonic grin on his face. "Make me."

It was Pete.

She was still immobilized by shock when the image of Pete dissolved and in his place stood a small boy. Somehow, she knew he was getting ready to go outside and play. "Put on your coat," she said, "it's cold outside." She guided the little arms into the coat, then buttoned it up. The boy calmly unbuttoned it and took it off.

She put it back on again.

He took it off again.

Over and over they performed their pas de deux, and every time the boy took off his coat, he grew taller. While he had had to look up to her at first, he soon was eye-to-eye with her, and then she had to look up to him.

The tall boy took off the coat one last time. He dropped it at her feet, saying, "Keep it, Maxine. I never liked it anyway."

Ernie.

He turned away, and she tried to follow, but she couldn't get out of the center of the merry-go-round. She struggled with the bar that surrounded her, then looked up to see where Ernie had gone.

And found herself face to face with a scarecrow. The outline of the cloth-covered head was familiar and somehow dear, but the rough cloth sack that covered it was featureless.

"Who are you?" she cried, frightened at the ominously blank visage.

The scarecrow chuckled low in his throat but didn't answer.

Frantically she grabbed at the box of crayons that had appeared at her side. She knew how to get rid of the fear. She would draw the face she loved the best. She pulled out a crayon and began, but the line wouldn't stay put. The eyebrows thinned and thickened as she watched in horror. The mouth stretched open, then closed prissily. The face was by turns comical and cruel, tender and terrifying. She couldn't make it be what she wanted it to be. She couldn't make it look like her father.

Then she knew. The scarecrow was Will.

Suddenly the merry-go-round began to pick up speed. Frightened, she grabbed the scarecrow with her left hand. She put her right arm around Ernie and, with that hand, managed to reach out far enough to grasp Pete by the collar. She hung on desperately as the merry-go-round went faster and faster, until she felt her cheeks being pulled away from her jaw by the force. It pulled at the men, too, prying them loose from her grip. Her mouth opened in a soundless scream as the force flung first Pete, then Ernie, and finally Will off into the blackness of the void surrounding her.

They were there – then they were gone, and she was alone.

In the deep, drug-induced sleep, Maxine whimpered. There was no one to hear.

23

Upon awakening the next morning, Maxine realized the emergency room doctor's prognosis had been correct. The headache was gone. In its place was a slightly raw, tender feeling that prompted her to move very carefully as she swung her legs over the side of the bed. When she stood and realized that the world was going to stay in focus, she felt stupid at having created such a fuss. She reluctantly took the information about the different causes of migraines her own doctor offered her later in the morning, assuring him that it was a one-time occurrence. She accepted the prescriptions he wrote for her with even greater reluctance. She herself would not have had them filled, but Ernie insisted on taking them down to the hospital pharmacy before he checked her out and drove home. Once there, he gently helped her up to their bedroom. "You don't have to treat me like I'm going to break," she said. "There's nothing the matter with me."

Despite her bravado, Maxine woke the following morning in a state of tense readiness. She relaxed only when she clearly felt the absence of the pain, the numbness, the art-deco flash, and the broken-glass visual distortion that had accompanied her attack. Once assured that she didn't have any of those symptoms, she would carefully get out of bed, carefully walk to the bathroom, and carefully do her morning routine.

She was in no hurry, however, for she had decided to take it slow and easy for a few days. And she could. With the first weekend in November behind her, her obligations were much fewer. She still planned to have her regular Thursday night Pure Organics meetings, but business was usually slow in November and December. People were too busy buying presents to think about nutrition and health. As for Woman's Day, she had begged off going to the evaluation meeting. Even Martin Development Corporation could do without her for a few days, so why not take the vacation her doctor had suggested?

At least, that was what Maxine Heffelfinger told herself. The truth was, she was scared. She had enjoyed good health all her life. Beyond taking the numerous Pure Organics vitamin and mineral tablets and the protein supplement that were part of her morning routine, she had never given it a second thought. The suddenness of the migraine attack had shaken her profoundly, putting in question everything she had taken for granted.

It was as if she had been in an earthquake, a strong earthquake that had shaken to the floor all the assumptions she had put into neat little boxes and stored on the upper shelves of her mind. She didn't want to acknowledge what had happened, however. She carefully tiptoed through the rubble, avoiding the necessity of actually picking them up, examining them, and deciding whether to put them back on the shelves or throw them away.

A clear indication of her fear was the fact that she was following all the suggestions on the list her doctor had given her. She had stopped eating dairy products and drinking any kind of pop with caffeine in it. She had thrown away all the things in her kitchen that were fermented or cured. Out went the smoked ham. Out the pickles.

Now if she could just throw Ernie and Pete and Will out as well.

That, thought Maxine as she sat down to a late breakfast one morning, would fall under the heading, Getting Rid of the Stress in Your Life. And the doctor had said she should do that as well.

"Take it easy," he had advised. "Let your business ride for

a while. Go on a vacation. Ernie and Pete can take care of themselves."

"I can't."

"Why not? They're two grown men."

"I don't know . . . "

"Don't you trust them?"

She hadn't answered that question, because she knew the truth would sound awful. The fact was, she wasn't sure if she could trust them to do what they were supposed to do without her reminding them.

She had always told them what to do. Wasn't that her job as wife and mother? Weren't women the civilizing influence on men? Weren't they supposed to set the tone in the home and prod their husbands and children to good works? Many a time she had heard a speaker say, "I'm grateful for my wife, who keeps me going in the right direction."

All she had ever tried to do was to keep Ernie and Pete—and then Will—going in the right direction. That hadn't been easy, lately. No wonder she had had a migraine.

Such reflection didn't do much for her state of mind, however. She drank the last of her orange juice and was about to put the glass in the dishwasher when she heard a knock at the patio door. "Come on in," she said, knowing it was Will. He had shown up every morning since her return from the hospital to see how she was doing. That was a surprise. She had never felt any tenderness or concern from him before. Something had changed since the morning he had driven her to the hospital . . .

She felt a little tug in her mind, but ignored it as Will stepped in the house.

"How are you doing?" he asked, sitting down at the table.

"Fine. I'm just being lazy."

"Good. Why not? The world won't stop just because you don't wind it every morning."

"Are you sure?"

Will grinned, then accepted her offer of orange juice. "I'm glad to hear you're feeling better. You scared me the other day. I wasn't exactly sure what I should do."

"Really? You seemed to know exactly what to do . . . " The tug was even stronger this time, and her eyes widened as she realized what had been bothering her. " . . . including how to drive a car! Will! You haven't driven since your accident."

"*His* accident."

In her excitement, Maxine ignored his words. "But you remembered how to. That's wonderful! If you remembered that, maybe you'll start remembering other things."

"I didn't remember."

"What?"

"I didn't *remember* how to drive a car. I *learned* how. Ren and Pete taught me."

She looked at him blankly.

"They've been taking me out after school. We drive on the back roads."

"But . . . you don't have a license."

"He did."

"I don't understand."

"Ren figured it out. She said if I got his license renewed before it expired, I wouldn't have to take the test. I got it renewed in the nip of time. See?"

He opened up his wallet to show her. *William H. Martin,* it stated. The likeness showed a man with thinning gray hair, and a broad, graceless face.

It was Will. *How can the same face look so different?* she wondered. Her father had had a look of confidence and power that had marked him as someone important. This was only an old man.

"I don't think you're being exactly honest, Will."

"What do you mean?"

"You haven't taken driver's training. You haven't passed the test."

"They don't know that."

"That's what I mean. You can't insist you're Will one day and pretend to be Bill the next."

"Why not? As you say, I've got his name, his face, his fingerprints. The only thing I don't have is his memory." He scrutinized her in a way that made her very uncomfortable. Then he added, "And his money."

Maxine distractedly rubbed her temple with her fingertips. "I give you some money every month."

"Yes, you do. You dole it out bit by bit. Tell me, how did you get control of it?"

"Helmut did all the legal work when . . . " Maxine paused to clear her throat. "When you were in the coma. We had to do something. There were bills to pay. A company to run. Mom's funeral . . . "

Will handed her a napkin and watched as she wiped the tears from her eyes.

"It must not have been easy."

It was the first time he had ever expressed sympathy for what she had gone through during that time. "It wasn't," she said, taking a deep, shuddering breath. "But I survived. Watching you lie there day after day was worse, much worse. I was so excited when they called to tell me you had opened your eyes."

"Sorry to disappoint you."

She made a fatalistic gesture.

"There's a lot of money involved, isn't there?"

She nodded. "There's the stocks and bonds he acquired over the years, the rent from his condominium, and the business."

"Where does all the income and interest go?"

"The same trust fund Helmut and I drew on to give Ernie and Carl the loan."

"Hmmm. Tell me how the business is doing."

"It was rocky at first, but it weathered the crisis. When your people realized I wasn't going to dissolve it, they pitched right in. Your vice-president runs it on a day-to-day basis, but I go in a couple of times a week to make final decisions on things and sign papers."

"Interesting." Will leaned back in his chair. "When do you plan to go in next?"

"Why?"

"I'd like to go with you."

"Oh, I don't think that would be a good idea," said Maxine, endeavoring to be calm. Her pulse throbbed behind her eyes, and little waves of nausea were beginning to rise.

"Why not?"

"Why not? You . . . uh . . . Nobody would know how to act around you. You wouldn't understand a thing that was going on."

"I can learn."

"Will, you don't understand. The business is complicated. There's a lot of money involved. *A lot.*"

"Like how much? Thousands?"

"More than thousands."

"That's what I thought. I'm a rich man."

Maxine pressed the heels of her hands against her temples. *I didn't hear that,* she tried to convince herself.

"Listen, Maxine, I want some control over that money."

"No!"

"I don't mean all of it, and I don't intend to squander it."

Maxine rose, trembling. "You listen to me, Will Martin. My father made that money. You don't have any right to it."

"I don't know about that. I think he owes me something. It's his fault I woke up a fifty-nine-year-old man with no memory." Will grinned as he added, "A half-a-million or so might just be enough to compensate for my mental suffering, don't you think?"

But Maxine was in no mood to joke. "You wouldn't even know what to do with that much money."

"I've been thinking about it a lot. Remember when you took me to the Epcot Center?"

Maxine nodded. It had been her idea of a short course in world history, a drive-in order of culture.

"Well, it seems to me that if I really want to know what the world's like, I need to see it for myself. I'm thinking about a round-the-world trip. If I go slow enough, I ought to be able to use up all the money before I die."

Again she pressed her hands against her temples. "I don't want to talk about this now."

"Okay, we'll pick it up later. I'm in no hurry," said Will calmly. At the door he turned and added, "But I do think we ought to let Helmut in on the discussion. He helped gyp me out of my money—he can help me get it back again. Maybe we can talk to him when he comes for Thanksgiving dinner."

Maxine's hand was shaking as she dialed Helmut's number. Avoid stress? What a laugh. When Helmut answered, she said abruptly, "We've got a problem."

"Good morning, Maxine." The cool, well-modulated voice coming smoothly across the line instantly calmed her rapid breathing. There was at least one sane person in the universe. Thank heaven for Helmut.

"I'm sorry if I sounded rude, but we've got a problem with Will. He's got some crazy idea about wanting control of his money. Of Bill's money. Oh, you know what I mean!"

"Hmmm."

"You've got to stop him."

"Why?"

Momentarily stunned by Helmut's question, Maxine said in a shaking voice, "You know what he's like. He's not capable of that kind of responsibility."

"What makes you think that?"

"For your information, he's already told me he's planning to squander all the money on a trip around the world."

A low chuckle was Helmut's response.

"It's not funny! We've got to do something."

"What do you have in mind?"

"I was hoping you might be able to talk him out of it when you come for Thanksgiving dinner. He's already got the idea of bringing it up then."

"And if I can't?"

Maxine squeezed her eyelids shut against the pain. "I'm Will's guardian and the conservator of his estate. That would have to change before he could have direct access to the money. Am I right?"

"Yes."

"That could take some time, couldn't it? A long time?"

"Yes," said Helmut dryly. "Unless he's got a top-notch lawyer. And even then, there are legal maneuvers enough to block it for a considerable length of time. Is that what you have in mind?"

"I . . . I'm not doing this out of greed, Helmut."

He didn't respond.

"I haven't asked to be paid for all the work I do. I could, you know."

"I know."

"I just don't want to see everything my father worked for go down the drain. You can understand that, can't you?"

"Yes, but I also think that Will is entitled to something."

"He gets his allowance."

"You *give* him an allowance."

"Same difference."

"Not quite."

"The important thing is, we have to keep the estate intact."

"In other words, we have to keep Will's hands off it."

"Yes."

"You don't like him much, do you."

Maxine bit on her lower lip so hard she drew blood. "He's a poor substitute for my father." When Helmut didn't respond, she added, "I'm going to hang up now. I can't talk any longer."

"I am still invited for Thanksgiving dinner, am I not?"

"Yes," she murmured through her teeth. "Helmut, promise me you won't talk to him about the money."

"I won't bring it up."

The moment she hung up, she dashed to the medicine cabinet, where with shaking hands she reached for her bottle of cafergot. Nonaddictive, the medicine was supposed to dilate the small blood vessels in her head, thus eliminating a major source of migraine pain. *If* it was taken at the first sign of trouble, that is. She swallowed two of them with a gulp of water and a prayer.

24

It might have been easier for Maxine if she had had someone to talk to, but she didn't. The aspects of her personality that worked to her advantage in Pure Organics worked to her disadvantage when it came to making friends. She was relentlessly upbeat around other women, for to admit that she was sad, sick, or otherwise distressed would cast doubts on the efficacy of the products she touted as cure-alls. She tended to view everyone she knew as either someone who could (and should) buy her products or as a possible addition to her downline. She was used to making business decisions and routinely made personal decisions for those around her with little consideration for their feelings.

Partly because she had no group of intimates who could offer commiseration or comfort, the bottle of cafergot prescribed by her doctor was emptied with disconcerting rapidity in the days preceding the Thanksgiving Day celebration. Each onslaught of stabbing pain brought Maxine to the medicine cabinet. After taking another pill, she would lie down in her darkened bedroom, her tears slowly seeping into the pillow she held tightly clasped to her.

To anxious expressions of concern from Pete, Ernie, and Will, Maxine replied, "I'm all right. I just need some peace and quiet." They took her at her word and left her alone, which only increased her misery. She wanted someone to hold her, to tell her she was loved, to make things better, but she couldn't bring herself to ask.

The Tuesday before Thanksgiving, Pete approached her tentatively as she huddled in the corner of the family-room couch, an afghan cocooned around her.

"How are you feeling this morning?" he asked.

"I'm okay."

"No headache?"

"Not yet. What do you want?"

The tone of her voice took him aback. Reluctantly he said, "Uh . . . I just wondered if you remembered you gave me permission to invite Ren over for Thanksgiving."

"Yes," she sighed, regretting the momentary impulse that had resulted in her acquiesence.

"Well, that's the day after tomorrow." When she didn't respond, he continued hesitantly, "I mean, is there anything I can do to help you get ready?"

"No."

"Are you sure? Ren said Sally wouldn't mind making some pies or rolls before she went to her sister's."

"I don't need anyone to make pies for our Thanksgiving dinner, thank you very much."

"That wasn't meant to be an insult. Ren knows you haven't been feeling well lately. She thought you'd appreciate a little assist."

"Okay. I'm not insulted. But I don't need any help, and I will get everything done by the time your precious Ren gets here. I won't embarrass you."

"Don't start in on your martyr act. We can help, if you'll let us," Pete said. When she didn't reply, he walked from the room.

"I'm not being a martyr," she muttered to his retreating back. "Never mind how I feel, as long as there's a turkey on the table." She knew she was being unfair, but justified herself with the thought, *So what? Life's unfair.*

True to her word, she spent the whole next day cooking and cleaning. She did it with determination, but the usual spark of anticipation was missing. She didn't relish spending the day in the company of Pete the Punk, Ernie the Hush

Puppy Man, and William H. Martin, whoever he was. She only hoped that Helmut would hold to his promise and not talk to Will about the estate.

When Maxine woke Thanksgiving morning, the brightness of the sun streaming through the window stabbed her eyes. Instantly, fear gripped her. She squeezed her eyes shut and held her breath while she assessed the state of her body. Then she opened them just enough to ascertain that there was no visual distortion. The brightness was not the signal of an incipient migraine, but rather of something vaguely familiar, something she felt she should recognize but didn't. The brilliance of the sun was unusual, and the sky through the window was a lighter, clearer blue than it had been the day before. She rose carefully so as not to awaken any slumbering pain and went to the window.

Snow covered the ground, which had been bare and brown the day before. It capped the fence posts and lay heavy on the evergreen branches. The sun in the cloudless sky glinted off a million crystals, and the whole landscape was clean and still.

Of course. She should have remembered this peculiar quality of light that she always associated with the first snow of the season. Into her head popped the words of the song, "Over the river and through the wood to grandmother's house we go. The horse knows the way to carry the sleigh through the white and drifted snow. . . . "

The stillness was shattered by the sputter of an engine. Once, twice, and then it caught. Out from the garage came Ernie, maneuvering the snowblower in his first pass down the driveway. His cheeks were already reddened with cold, and watching him, Maxine was glad to be inside where it was warm and comfortable and smelled so good.

Years earlier, she and Ernie had made a deal that she would do all the baking and get the house ready for Thanksgiving if he would get up early Thanksgiving morning, make dressing (à la Brownberry dressing mix), and put the turkey in the oven. He had not forgotten. The smell that was slowly working its way into the far recesses of the house was evidence of that.

Watching him move slowly forward, the heavy snow arcing through the air to make a high pile next to the drive, she smiled. He was not so changed after all, her Ernie. Things were not as bad as she had thought they were. After all, did it make a critical difference whether he was a carpenter or a builder? Whether he wore gray or brown?

Part of her knew it didn't, but part was consumed by a dreadful fear that if she didn't manage his life, he would make a terrible mistake. And underneath that fear crouched the even darker fear that if she ever let loose of him, he might leave her. That recognition was like the flash of light through a door that is opened a mere crack and then quickly shut, the momentary illumination snuffed. It was not something she wanted to know.

The brightness of the day remained, however. The snow outside and the warmth and the smell of roasting turkey inside gave the house a cozy air. Maybe it would turn out to be a good Thanksgiving day, after all.

She had barely gotten dressed when the doorbell rang. Her eyes flashed to the clock. It was already eleven, and Ren was right on time. It was a good thing she had done all the preparations the day before, she thought.

Pete had let Ren in and was taking a tray from her when Maxine came into the kitchen.

"Didn't Pete tell you not to bring anything?" she asked reproachfully.

"I told her, Mom."

"Don't blame Pete. It was Sally's idea. She couldn't bear to send me off without something." Ren picked up an edge of the foil that covered the tray. "She made stuffed mushrooms and shrimp toast. All you have to do is broil them."

"How long?"

Ren shrugged apologetically. "Sorry. I don't remember."

"That's okay. I'll keep an eye on them," said Maxine, taking the tray. "Pete, help Ren with her coat."

"Thank you, Mother. I wouldn't have thought of that on my own," said Pete sarcastically, taking the long men's overcoat that Ren shrugged out of.

For the first time since Maxine had known Ren, the girl was wearing something colored. Topping her black skirt was an oversized sweater in soft lavender. Even for oversized, it was too big. It hung down almost to her knees, and she had pushed the too-long sleeves up to her elbows. It made her look like a waif, but the color enhanced her delicate complexion. Maxine, deciding to ignore the matching streak in Ren's hair, exclaimed, "My, you look pretty in that! Lavender is a good color for you. Much better than black."

Ren smiled. "Thanks. Just don't tell my folks you saw me like this. They might think it's a sign of the Second Coming."

Maxine raised her eyebrows a bit, but she smiled as she did so. "No. For that, you'd have to be wearing a pleated plaid skirt and a sweet little sweater."

"Probably." A funny look crossed Ren's face, and when she spoke again, her voice had an oddly shy quality. "Thanks for letting me come over today. I wasn't sure I should come when Pete told me about the migraines."

"I'm doing all right."

"I hope so. I wouldn't want to cause you extra trouble."

"You're not."

Ren relaxed. "I'm glad. Sally was planning on taking me with her to her sister's, but it would be boring over there. I can't imagine watching a football game with two old ladies."

Maxine had forgotten about the football game. She had been quite happy to have the play-offs and the World Series over and had been looking forward to a quiet day. The chances of that faded rapidly when Pete said, "You had to come. You and me and Dad and Will are the lucky foursome. The team we're rooting for has to win when we're together."

"Will and Ernie are watching the parade," Maxine said, resigned to a day of TV. "You can go join them if you want to. I'll bring the hors d'oeuvres in when they're ready."

"Can I help you with anything?" asked Ren.

"No, thanks."

In one swift motion, Ren rose on tiptoes and kissed Maxine on the cheek. "Oops! Now I've made a mess," she said with an embarrassed giggle. She fished a tissue from the pocket of her skirt, and before Maxine could move, Ren wiped the scarlet lip-print off her cheek. Then Pete put his arm around Ren, and the two of them went into the family room.

Noticing their unself-conscious intimacy, Maxine felt only relief. She tried to keep busy in the kitchen, only to find herself drawn now and then to the family room. Ernie and Pete were watching the football previews while flopped on the floor, but Will and Ren had chosen to sit on the couch. Will's arm was around her, and she had snuggled comfortably next to him. At the sight of them, Maxine felt even lonelier. She wished she knew how to be a part of their easy companionship.

At least she had one thing to be happy about. To her relief, Helmut delayed his arrival until just before dinner, which meant that Will didn't have time to ask him about the money before they all sat down. She crossed her fingers. So far, so good.

The last thing she had to do before they could eat was put the traditional three kernels of parched corn on each of the plates. As a descendant of the *Mayflower,* Maxine had adopted a tradition of beginning the Thanksgiving meal with three kernels of parched corn, representing a day's ration of the meager supply of grain the Pilgrims were reduced to before the first harvest. Then she adjusted the angle of one of the cloth napkins and called them in.

They came laughing, in high spirits. None of them except Helmut seemed interested in listening to Maxine's reading of the *Mayflower* story, and they chewed their three kernels of corn dutifully, but without much enthusiasm.

"Ugh. Not what I would choose to eat," said Ren. Then she looked apologetically at Maxine. "But it does make me appreciate all the yummy things you've cooked."

Ernie prayed, Maxine brought the turkey in, Helmut carved, and they ate.

"I hear you drove Maxine to the hospital when she had her migraine crisis," said Helmut, laying his fork on his empty plate and dabbing at the corner of his mouth.

"My first venture into heavy traffic," said Will, his mouth full. "But I did okay."

"You're a great driver," offered Ren.

"You and Pete are great teachers."

"I don't think we taught you anything. You seemed to know exactly what to do, including how to shift."

"It's odd," agreed Will. "Although I have lost my memory, it seems that my muscles have a mind of their own."

"Kinesthetic memory," supplied Helmut.

"Whatever. I am pretty good at it."

"Do you want to see if you can remember how to drive in snow?"

Maxine, sure that Will would make the most of such an opportunity, tried to signal Helmut, but he seemed oblivious to her efforts. Before she could change the course of conversation, Will said, "Sure. Why not?"

"It will also give you a chance to drive a Mercedes. You used to drive nothing but Mercedes. Said it was the only car worth buying."

"I guess I had pretty expensive tastes."

"You could afford to indulge them."

"I can't afford it nowadays," said Will pointedly.

"Uh, should we go into the living room or the family room for dessert?" asked Ernie, who had sensed a change in the atmosphere and was trying to avoid unpleasantness. He wasn't successful, however, for everyone had eaten too much, and the consensus was that pie should be reserved for later in the afternoon.

"That gives us time to go for a little ride, doesn't it, Will?" said Helmut. "Unless you are committed to watching the football game."

Maxine started half a dozen things in the kitchen after Will and Helmut drove away, only to leave them unfinished. She was so worried about what Will might be saying that she found it impossible to concentrate. On top of that, she could feel a headache coming on. Why had Helmut orchestrated this time together with him? She had thought he was her ally. "I'll kill him," she said through gritted teeth.

"Did you say something?" asked Ernie, coming in for pop and ice cubes.

"Just what is your father up to?"

"What makes you think he's up to something?"

"He knows that Will wants to talk to him about the estate today. So instead of avoiding Will as I asked him to, your father invites him to a little tête-à-tête."

"They might just be taking a ride, Maxine."

"They're not. I know what they're talking about, and it's not fair for them to go behind my back."

Ernie put his arm around her, but she stood stiffly in his embrace. "Don't try so hard, Maxie. Things are going to work out fine with Will. He's really an okay guy. And he and Dad aren't going to do anything without talking to you first. Even if they wanted to, they couldn't."

That was slim comfort to Maxine, as she watched the minute hand advance. A full hour passed before she heard the car pull into the driveway, and by then, the pressure in her temples was building painfully. From the window she watched Will and Helmut get out of the car and walk toward the house, talking convivially. They had just entered the kitchen when the three watching football burst into whoops of delight.

"What's happening?" cried Will, rushing into the family room to see who had scored.

Maxine had a question of her own. "How was your ride?" she asked Helmut.

"Very pleasant, thank you. Will is, as Ren and Pete attested, a very accomplished driver. He says he's had his license renewed; I think that was a good idea."

"I suppose he talked to you about what he wants to do?"

"Yes."

"Some help you are. You played right into his hand."

"For your information, Maxine, never once did the conversation touch on the subject of money."

She stared at him. "Then what did you talk about?"

"Many things. Are you aware of the fact that Will is highly intelligent and articulate?"

"Not the Will I know."

"Perhaps he doesn't deign to reveal himself to you. You don't make it easy for him, you know."

"Or maybe he was putting you on by quoting something he's heard in some public television program."

"You are making a very serious mistake if you assume that what you see is what you get in the case of Will Martin. Remember, he's trying very hard to discover who he is. If he does things that irritate you, it's much the same as Pete dyeing his hair red – a search for identity. Only it's much more critical for Will than it is for Pete."

"Search for identity, ha!"

"Consider the situation carefully, please. Here you have a grown man whom you have been treating as if he were a child."

"He was, at first. I had to teach him everything all over again."

"Be that as it may, he's a child no longer. He is, in point of fact, a competent adult. And I think that if he should choose to press his claim for more control over the estate, we would have a hard time convincing a judge that he wasn't capable of handling it."

"He doesn't know a thing about finances!"

"He's not entirely ignorant of financial matters, Maxine. In any case, he is a rational adult, capable of weighing options and taking considered advice."

"You aren't suggesting – "

"No, I don't think Will should try to go back into the business actively. Nor does he want to. He has only limited time, and he wants to make the most of it. It's a sentiment I appreciate."

Maxine sank into the nearest chair. "You're on his side."

"Yes, I am. In fact, I'm quite fascinated by the fellow. You know, I was as close to Bill as I have been to anyone, and I have been very disappointed to find that Will doesn't share an interest in the things I used to enjoy with Bill. Opera, the Saint Paul Chamber Orchestra, fine dining. But I have found to my extreme surprise that we do have something in common."

"I can't imagine what."

"The need to find something to fill our last years." He put his unlit pipe between his teeth and pulled on it, considering.

"What are you thinking?"

Helmut raised his eyebrow. "I'm thinking, my dear, that a round-the-world trip might be just the thing."

25

When Maxine called in for a renewal of her cafergot, the pharmacist said, "I'm sorry, but your prescription didn't give orders for a refill. You'll have to talk to your doctor."

"But I need it now." Maxine's voice held a note of panic. "I've got this pain—"

"I'm sorry. There's really not anything I can do for you. If you talk to your doctor and he calls us with an okay, I'll be glad to make up the refill."

Frustrated, Maxine slammed the receiver down. She didn't want to talk to her doctor. She didn't want to tell him that in a few weeks she had gone through a vial of medicine he had expected to last her several months. It would reveal the increasing frequency of the migraine attacks, something she was too frightened by to discuss with anyone, even him.

Why wasn't it working, the doctrine she had preached so successfully for so many years? She had been taking her vitamins, her energy-giving herbs, and her cleansing herbs, hoping they would build her up. She had been taking extra of the vitamin B capsules, hoping they would calm her down. She had been praying and reading her scriptures. What more could she do?

At least she still had a few pain killers with codeine. She shook two out into her palm and stared at them with revulsion. The very thought of trying to swallow them made her feel like retching. Somehow, she got them down, then crawled into bed.

She was feeling somewhat better when Ernie quietly entered the bedroom. "Oh, Maxie. Not again," he said, his voice full of concern.

She moaned in reply.

"Have you taken a pill?"

She nodded, not telling him that the cafergot vial was empty. "I'll feel okay in a while."

"Is there anything I can do to help you?"

"No."

He sat down on the bed, careful not to create any unnecessary motion. "This is getting out of hand. We need to get you some help."

"No one can help me."

"Maybe we can make it a little easier on you. I know you've been trying to do all the things you usually do for Christmas. Why don't you forget all that this year. Don't make it into such a big deal. Pete and I can put up the tree, and I'll buy some Christmas cookies at the bakery so you won't have to worry about making them yourself. And as for Christmas dinner, I'll put in a roast. How does that sound?"

Awful, thought Maxine. The very idea of store-bought cookies was enough to get her out of bed. Sitting up, she said, "Thanks, but I'm not an invalid. I can get everything done."

"I never said you couldn't. But you're supposed to avoid stress."

"Christmas is a stress," she murmured, but Ernie was taking off his work boots and didn't hear. It wouldn't have made any difference if he had heard. He didn't understand her need to have everything just right for that special season. He didn't need a perfect Christmas to make him happy.

She had set up almost impossible criteria for the perfect Christmas. The house had to be cleaned from top to bottom, then decorated. Decorating was a week-long project going far beyond the simple setting-up of a tree that would have satisfied Ernie. Every nook and cranny became the repository of some bit of Christmas cheer: a stocking-capped elf, a trio of singing angels, an arrangement of greens and bows, an array of different-sized brass candlesticks with red candles.

The baking was done with the same determination and attention to detail. It amazed Maxine that Ernie could think his offer to stop at the bakery for a boxed assortment of spritz cookies would take the place of the elegant assortment she produced every year. She wondered if he had ever looked at them before putting them in his mouth.

In addition to cleaning, decorating, and baking, Maxine had always made a new pair of flannel pajamas for each of the men and a nightgown for herself every year. Solid red or red and green plaid, the nightwear came complete with matching nightcaps. It took time but was worth it, if only for the effect of their color-coordinated outfits in the Christmas-morning photographs.

Finally, she had always prided herself on picking out the perfect present for each of her family members. Not only did she know what they wanted, she knew what they ought to want. Most often, her purchases fell in the latter category.

Such had been the extent of her Christmas preparations in years past, and she was determined that no matter what, she wouldn't let down this year—certainly not because of a headache. At least she had already made some of her purchases. She determined that after Ernie and Pete had left the next morning, she would wrap them.

It never happened.

She did fish them from the back of the family room closet and line them up on the floor before the hearth. She also laid out the paper she had bought during the after-Christmas sales the January before, along with the necessary scissors, tape, and ribbon. That was as far as she got, however.

The first box she picked up was a hat box marked "Ernie." She opened it and took out a beautiful gray touring hat meant to go with the gray overcoat that was in the bigger box bearing her husband's name. Both of these were meant to coordinate with the suits she had purchased for him.

Except Ernie didn't wear gray anymore. She laid the touring hat back in the box and put the lid on.

In the box marked "Pete" was a navy blazer with brass

buttons and tan cotton pants. Maxine ran her hand over the smooth fabric. He would look so sharp in that blazer, especially if he got rid of the ridiculous hair. But he wouldn't wear it. The blazer would molder in his closet, Maxine thought, remembering Ren's laughing description of the fate met by the clothes her mother bought her.

She herself had always worn the outfits picked out for her by her father. Bill Martin had enjoyed going shopping for his "girls," as he had called both Maxine and her mother. The clothing he chose for them was always beautiful, expensive, and conservative, as was befitting his way of life.

He had wanted to be proud of his girls, not only in how they looked, but in what they achieved as well. So Maxine, wanting to please him, had achieved. Thinking about it as she sat on the floor surrounded by boxes and paper and ribbons, she smiled sadly. Cheerleader, student body vp, salutatorian. She had given him something to be proud of.

He had been happy when she told him she wanted to marry Ernie, but at the time, Ernie had still been in law school. He had done little to mask his disappointment when Ernie dropped out, announcing his desire to be a carpenter.

"A carpenter? That's nothing to strive for. A carpenter is what you become when you can't do anything else. I ought to know. I employ carpenters."

"He really wants to be a cabinetmaker, Daddy. That's not the same."

Although he could have helped them out by offering Ernie a job, he didn't. He wanted his son-in-law to understand how tough things were going to be in his new choice of career. However, he insisted on contributing to Maxine's monthly food, clothing, and household budget. "I don't want Ernie to think I'm supporting him in this craziness, but I won't have you living like a gypsy."

She remembered how torn she had been at that moment, needing to support Ernie, whose total, undemanding acceptance of her was a precious gift, but needing also to be her father's daughter.

How funny, she thought. *When Ernie was going to law school, Daddy was pleased. When he started working with wood, Daddy was furious. If he were here now, he'd be pleased again. But Ernie hasn't changed since the day I met him. Law student, cabinetmaker, builder, he's just plain Ernie.*

Plain Ernie hadn't been overwhelmed by his first Christmas with the Martins. Attending the *Messiah* on Christmas Eve and then having a traditional late supper of oyster soup wasn't his idea of fun. He preferred to stay at home, playing games and eating popcorn balls and fudge. In the early years of their marriage, however, her father's traditions had triumphed over Ernie's preferences. If Ernie was miserable, nobody noticed or cared. Maxine had hoped that Pete, having grown up with the Martins' kind of Christmas, would accept it as right and proper.

But since the accident . . .

How many things had changed since the accident! Not only didn't she know who her father was, she also didn't seem to know who she was anymore. One day Will had said to her, "You want me to be Bill so you can be comfortable being who you are." Perhaps he was right. She had made her choices to please her father, and now her father was gone.

She picked up the box meant for Will. In it were a pair of Bushnell field glasses and an Audubon book on birds of North America. She had bought them because bird watching had seemed an appropriate activity for an older, retired man to engage in—which was all well and good except for the fact that so far as she knew, Will didn't like bird watching.

In a burst of insight, she knew that with these gifts, she was doing to her family what Bill had done to her every Christmas she could remember. He had bought her what he wanted her to have, not what she wanted. The thought was inexpressibly sad. Surrounded by her presents, she wept soundlessly, the heavy tears splashing onto the bargain Christmas paper.

That was how Ren and Pete found her.

"What are you doing home?" she sniffled, wiping her cheeks with the back of her hand.

"The boiler broke down, so we don't have any school today. Are you okay?" said Pete.

"No, actually I'm not," said Maxine through her tears. "I was going to wrap these presents, but I've bought all the wrong things, and now I've bawled all over the paper . . . "

"Ah, Mom," said Pete awkwardly. He made a move toward her, but he didn't know what to do.

"Let me take care of it, Heffelfinger," said Ren. "Women are better at these things than men."

Maxine shook her head. "No," she said in a thick, muffled voice. "I want to be left alone."

But Ren didn't pay any attention. "Go on," she told Pete. "I'll come up later." As Pete reluctantly walked up the stairs, she sat down on the arm of Ernie's recliner, an uncertain smile on her lips.

Maxine turned her tear-streaked and swollen face away from the girl. "You can't help me. What do you know about life? You're only a kid."

"You're right there," agreed Ren. "But then, I didn't plan on solving your problems or telling you what to do. I just thought I'd sit with you for a while. That's what Sally does with me when I'm in a funk."

Maxine gulped down a sob.

"Don't stop crying on account of me. Scream. Yell. Have a tantrum. It'd probably do you good."

A half-sob, half-laugh issued from Maxine's throat. The pain that had settled in the region of her heart (was that—not the migraines—the real pain after all?) was so great, she thought she couldn't bear it. But the simple acceptance of the girl loosened something. Deep, long-held grief flowed up the newly opened channel, and sorrow fell like rain on the uncut wrapping paper.

"Good. Cry as long as you want to," said Ren. She moved to a cross-legged position on the carpet and leaned against the recliner. "That's what my shrink told me after Chris killed himself. Only I couldn't, not for a long time. I was too mad at my parents for pushing him so hard, for caring more about their house than their son."

Maxine's resistance to Ren's presence was no match for her curiosity about what the girl was saying. Although she still refused to look at her, she began to pay closer attention to what Ren was saying.

"I was mad at Chris, too," Ren mused. "The creep. Who did he think he was, checking out and leaving me alone with them? He could have fought. He could have run away from home. He could have gone punk like me and told them where to . . . well, you know.

"It's a conspiracy," she continued, talking to herself as much as to Maxine. "You guys will do anything to make us turn out like you, and you know what? You're not even happy. It's so stupid."

Maxine felt something click inside. Ren was speaking the truth, and she knew it. Although he had loved her, her father had also laid out his expectations for her, allowing no options, and she had tried to fill them. Unhappily, resentfully, but with no thought of rebellion. And in turn, she had held up her own expectations for Ernie and Pete. Only they weren't as compliant as she had been. The red hair, the Hush Puppies, the new job . . . It was their way of saying, "No more."

Maxine drew a shuddering breath as she felt the last of her resistance go. She picked up a piece of ribbon and ran her finger along the smooth length. "Do you know what I always wanted for Christmas?" she asked Ren.

"No," said Ren, who relaxed visibly at the change in Maxine's voice.

"A pet. Every year my Daddy would ask me what I wanted. Every year I asked for a pet. First I asked for a dog, but he said no, dogs were too big and rambunctious. So I asked for a cat, but no. Cats shed too much. Nix on a hamster and a bird. He wouldn't even buy me a fishbowl. He bought me . . . " Maxine's voice shook as she finished, "what he thought I should have."

Suddenly she picked up the hat box and threw it across the room. The lid flew off and the hat landed on the floor near the fireplace. Ren made a move to retrieve it.

"Leave it," said Maxine. "Nobody wants that hat. It's going in the trash anyway." Then she shifted so that her back was against the couch, and for the first time that morning she looked directly into Ren's face. Ren was smiling, an odd, pathetic smile, and her tears had carried mascara in dirty rivulets down her cheeks.

"Why, Ren." An unexpected surge of warmth and compassion moved Maxine to do something she would not have considered moments before. "Come sit beside me," she said, patting a spot on the carpet next to her. "I won't bite."

Ren moved tentatively, a mixture of need and doubt in her face. When she sat down, she left an arm's length between them.

"You don't trust me, do you."

"I don't trust adults as a matter of principle. Except for Will and Sally. And Ernie."

There was an awkward silence, in which Maxine contemplated her exclusion. She wanted to be someone Ren trusted, yet she realized that she had never given Ren any reason to. In spite of that, the girl had reached out to her when she needed someone. There was genuine emotion in Maxine's voice as she said, "Thank you for staying with me."

"No biggie."

"I think it was." She ran her fingers lightly down Ren's cheek, then let her hand rest on the girl's shoulder. Ren made no move away from the contact. "You took a real risk, especially considering the fact that you don't like me all that well."

Ren smiled. "It wasn't so hard. You're Pete's mother, not mine."

"I'm sure your mother wouldn't turn away from you."

"Probably not."

"It's Christmas, the season of good will. Why not try to reach out to her?"

"She won't be here this Christmas. She and Dad are going to Gstaad. Sounds just too perfect, doesn't it. Skiing in the Alps for Christmas."

"And you're not going with them?"

"No. I didn't want to."

"I can't believe that!"

Ren's shoulders dropped. "The truth is, I did want to, and I think Mom wanted me to come, but Dad . . . He can't stand to look at me anymore."

"Oh, Ren. What are you going to do while they're gone?"

"I dunno. Hang around and irritate Sally. She was hoping to visit relatives during the holidays, but she has to baby-sit me instead."

"Do you want to come and stay with us while your parents are gone?"

Ren's whole body stilled. She seemed to have momentarily ceased breathing. "Do you mean it? Sometimes I get the feeling I'm not your favorite person."

Deciding to take a risk of her own, Maxine slid closer to Ren and put one arm around her shoulder. "I admit I have a hard time with some things you do and say, but I think you're a very nice young lady."

"Nice?" Ren groaned. "I must be slipping."

"Will you come?"

"Sure. What did you think? I'll help out so you won't have to do so much."

"I won't be doing much," said Maxine slowly, "aside from returning those things and doing a little shopping."

26

Taking it easy wasn't easy, Maxine discovered. And she probably wouldn't have managed it at all if it hadn't been for the appointment she made with her doctor. Before authorizing a refill of her prescription, he had a long talk with her about stress and the relative importance of things. Time and time again during the two-week vacation that followed, she had to remind herself of what was and what wasn't important in the long run.

It wasn't important that she have a Christmas open house for her Pure Organics down-line. It wasn't the end of the world if she didn't give her visiting teachers a plate of seven different kinds of cookies, and take the same intimidating assortment to the sisters she herself taught. It didn't make Christmas less festive if they didn't go to *The Nutcracker* at the Northrup Auditorium or *Scrooge* at the Guthrie. Nor would she be fired as wife and mother if there was a cobweb in the corner by the fireplace.

She did return the gifts, however. That *was* important. In place of the binoculars, she got Will a set of good luggage, her way of saying bon voyage. Ernie's new present was a capacious cardigan of nubby brown wool with bone buttons. At Ren's suggestion, she bought Pete a Pink Floyd album and *Greatest Hits of Simon and Garfunkel.* "At least I can listen to one of them without tearing out my hair," she told Ren. "You may think you discovered Simon and Garfunkel, but I grew up with them." And she bought Helmut two tickets to a spring performance of Itzhak Perlman with the Saint Paul Chamber Orchestra.

"What should I get Ren?" she asked Pete. "I can't imagine anything she would like."

"She likes stuffed animals."

Maxine was doubtful, but she bought Ren a wonderfully squeezable koala bear, which she dressed in a Twins cap and christened "Kirby" in honor of Ren's favorite Twins player.

Three days before school vacation, Maxine answered the phone to find Mrs. Dykstra on the line. After a few words of introduction, the woman said, "I understand from Ren that you have invited her to stay with you during vacation."

"Yes. I hope that's all right."

"We don't want you to go out of your way. We had planned on having our cook and housekeeper here during that time, so Ren really doesn't need to impose."

"She's not imposing. I invited her."

"So she said. It's up to you then."

"We'll get along fine."

There was a long silence, then Ren's mother said tonelessly, "That's more than I can say for the two of us."

"I understand it hasn't been easy."

"Don't believe everything Ren tells you. She has a very colored viewpoint of what has happened in our family."

"Kids do, I understand that. But I'm beginning to understand that adults do too."

After a slight hesitation, Mrs. Dykstra replied, "You're right, of course, but knowing that doesn't make a difference."

"It could."

"Perhaps . . . "

Ren arrived a few days later with her car full. She had brought over fancy cookies, fruit cake, caramels, and fudge, all from Sally's kitchen. She had also brought a box of records. Maxine could tell from the covers that they would set the house reverberating. It made her shudder to think of it. Ren's sometimes screechy, abrasive voice, her lapses into swear words, her way of always touching Pete . . . all of those things would be enough to make her scream if she let them get to her.

The best way to avoid that, she concluded, was to keep everyone busy. So the first couple of days Ren was there, Maxine tried to organize the way time would be spent. Her suggestions fell flat. Finally Pete said, "Mom, why do we have to *do* something. Why can't we just hang around?" She couldn't understand how they could do nothing all day long, but they quite happily did, except for the chores she assigned them.

It was during this time that Maxine first learned about Ren's pen and ink drawings. She found Ren at the kitchen table one afternoon working on a copy of a classic illustration.

"My goodness! I didn't know you could draw."

"I didn't draw this," Ren admitted. "I traced it from a book. I do that a lot; then I try to copy the kinds of strokes the artist used."

"You're doing a beautiful job. I'd like to have one, if you wouldn't mind giving it up."

"What would you like? A cartoon or a landscape?"

Maxine looked at the intricate medieval scene Ren was working on. "I like this one."

"Then it's yours."

And Maxine flushed with pleasure.

They did do two things as a group that Christmas. They went on a sleigh ride, and they attended the Christmas party at the ward.

The sleigh ride came about because Will wanted to see what it was like. At first only Ren and Pete were planning to go with him. Then Ernie said, "I'd like to come. I've never been on a sleigh ride either." So they all went. For an hour they rode over the hills and valleys of a farm to the north of the Twin Cities, snuggled under plaid wool blankets and fortified by hot chocolate. Afterward, Pete started a snowball fight, which didn't end until they were freezing.

Going to the church Christmas party was the one suggestion of Maxine's that they actually followed through on. The party was to be a Christmas carol sing-in, followed by a visit from Santa Claus for the little children, and refreshments. "Naw," said Pete, who thought the Santa Claus part sounded too childish. But Ren said wistfully, "That sounds kind of nice. Why don't we go?"

"Are you going to be okay with this?" Ernie asked Maxine as they got ready. "You know that people are going to stare at Ren."

"I'll just have to get used to it, won't I."

He hugged her and whispered into her ear, "You're a real trooper, you know that?"

Coming from Ernie, this was high praise indeed.

Still, getting through the vacation wasn't easy. Maxine often caught herself gritting her teeth. At times she could feel the irritation rise up the back of her neck and her mind clench. Then she would shut herself in the bathroom or go for a walk. She spent a lot of time in the bathtub with a book, and twice she took a pill from her prescription and went to bed early. She felt a great sense of accomplishment when Christmas Eve arrived without a crisis.

Helmut joined them early in the evening. They played some games and sang a few carols, and Ernie read the Christmas story while the fire flickered. Maxine had been worried that Ren would be uncomfortable with that part of their celebration, but she did nothing to dampen others' enjoyment. Neither did Helmut.

On Christmas morning they exchanged gifts. Maxine could hardly contain herself, waiting for her family to open the presents she had purchased, for they were a message from her to each one of them. She hoped they would recognize it and appreciate it.

"Good deal, Mom!" said Pete when he saw what records she had given him. "I won't play them too loud, okay?"

She nodded.

Ernie put on his sweater immediately and wore it every day the rest of the week.

Ren cooed over the stuffed bear. "Oh, cute. He looks just like my Kirby!" She was equally pleased with the lavender scarf Maxine had added as an afterthought.

And Helmut said, "What a wonderful gift. These tickets must have been hard to come by."

But Will was the one most moved by the implications of his present. "Are you sure you'll trust me to take a trip on my own? You don't even trust me to go downtown without getting into trouble."

"I think you'll do fine, Will," she said, and for the first time, she gave him a hug. He returned it shyly. To cover her embarrassment, she said, "Ren! Pete! What are you two doing? Either go out or come in, but don't stand there with the door open!"

They giggled conspiratorially. "Ready?" Pete asked.

"Yes," Ren said.

Suddenly there was a flurry of tawny fur and flapping ears. A cocker spaniel puppy dashed into the room, attacking Helmut, Ernie, and Maxine alternately with dripping tongue.

"What!" cried Maxine, laughing. She captured the wriggling puppy and held her up. The puppy, of course, took the opportunity to slobber on her cheek. "Where did this cutie come from?"

"She's from all of us," Ren said. "I remembered what you said that day about wanting a pet. Merry Christmas."

Maxine buried her face in the warmth of the wriggling puppy's fur. It seemed to her that she had never had a nicer gift.

WINDING DOWN

Looking back, Maxine wished there were a way to capture the essence of such moments, to make tangible and enduring the extraordinary sense of connection she had felt with those who had gathered around her as she held the puppy that Christmas morning.

But there wasn't. Time moved inexorably forward, its necessities intruding upon the delicate awareness she had experienced, forcing it into the background where it faded away. Yet she knew it had been real and that she wasn't the only one who had felt it. That knowledge gave her hope, which she held as a shield against uncertainty when the vacation ended and life fell back into the familiar pattern.

It wasn't a pattern Maxine could be completely satisfied with anymore. Too much had happened, and to go on as before would be a negation of her pain, a rejection of lessons learned, a loss of meaning. Nevertheless, there were certain things that were givens in her life. She couldn't change them all with one wave of a magic wand. She would have to find within the givens a new way of being.

I can do it, she thought, gazing out the frosted window onto the frigid January landscape. *I can, if I hold on to that moment and what it meant.* For in that split second, everything had been both the same as in the moment before and yet different. The way she had felt had changed the way things seemed. If she could hold on to that new way of feeling, it would guide her. And then maybe, just maybe, that moment of revelation would gradually become manifest in reality.

Tuned in to her feelings in a way she had never been before, she became aware over the next few days that they demanded something of her that up to now she had been unwilling to do. She had to accept Will as *Will.* The old resistance and anger were still there, however, hard as a brick wall, blocking her forward progress. It occurred to her then that she couldn't wait for those feelings to dissipate. Like the children of Israel who had had to wade into the Red Sea before the Lord parted the waters, she would have to decide on a course of action and then follow through with it, hoping grace would come as a result. Before she had a chance to change her mind, she made two phone calls: one to Helmut, asking him to begin the paperwork necessary to give Will financial independence; the other one to her ward clerk, requesting an interview with the bishop.

The interview was actually for Will, although Maxine went with him. The bishop listened to his story sympathetically, but he had never faced a situation like Will's before, so he referred them to the stake president. The stake president listened, then said he thought something could be worked out, but that he would need to check with Church headquarters in Salt Lake City. A few weeks later he called to tell Will he could be baptized. They would simply not record the ordinance, since there was already a record of William H. Martin's baptism.

Will's joy was expressed in his brilliant smile and calm sureness. He shook hands with Pete and Ernie, then stood before Maxine. Resting his hands on her shoulders, he said simply, "Thank you. I don't think this would have happened without your support."

Tears pricked her eyes, and she kissed the dry, thin skin of his cheek. "Merry Christmas again. And a Happy New Year."

"I think it will be," he said. Then he asked his grandson if he would perform the ordinance.

"I've never done that before," protested Pete.
"So this will be the first time."
"Can I think about it a little?"

The idea of baptizing Will was sobering. It prompted Pete to consider what his commitment to the Church really was, for he knew he wouldn't feel good about doing the ordinance if he couldn't say truthfully that he believed it was important. In the quiet of his room that night, he picked up his long-neglected scriptures and opened them to the places he had marked for scripture-chasing. The words had a sweet familiarity that called up a warmth he hadn't felt for some time.

When he finally closed the book, he knew that the gospel was precious to him, and that he could baptize Will with complete faith in the ordinance he was performing. But he wasn't quite ready yet. Knowing that Will's baptism was a sign of his commitment to Christ, Pete wanted to do something himself that would indicate his own commitment.

"I knew you were about ready to make a change," said Ren. "Can I make a suggestion? Get an appointment at Horst's school downtown. They're really good, and they don't charge much – relatively speaking. They'd give you a great cut, something with a lot of style."

"Maybe."

She put her arms around his waist and tipped her head so she could look into his face. "If you think it's going to change anything between us, forget it. I don't care what you look like, Heffelfinger. Don't you know that by now?"

The stylist at Horst's cut the sides and back of Pete's hair even shorter than it was, sculpturing outward as he worked upward. He then opted for a modified flat-top, leaving somewhat longer hair in front. Almost all of Pete's latest color lay on the floor when he was done. Pete was back to brown hair, except for the tips of his bangs, which were combed to one side.

"I love it!" said Ren.

"You've got great hair," the stylist enthused. He called the supervisor to come see what he had done to Pete.

The supervisor ran a comb through what was left of Pete's hair. "Very uptown. Good job. Do you think you might want to come model for us?"

Pete guffawed. "I don't think so."

That night he and Ren spent an hour at Will's going through the boxes and closets. This time they were in search of only slightly dated country-club attire. "I can't believe I'm doing this," Pete said, shaking his head. "If I don't watch out, I could end up being a Drew Conzet clone."

"A new year, a new look," said Ren.

"How about you? Are you going to try something different?"

"Haven't you noticed that I've been wearing the scarf your mother gave me?" she demanded, flipping the fringed ends in his face.

"You have, haven't you. That's a start." He hesitated, then asked, "Are you coming to the baptism?"

"Will asked me to, but I'm not sure."

"It's no big deal. Nobody will be there but me, Mom and Dad, Will, and Helmut."

She hesitated, considering.

"Would you come if I asked you to? It would seem strange not having you with us."

The little group gathered in the church the second Saturday of February. Besides the family and Ren, the missionaries and the Heffelfingers' home teachers were in attendance. It was a quiet, simple ceremony, but there was a tangible sense of power and purposefulness about the ordinances taking place. Helmut, who had never come to witness any ordinance involving his family, had a contemplative air about him as Pete said the words, immersed Will, and brought him up out of the water.

Ernie put his hand on his father's shoulder. "How come you're so solemn? Have you changed your mind, maybe?"

"No," said Helmut. "I don't have Will's faith. Yet I feel sad that I don't."

Ernie gave Helmut's shoulder a squeeze; then they stood together in a moment of rare oneness while waiting for Will and Pete to return from the dressing room.

Ren was the first to give Will a congratulatory hug. "There's something special about this," she said. "I feel . . . I don't know how to explain it." Keeping one arm around Will, she put the other around Pete. "You guys are my family," she said to those circled about Will. "I love you all." Then several minutes passed as tissues were handed out and everyone hugged everyone else. "Sally would groove on this," Pete whispered to Ren as he held her.

After the service, they went to Chi-Chi's for a celebration supper of Mexican food. They lingered over their choices, laughing and talking, unwilling to bring the afternoon to an end. By the time they pulled into the Heffelfinger driveway, the pale February sun had begun its slide down the western sky.

"Guess I'd better be on my way," said Helmut. He shook Will's hand once more, then got into his Mercedes and pointed it in the direction of Stillwater.

"Brr! It's freezing!" said Ren through chattering teeth. She stamped her feet as she waited for Ernie to unlock the kitchen door. When he got it open, they all tumbled in behind him—all except Will, who had hung back and was standing by the car, an odd look on his face.

"Hurry, quick!" Maxine called to him. "You'll catch pneumonia if you stay out in this any longer."

"There's something else I want to do," he said.

"Come into the house first and then tell me," said Maxine, shivering in the cold.

"No. I want to go someplace, and you have to come with me."

She hesitated, then called to the others that she and Will would be back soon. "Where are we going?" she asked, pulling her coat collar up around her neck.

"You'll see. May I drive?"

She hesitated only a moment before holding out the keys.

He didn't say much as he drove, and Maxine racked her brain, trying to think what he might be up to. She drew a total blank when he turned into the parking lot of the nearest elementary school.

"You wanted to go to the school? Whatever for?"

He opened the door without answering her. "Everybody out," he said.

She did as he asked, following him around the building to the playground. Her heart stopped when she realized he was headed for the merry-go-round. It stood off to one side in a moat trodden in the snow by booted feet, the dull metal disk shining coldly in the last rays of the sun.

He motioned to her. "Come on. It's okay."

Slowly she walked to the merry-go-round.

"Get on," he encouraged.

"I don't understand."

"I'm going to push you, the way your dad used to."

"Why?" she choked.

"Look at it this way. We're stuck with each other, you and I. I might get my memory back sometime, who knows. Until then, I can't be your father." He gazed at her, his expression full of love and longing. "But maybe, if you'll let me, I can be your friend."

The tears starting down her cheeks were warm, but her flesh felt like ice in their wake. Half-blinded, she sat down on the merry-go-round and put her arms around her knees as she had when she was little.

"Ready?" Will asked.

She nodded, and he began to push.